burn

Celestra Series

Book 3

ADDISON MOORE

BURN © 2011 ADDISON MOORE

Edited by: Sarah Freese
Cover Design by: Gaffey Media
Interior design and formatting by: Amy Eye of
www.theeyesforediting.com/

Copyright © 2011 by Addison Moore
http://addisonmoorewrites.blogspot.com/

This novel is a work of fiction. Any resemblance to peoples either living or deceased is purely coincidental. Names, places, and characters are figments of the author's imagination. The author holds all rights to this work. It is illegal to reproduce this novel without written expressed consent from the author herself.

All Rights Reserved.

Books by Addison Moore:

New Adult Romance

Celestra Forever After (Celestra Forever After 1)
The Dragon and the Rose (Celestra Forever After 2)
Perfect Love (A Celestra Novella)

Someone to Love (Someone to Love 1)
Someone Like You (Someone to Love 2)
Someone For Me (Someone to Love 3)

3:AM Kisses (3:AM Kisses 1)
Winter Kisses (3:AM Kisses 2)
Sugar Kisses (3:AM Kisses 3)
Whiskey Kisses (3:AM Kisses 4)
Rock Candy Kisses (3:AM Kisses 5)

Beautiful Oblivion (Beautiful Oblivion 1)
Beautiful Illusions (Beautiful Oblivion 2)
The Solitude of Passion
Burning Through Gravity

Young Adult Romance

Ethereal (Celestra Series Book 1)
Tremble (Celestra Series Book 2)

Burn (Celestra Series Book 3)
Wicked (Celestra Series Book 4)
Vex (Celestra Series Book 5)
Expel (Celestra Series Book 6)
Toxic Part One (Celestra Series Book 7)
Toxic Part Two (Celestra Series Book 7.5)
Elysian (Celestra Series Book 8)
Ethereal Knights (Celestra Knights)

Ephemeral (The Countenance Trilogy 1)
Evanescent (The Countenance Trilogy 2)
Entropy (The Countenance Trilogy 3)

Preface

The future wafts in and out of my world like a ghost—like a lumbering beast, begging to be tamed. For so long it sat locked in mystery, surrounding me, fickle as the wind. I see it now for the noose it is, the game that never satisfies, the warrior that always kills.

The past proved to be set in stone, the immovable rock of my existence that cast its shadow into the valley of death. But it is the future's bright light that draws me in, the blinding rays that pull me forward with bionic, magnetic, force. They row me toward my destiny with indescribable power, to a fate questionably determined—washed in the patina of hope.

1

Chloe's Diary

Brody the Nitwit,

You so much as turn another page, and I will let Mom, Dad, the Fosters, and the entire population of Paragon in on the fact that Carly left school in April to give birth to your quadruped spawn in New York, where it will be raised as her brother, by her drunk of a stepmother and questionably employed father. If you haven't scampered already, I'll make sure your son, whom I shall affectionately refer to as the 'bastard', knows what a coward both you and his mother are when the time is right, and trust me, that day will come, ready or not.

-Chloe

I close the covers and clutch the book near my chest. Carly has a baby? Bet Logan doesn't know that.

I rub my finger against the hard lines of the plain powder blue diary—the pages glued shut long ago by Chloe herself. It's like holding dynamite—an entire explosion of secrets—the shards refracting into people's lives.

I pick up the personalized message Chloe left me that slipped out after the first page.

Dear Skyla,

This changes everything.

I must admit, I'm pretty happy with the changes so far. I mean, I don't know Chloe's brother at all, he graduated last year, but I know Carly plenty. Carly was the sole reason I was able to channel my hatred into a perfect funnel of angst and kill a Fem. Just the thought of her with Logan sends a rush of heated adrenaline up my spine.

I hop down out of the butterfly room and head over to bed. I cradle the diary as I get under the covers and pull my pillow up behind me. How am I going to read Chloe's diary—thick as a bible, knowing she wanted Logan as much as I do? I guess my one consolation is the fact she's dead, for now anyway.

I pull back another page, slow and careful like peeling off skin from a sunburn.

June 26,

Am I supposed to say Dear Diary? I think diaries are stupid. I think diaries belong in a thirteen-year-olds bedroom, tucked under the bed, with a balding one-eyed teddy bear keeping watch.

Let the record show, that this diary was forced upon me because my mother thinks it will help to get my feelings down on paper. I believe the word she used was cathartic. I told her I'd write down my genetic code in Latin, burn my soul onto parchment, like the Shroud of Turin, in exchange for never setting foot in Dr. Booth's office again. If I never see that man's face again it will be too soon. Nothing was a bigger waste of time than sitting in his overstuffed chair staring past him out the window for an hour straight.

It wasn't helping, so I just stopped going. My mom even tried dragging me to the car. So Dr. Booth caved a little and suggested the diary. My mother picked it up on the way home from their private pow-wow, and now here you are, rubbing against my bare knees, a place Ellis would give his left testicle to be.

But I'm glad you're here. I'm glad I can finally write down how I feel about things, like the love of my life, the friends that stab me in the back at least once a week, the reason I never forgot the way my hands looked that night last spring covered in blood. That last one still gives me nightmares. But I'm about to unlock all the secrets to this shithole, and I won't have to die like she did. I'll do anything not to die like that.

June 27,

So the day started with Michelle bitching about Lexy again. Honest to God, if she can't figure out how to get a guy of her own, I'm going to feed her to the next rabid Fem that lands in front of me. I tried explaining girl code on the way to the mall where I picked up a hot pink two-piece that glows on my body. It's straight up practically a g-string in the back, but it has this sort of whale tale thing—anyway, Michelle is on hormonal overdrive and I'm about to give her two black eyes to accessorize that horrific mono-kini she stuffed herself into. It makes her ass look twice its size, and her waist cinch abnormally, like you could stick a ring around it. Just looking at her in it, made me feel like I was staring in a fun house mirror. Maybe that's why Michelle can't get Logan away from Lexy? Maybe, it's because she's got friends like me who tell her she looks great in whatever her goofy sense of fashion dictates for her to wear.

I go back and reread Logan's name twice. I'm pretty sure she meant someone else, like maybe Ellis? Although, Lexy with anyone is news to me.

So he was there. Of course he was there—it was at his house. I love going behind the gates, especially to the Oliver's. I love Emma and Barron, Dr. O as I call him. I can't wait until they're my in-laws. They already feel like family since I've known them forever. Sometimes you just know who you're going to be with. For me, it's been the same person my entire life. I've grown up with him, hung out at parties and games, swam in the ocean with him brushing up against my skin. I want nothing more than to live out my days, safe, and loved by no one else but Gage.

2

Let's Dance

Gage needs more time in the morning and asks if I can catch a ride to school with Drake and Brielle. I'd rather be late than have to listen to all the cooing that goes on between the two of them. They're sickeningly in love and seemingly the perfect couple except for the fact Brielle seems to think it's totally acceptable to cheat on him whenever the opportunity presents itself. I guess I should feel a little protective over Drake considering he's my stepbrother, but something inside me can't accept this new family— this new life without my father, so knowing that Brielle routinely sleeps around doesn't seem to faze me much.

Brielle parks in the gravel overflow of the student parking lot and shoos Drake out of the car.

"Skyla and me have some serious girl talk to do." She flutters her hand in the air until he scatters like a pigeon in the direction of the gym.

"What's up?" I ask getting out of her blood red jeep, dirt high up on the sides. "I bet Drake would wash your car if you wanted him to," I say adjusting my backpack, taking in a lungful of dewy morning air. Maybe that simple act of kindness on Drake's part will help Brielle turn the corner and respect him a little bit more.

The evergreens stand tall around the periphery, dark and guarded. This island is rife with secrets. The thick black forest surrounds it like a garrison, the never-ending trail of fog lifts for no one—it attests to the island's truths like a well-worn testimony.

"Yeah, I bet he would." Brielle traces a heart with her finger onto the hood of the jeep, then rubs the muck off on her jeans. "So guess what?"

"What?" For a moment I think of telling her about Chloe's diary, about Carly, and how Chloe obviously mixed up Gage and Logan's names.

"Mr. Dudley offered me a job on his ranch, and I took it."

"Great." My lips twist as I contemplate the unholy arrangement. "So when do you start?" I don't bother asking what she'll be doing. I already know it has nothing to do with horses or any other scam he's running while trying to look perfectly human.

"Saturday, and I want you to come with. I made him promise we could work all the same hours and days. It'll be a total blast."

"Plus, Drake won't catch on about you spending too much time over there all by your lonesome." Marshall, a.k.a. Studley Dudley, takes good looking to a whole new level.

She clicks her tongue and pushes hard into my shoulder as we head to first period. "You're so funny. And did I ever mention, smart?" She shakes out her hair until it falls around her shoulders in dark copper waves.

"Yeah well, I don't want a job at the ranch." In truth, I want to stay as far apart from Marshall as possible. I've been a little weirded out ever since he confessed to wanting to procreate with me.

"Please Skyla." She steps in front of me creating a barrier between me and the entrance to the English building. "Just the once and if you hate it, I'll totally understand, and I won't say another word." She holds her hand in the air, pleading.

Something about Brielle, her bright green eyes, the open look of mischievous behavior written all over her face, everything about her draws me in. Well, everything except for the fact she's a Count, and the Counts want my blood. I should never trust anyone even remotely associated with the Countenance. They're the last people I should be hanging out with, or catching rides to school with, or even time traveling with like I have been with Ellis.

But all those things aside, I'll do anything for Brielle.

"OK, I'll go."

Gage doesn't show up for first. I'm anxious and keep checking my cell to see if he's called or texted, but nothing. I stroll into second without bothering to acknowledge Marshall sitting at the desk impatiently tapping his fingers as if he expects me to be so enthused to be in his presence I should spontaneously break out into cartwheels or something.

"Hey," I slide in behind Ellis. His dark blonde hair is slicked back in soft waves. He looks slightly more lucid than usual, which means he either got up too late to get stoned or he's already burned through his stash.

“What’s up with Gage? You zap him back to the past?”

“Very not funny.” I lean forward to continue our conversation just as the bell rings.

Marshall claps his hands and strides into the center of the room in order to get our attention.

“Homecoming is upon us.” He gives a broad smile in my direction. *I’ve got dibs on the last dance, Skyla.*

Right. Like that’s going to happen. And what’s this ‘upon us’ business? Homecoming is not for like three weeks.

“On behalf of the school, I’ve taken the liberty to reserve the Paragon Beach Resort Hotel. This means no party at Ellis’s this year.” He says the word *party* and *Ellis* as though they were vile. “I’m sure you’re all aware of the tragic events that marred last years event.” He rasps his knuckles against the desk of an unsuspecting student.

Chloe. He’s talking about Chloe, how they, the Counts or Fems, kidnapped her during Ellis’s party, and a horrible feeling washes over me as though I were somehow responsible.

“There is a dress code for this event,” he continues. “Formal wear for ladies and suits for the gentlemen.”

Gage walks in interrupting Marshall’s dissertation on fashion. His dark brows lock in on me as his face breaks into a gentle smile that pushes in his dimples on either side. I clasp his hand briefly as he sits down behind me.

“So, for instance, Mr. Oliver,” Marshall directs his speech toward Gage. “Someone like you, whose wardrobe is comprised of football uniforms, jeans, overalls and Speedos, what have you.” The class explodes in a fit of quiet snickers. “You are going to have to don a dress shirt and slacks, shoes without those spikes you use to gain traction in God’s green earth, and, most definitely, a tie." *Which could double as a noose quite easily*, he adds for my benefit. "And if you've outgrown the one you wore to the family's latest and greatest funeral, perhaps your father would be kind enough to let you strip a corpse for the night." The laughter morphs into gasps. *He could dig up the entire cemetery in search for that perfect designer look.* Marshall winks in my direction. *Lord knows he's an expert at unearthing the dead. And by the way, Skyla, I have the perfect dress for you.*

Like I'm going to let some six thousand year old Sector dress me. Dream on. It's probably some white robe that drops down to my ankles, fully equipped with a golden sash. No thanks. Or better yet, a tube top and Angel wings, probably sans the tube top this time. I bet he'd be thrilled to see me running around half nude.

I pull a face without meaning to.

He folds his arms across his chest, and bullets his gaze right at me.

It's black, short, has chains, and is sexy as hell.

I shrink in my seat a little. I'm still not sure this whole telepathy thing is a one-way street with him.

3

Ride

Since Logan and Gage drove to school together, it means I get to drive home with both Logan and Gage. Even though Gage mentioned it in passing, this information buoyed my mood all day long.

I didn't even respond to Michelle during cheer when she called me a bitch-faced snot for accidentally landing on her walking cast during one of our routines. I could hardly wait for that final bell to ring.

Logan's already leaning against his white truck, waiting. He's got on a faded red sweatshirt and jeans. His hair is wet, combed back in dark blonde strands from either the early onset of dew or showering after practice. I walk up and give him the world's quickest hug. The strong scent of soap clings to him and his skin is polished to perfection—definitely shower.

"Hi," I say. It comes out a little too eager.

"Hi." There's a slight sorrowful edge when he says it. I can't find it in me to appreciate our game of keep away in public. It heightens the intensity of the time we get to spend alone—makes me long to be with him a thousand times more concentrated than the sun. I let that dull ache burn through me all the while we're apart. Let it needle into me until I want to cry out from its smoldering oppression.

Gage pats me on the shoulder as he helps me inside, sandwiched in between the two of them. Suddenly it doesn't feel so great anymore. There's nothing in me that doesn't like Gage any less than Logan, and even though I know this is wrong, strangely I don't feel too horrible about it.

It's the Count's fault I'm sociopathic when it comes to love. If they weren't after me, I could openly be with Logan and would never have even gotten involved with Gage.

"I have a surprise for you." Logan digs into his cheek with a wicked grin. His brow arches into a perfect curve, and he takes my breath away with his beauty.

"Really?" I try not to sound like I'm flirting while Gage sits dutifully by my side. I'm never going to hurt Gage. I swear to myself I won't let this happen. "Is that why you guys were late? What is it?"

"Yes, but it was worth being late. And let's see..." He looks skyward for a second. "It's big and hot, and desperately wants you to have your way with it."

OK, so Logan is not against the idea of flirting in front of Gage. I face forward trying to ignore him, watching the scenery bleed by.

Gage places his hand over my thigh and shakes it as if letting me know it's not a big deal.

"Please take your hand off her," Logan says with a restrained anger, his eyes never leaving the road.

We drive another five minutes to the bowling alley.

Gage doesn't listen.

"OK, close your eyes." Logan's enthusiasm has returned. He takes me by the hand and leads me through the parking lot. I keep my lids cracked so I don't feel like I'm about to fall off a cliff with each step and let him take me around the building.

"Open," he whispers.

The air is frosted with a milky layer of fog, coupled with the fact I'm creating a steady stream of smoke from my nostrils with each breath of anticipation.

"Where is it?" There's nothing but a dumpster back here, a fractured bucket rolling around in the dirt, and some old car.

"This is it." He glides into a huge grin, pulling me toward a dilapidated piece of junk. "Surprise." He gives my shoulders a squeeze as he leans in and kisses me just above the ear.

"Surprise?" It's a dull faded orange and as old as like Tad and my Mom combined. Wow, Logan's lousy at surprises. I totally won't hold it against him though. "What are you going to do with it? And why would I be surprised to see it?" Maybe it's a monument, and it belongs in a museum somewhere? Obviously it must have some historic value that I'm not aware of.

"It's for you. An early birthday present." He wraps his arm around my waist.

"Oh no—that's OK, you don't have to do this. I don't even have my license." Dear God, just being seen in that thing could socially isolate me. Maybe that's the point?

"Well, you'll get it eventually." There's a mixture of hurt and hope in his eyes. "I can teach you. Besides, with a car of your own, you won't need to rely on Gage to take you everywhere." He leans in almost pleading.

"Oh, I get it." It's the keep-away-from-Gage-mobile. "I'm not sure," I say, opening the door. It's heavy—feels solid, not all light and plastic like new cars. It smells like cigarettes and bunch of illegal stuff I'm not even aware of. Who knows what people have done in this car—it was probably known as the sex-mobile.

I back up a notch.

"I sort of envisioned my first car as something..." I scratch at the back of my head searching for answers.

"Something more this century?" Gage interjects as he walks around the vehicle. "Nice ride, but it's not you Skyla. And if you're not ready to drive, don't let this idiot bully you into doing something you don't want."

I'm not so sure we're talking about cars and driving anymore, and, for sure, I've never heard Gage refer to Logan as an idiot before.

I look from Logan to Gage. There's so much anger locked up in their eyes, so much newfound hate filling the gap between them. I feel horrible knowing it's all because of me.

"So where did it come from?" I'm almost afraid to ask. Judging by the rust spots around the wheel well, it's safe to say it could have been abandoned for years somewhere on the island.

"It was my dad's," Logan says rubbing the top of the car as though it were flesh.

"This belonged to your dad?" I step forward and pull him back gently by the shoulder. My insides melt at the thought he wants to give me something so special.

He pinches a smile and nods with glimmering eyes.

"I love it." I pull him in. "Can I paint it pink?"

"No." Both Logan and Gage answer in unison.

At least they agree on something.

4

Oh Baby

We leave Logan at the bowling alley and Gage drives me home. By the time we slide in at the bottom of my driveway, I'm pretty psyched about having my own set of wheels. Gage said it's a 1966 Mustang with original paint and body, so I guess that was his nice way of letting me know why it wouldn't really be a good idea for me to paint it pink or even reupholster the inside to that cool patent purple with glitter that my bicycle seat used to have. Evidently after Logan's father died, it sat around collecting dust in the Oliver's side yard, and Logan is more than happy to gift it to me. That, and it cuts down on my interaction time with Gage, which I know for a fact I don't want to do.

Gage hops around and helps me out of his truck. My knee is still pissed off about that fall I took a few days ago out of a two story window trying to get Ellis and Gage back into the right year. That whole time travel thing has definitely bit me in the ass, knee, and quite a few other places—I'm not so hot on cruising around the time continuum anymore.

Gage takes my backpack and secures it over his shoulder. He tilts his head into me, his features lost in shadows. It's only five-thirty and already it's pitch black outside. I love autumn nights on Paragon. A dense layer of fog lies across the island like a thick blanket of sorrow. I love to let my emotions bleed into the weather here. It leaves room in my heart for the joy of having someone as spectacular as Gage around.

He wraps his arms around my waist and rubs his cheek softly against mine. I want to tell him to stop, not to get so close, but I can't find the words or actions to go along with that rationale.

He brushes along my face until his lips find mine and offers a deep, luxurious kiss. My stomach bottoms out over and over until he gently pulls away.

I want to say it's wrong, but my tongue is tied up in knots at the moment.

"I know," he whispers. "I'm going to talk to Logan and tell him how I feel."

"I think he's got a pretty good idea." This is going to end up in a pile of crap. I can feel it.

"I need to do it." He chews the inside of his cheek and gets lost staring into the forest behind me. His black hair blends into the shadows. The deep blue of his eyes, glow in the night like luminaries. "I'm not trying to put you in any kind of weird position, but I need for Logan to hear what I've got to say."

"OK." I tighten my arms around him and sigh into his chest.

He leans in and offers me another kiss, slow at first as though he were asking permission this time, waiting for me to shove him away, tell him it isn't right. Then comes the strength, the wave—an entire ocean of kisses, a circle that never ends, a seamless loop that could easily slide us across eternity.

Something's got to give. I already know this.

The house glows an eerie orange. I race inside and toss my backpack on the floor. Everyone is seated at the dining room table, which is suspiciously complete with pressed linens, my mother's wedding china from her marriage to my father, and my grandmother's good silverware—never a good sign.

"Just in time for dinner!" My mother takes me by the shoulders and guides me to an empty seat at the end of the table.

"What's going on?" I examine the gourmet offerings. Looks great. "You make this?" I marvel at the Mexican food buffet sprawled before us.

"I went downtown to that cute restaurant we went to for Melissa's birthday and picked it up." She scoops some rice onto my plate before taking a seat.

It's quiet as we eat. The strange gaps of silence are filled in with the clank of our forks butting up against the dishes, the ice sloshing around in our glasses. I look over at Drake, and he shrugs as though he suspects something as well.

"Let's get to this, shall we?" Tad wipes his face while addressing my mother. His hair is fluffed out a good three inches longer than usual, and he's starting to look a bit more portly than when he first married Mom six months ago. I still don't see what drew my mother in. It's like he's got her under some sort of a spell. Now that I know I'm an angel from the Celestra faction, nothing seems outside of the realm of possibility.

"First, huge announcement," Mom taps her hands on the table doing her version of a budding drum roll. "Mia has decided to legally change her last name to Landon." She annunciates her point with an open-mouth smile.

"What?" I can't believe this. "You can't change your last name," I say examining her up and down. Mia has slowly morphed into the mirror image of me with wavy blond hair, grey eyes as clear as velum.

"Yes I can." She picks up a glass of water and starts chugging without elaborating.

"No, you can't." I leave off the part about our last name being the final connection to our deceased father. "You're a Messenger."

"And soon-to-be Landon." She shoots over a curt look. "Look, it's not a big deal, I'm tired of explaining to everyone why Melissa and me have different last names, and this way we can be real sisters. It's not like I'm keeping it forever, I'll change it again when I'm married. Relax, Skyla." She sets her glass back on the table hard. "You make a big deal out of everything," she adds, "drama queen."

"What?" I'm stupefied by this.

"Enough you two," my mother scolds, clapping her hands together once.

I haven't argued with Mia since before Tad and my mother started dating. It's like having Melissa in her life demoted me to a distant family member you don't really care about and pretty much ignore. I rather like that status.

"Next big announcement." My mother lets a lazy grin linger as she gazes over at Tad like a lovesick teenager. "You wanna?"

"No you." He motions.

They banter back and forth until Drake knocks his knife up against the rim of his glass.

"OK," my mother starts. "Your father and I have decided to conceive a child."

"You're going to have a kid?" Drake's face explodes with shock.

"Yes." She giggles into Tad like a schoolgirl. "What better way to bring this family together in a circle of unity than the two of us having a child together?"

"So when are you having the baby?" Mia is clearly overjoyed with the idea.

"Oh Honey, we're not having the baby yet, we're in the planning stages. As soon as it happens we'll let you know."

"So you're telling us," Drake cuts a look over to me briefly before continuing, "you'll be actively participating in the necessary relations in order to procure an offspring." Drake's features disintegrate into a clear look of disgust.

"Yes." My mother beams as she takes Tad's hand up in the air and waves it victoriously.

Oh gross.

"I'll have a brief ovulation window each month, and—"

I start hitting the air brakes with my hands.

"I'm going to go vomit now, thanks for dinner," I say, speeding down the hallway faster than my mother can react. Truth is, I wanted to bolt after Mia's big news, and now that my mom and Tad are trying to have a baby, it's sort of the last nail in the coffin of our old family—the one we had with my dad. I'd rather be alone in my room than celebrating, or pretending to smile while we discuss ovulation windows.

Drake comes up alongside me as we bolt up the stairs.

"You hear them rocking, don't come a knocking," he ditches into his room and shuts the door.

"Thanks for the visual," I shout as I pass his room.

5

Off with Her Head

I wake up to a dull, silent Saturday. In a few hours I'll be at Marshall's with Brielle. The only bright spot in my day, will be going over to the bowling alley afterwards to visit Logan and Gage, although if Gage had his little talk with Logan that might not prove to be such a bright spot after all.

I roll over in bed and pluck Chloe's diary from under the mattress. I must have read the last entry wrong. How could Gage be the love of her life when she was so into Logan? *Sleeping* with Logan?

I open it up again—nope still says Gage. I turn the page.

Days and days of boring hell. And this is something everyone was so worried about me reading?

July 4th,

The fireworks were beyond awesome! There was a bonfire tonight out by East so naturally there were too many people clustered in one tiny space. I can't wait to get off this island. As soon as I hit 18, I'm taking a boat to the mainland and never coming back.

So Lexy and Michelle got in a near fistfight over Logan—so stupid. I had to threaten Michelle to keep her claws to herself. I swear that girl is insane. I'm going to have to tell Lex I can't help her anymore. I know I had an "arrangement with her", that I'd keep Michelle as far away forever, but oh well. It's not like she delivered fully on her end of the deal. I'm still having HUGE problems with the brat pack.

I'm going to beg Gage for help. His dad's way more active with the faction meetings. My parents could give a shit less if I end up in a body bag dumped off at the side of the road. Anyway, didn't kiss Gage like I planned. Going over to his house tomorrow, see how it goes. Wish me better luck tomorrow!

With less than ten minutes to meet Brielle downstairs, I shut the book and hit the shower. The thought of Chloe kissing Gage turns my stomach. It's bad enough she was with Logan.

Before we head to Marshall's, I ask Brielle to drive me over to the mortuary where I give another pint of blood for project resurrect Chloe. It seemed like a good idea at the time, bringing Chloe back to throw her in Marshall's tank to see if he'll bite, but something about the whole thing is starting to make me uneasy. By the time we pull into Mr. Studley's palatial estate, I'm feeling completely drained and weak.

The fresh morning air cuts sharp into my lungs. It's heavily scented with the sweet smell of moist earth, the juniper bushes with their fragrant star shaped flowers expelling their sweetness.

We circle around back to the barn where Marshall instructs Brielle on how to shovel through hay and filter out all the horse crap. He pulls a giant waste bin between the stalls and lets her know there's another one out back when that one gets full.

"Looks like fun." I give a dry smile in her direction. It was her big idea to work here. She could have easily gotten a job at the bowling alley. I'm sure Logan would have been thrilled to have her—but no.

"And you, Ms. Messenger." His eyes twinkle when he says my name—for a brief moment I remember the dark reality that I'll soon be the only remaining Ms. Messenger in our leg of the family. "Follow me."

Marshall's not hard to follow anywhere. He's tall, impossibly gorgeous, and carries himself with an unreasonable amount of self-confidence that adds to his majestic flair.

He leads me out of the barn and over to the house. Marshall's home looks a little more like a bachelor pad today than during any of my previous visits, what with the discarded pizza boxes stacked on top of one another creating an unsteady tower, endless empty grocery bags floating around, and an assortment of drinks from fast food places springing up all over.

"You want me to clean the pigpen?" I'm not really offering. "Sorry, but I'm just here to support Brielle. I think a small part of her is actually afraid to be alone with you," I say, making my way into the den and flipping on the TV.

"Nonsense. You're here because you miss our alone time." He pins me against the wall and gives a quick peck behind my ear. An intense rush of pleasure only Marshall is capable of dispensing rushes through me.

"No, really I don't." I circle around just outside of his grasp.

"You haven't let me woo you yet."

"I'm not into wooing. Need I remind you I have a boyfriend? More than one—I've caught my limit."

Marshall moves forward with lightning precision and wraps his arms around my waist. Before I can react, I catch a blur racing past the window with my peripheral vision.

Carefully, I remove his hands from my hips. It feels so amazing to touch him—a relaxing, fibrillating sensation.

"Stop. Brielle's going to see," I hiss.

"Very well." He flattens his palms in the air. "But I'm going to win. You'll be spending time with me. I won't take no for an answer. Be sure to pencil me in for the downtime between the dolts. It'll be my pleasure to show up the both of them. I'm going to expose you to something so spectacular that they wouldn't be able to give you in twelve lifetimes." He presses into me an intense smoldering stare.

A loud clanging noise erupts outside, startling the both of us to attention.

"I didn't think she could hurt anything," he says, craning his neck in the direction of the barn. "Looks like Brielle is quite capable of defying the odds."

Marshall heads out toward the back.

She's probably writhing around on the floor due to a self-inflicted pitchfork injury. I know for a fact she had no intention of filling waste bins with horse crap while she was here.

Outside the front window I see a figure move into the bushes.

What the...

I head over to the front door and step outside. It's icy out today. A nasty wind is unleashing its fury on Paragon, ushering in a cover of storm clouds that have been lingering over the island for hours—dark clouds spreading like a slow malignant tumor.

"Brielle?" I ask, taking a cautious step out onto the porch. I crush a pile of fat maple leaves—they disintegrate under my feet in a series of dry satisfying crackles. The wind whips around my ankles as though it were alive, as though it were frantically trying to warn me of whatever it is I sense out here.

"Brielle?" I try and sing her name out as though I wasn't afraid of whatever that thing was ducking into the bushes, as though there were no possibility it could have been a Fem, or—

A hand plasters itself up over my mouth, muffling my cries as I'm knocked backward. The cold feel of metal pressing against my neck, ignites a whole new level of panic in me. I try to pluck it off me, and my finger slips through something sharp. I bring it up over my eyes to see the tip of my finger covered in blood. Then, the very distinct feeling of a clean slash runs from ear to ear.

Crap!

My flesh burns as I try to process what the hell just happened. I bite down hard on the hand slipping inside my mouth.

I'm lifted and pushed. A hard shove lands me face down in Marshall's entry and the door slams shut behind me.

I let out a guttural groan in lieu of a scream. My head spins with panic and a strong jolt of nausea rolls through me.

My blood sprays out like a violent splat of paint against the white marble floor.

I'm going to die.

I try to crawl up on all fours, but my hands slide out from under me, slipping in the never-ending torrent of red streaming from my throat.

Can't breathe.

Oh crap.

6

Breathing Lessons

Stark white walls are littered with my crimson fingerprints. A trail of thick red gloss runs all over my clothes, my hair—blurring my vision. I swing violently at the vases covering the sofa table, listen to them smash as they hit the floor in order to get Marshall's attention. The tiniest breath escapes me, igniting a sizzle of electric pain in my throat. I thrash wildly, knocking over a bench in the entry, plucking the mirror off the wall and smashing it to pieces against the grand piano. Only seconds remain before blacking out becomes a real possibility.

The world spins, the room turns a filtered shade of grey. From the back window I can see Marshall examining Brielle's hand and I pound erratically against the glass. His head turns sharply in my direction as he begins to sprint back over to the house. A look of intense worry crosses his face. The hard line of his jaw defines itself as he exerts himself to get to me. Suddenly it feels safe to melt into a black unconsciousness.

"Skyla!" He shouts my name loud as a gunshot, louder than any human voice is capable of, I'm sure.

I feel him scoop me up off the rug and jostle me across the room—many rooms.

"Stay with me!" He commands.

Brielle screams from somewhere in the distance.

"Call Dr. Oliver," he booms over to her.

"It's superficial. You'll be fine," he snaps as though he were angry.

The back of my head clunks down abruptly on a hard surface. My eyes struggle to briefly analyze the surroundings—kitchen counter—island to be exact.

Can't breathe. Shit. Shit. Shit.

I flex my hand just above my throat wildly. I sit up, and hit my head on a pot dangling from above.

"Relax," he barks, throwing down the copper pans that hang from the ceiling in a clanging fit of frustration.

The white-hot sting of the incision dances all the way across my neck as I try to take a breath. I clutch up at his chest and wrench his shirt in knots to get my point across.

"You can't breathe." It comes out calm. He reaches over me and snatches up something metallic, then picks up a plastic cup the size of a small bucket with a fat blue straw sticking out of it. "I'm going to cut you now." He pins my arms down with one hand and fondles my neck just below where I was sliced. "Easy."

I try to fight him, but it's like having a tractor lay over you. Lucky for the both of us he feels good to the touch. His soothing vibrations radiate through me and I end up clutching onto him rather than letting go.

A quick stab of pain flashes through me, forcing me to open my eyes.

He plunges the knife into my throat one more time and gives a quick smile of relief.

"There." He removes the blade and plucks the cobalt straw from out of the drink. A trail of brown liquid dispenses before he injects the straw into my neck. "Breathe, Skyla," he demands. "Right now, breathe."

I take in a breath—a ragged, feeble, interrupted breath, but a breath nonetheless full of sweet, sweet air. I clutch at his shirt again, and my lips curve in approval.

"Oh my, God!" Brielle screams so loud that the entire kitchen vibrates with her shrill cry.

"This isn't for you, leave the room," he says with relaxed authority.

Gage appears in the kitchen.

"Crap!" He stumbles backward. His face bleaches white as paper. I flail my bloodied hand out to grasp him. I want Gage to hold me, tell me everything is going to be alright as I lay here breathing through a fat, blue, straw, sticking erect from the center of my neck.

He steadies himself against the counter before turning and retching into the sink. A river of brown vomit spurts out of him causing me to dart my eyes back toward Marshall.

Dr. Oliver and Logan burst into the room. Dr. Oliver with his warm apathetic smile, Logan with his eyes rounded out in horror.

Logan comes up alongside of me and gently wipes the hair off my forehead.

"It's going to be OK," he whispers directly into my ear. I close my eyes briefly and let his voice wash over me.

"It looked superficial, and the girls insisted I call you," Marshall explains. "Brielle mentioned Skyla hates hospitals."

I look over at him, standing there with his hands waving through the air as though it were true. I had never told Marshall anything about hating hospitals before, had I?

"How's your breathing?" Dr. Oliver twitches a flashlight over my eyes.

I try to nod, but can't bear the pain.

Logan clasps his hand over mine. *Do you want to go to the hospital?*

Thank God for Logan. I can hear anyone telepathically if I touch them, but he's the only one who can hear me speak in return.

Not if I don't have to.

"She says no."

I need Marshall to touch me.

Logan compresses his lips. "Mr. Dudley, I think maybe it would help if you held her other hand." He increases his grip as he says it.

"Done." Marshall glides over with pride and picks up my injured finger. "This too." He holds it out for everyone to see.

"Good Lord, Skyla. What the hell happened?" Dr. Oliver plucks bottles of ointment, gloves, and an array of tools from out of his giant black bag of tricks.

You can't let on that you know Marshall's a Sector, I say to Logan in a mild panic. *That will drag this day into a whole other direction for me.*

Marshall threatened to capture me if I told. Of course I told, but Marshall's the last person who should be in on that secret.

I won't say a word. Logan looks to his uncle. "No use in asking her questions. You're only going to frustrate her." He returns his attention back to me. "I'll get you something to write on later."

Marshall squeezes my hand ever so slightly.

Fantastic, Marshall marvels. *Logan thinks that I don't know he's a Celestra. Go ahead and converse with him all you want. I'll play dumb.*

I squint over at him. It hurts to move even a micro millimeter. Not even Marshall's good vibrations are enough to quell this dull burning pain.

"I don't have the proper filament. All I have is black and it's going to stick out like a sore thumb against your ivory skin," Dr. Oliver says adjusting a spool of thread.

I look up in time to see a fat silver needle catch the light.

Oh God. A shiver runs through me and suddenly I have the urge to bolt.

He threads it with what looks like the thickest black chord known to man—a rope.

"I'm going to stitch you up now," Dr. Oliver announces.

That's what I was afraid of.

7

Out and About

Good thing Halloween is coming up.

I admire myself in the mirror while convalescing on the Oliver's couch. A row of uneven x's scissor across my neck in a very distinct Frankenstein-like fashion.

Dr. Oliver left to take Brielle home—Brielle who herself couldn't breathe due to the trauma. Speaking of breathing, Dr. Oliver removed the straw from my neck and coaxed me into taking slow deep breaths on my own. After I stopped inhaling my own blood and choking, everything was fine—everything but my voice.

I feel like I've run a marathon. I squeeze Logan's hand.

"You lost a ton of blood."

Gage sits next to me. "I want to talk to her too." He picks up my other hand and gives a weak smile.

"What's that Skyla?" Logan exaggerates his tone. "You don't want to speak to Gage? You wish he would disappear forever?" A sarcastic smile slides up the side of his cheek.

"Very funny," Gage shakes his head over at him, before directing his attention back to me. *Don't listen to him he's an idiot.*

"I can hear you, too." Logan shoots daggers at Gage. "See?" He holds up my hand. "We're all connected."

Enough. I glare at the two of them momentarily. *Who the hell slit my throat?*

"Skyla wants to know what the hell you're still doing here." Logan restrains a wicked grin.

Gage shakes his head over at him. *I know you're not thinking those things*. There's a gentleness in his eyes and it warms me. *I'm gonna run up and take a quick shower. I'll be right back. I don't want Logan upsetting you anymore than he has*. He glares over at him before heading upstairs.

"She says, she's glad you're gone," he shouts up after him.

You're not funny, I say.

Logan's features smooth out. He relaxes into a calm, measured nod. *I apologize*.

So did Gage have a certain conversation with you? I have an inkling.

Logan glances around with a heavy gaze.

I'm sorry I ever suggested he be with you. Does that make me selfish? There's a genuine sadness in his eyes.

Why would that make you selfish? You did it to protect me. I lean into his shoulder. It feels good to be here, safe at the Oliver's.

He picks up my hand and kisses my bandaged finger. *And now look at you*.

Did you give the book back to Ellis? I'm dying to know what names graced the pages of that bloated roll call of Counts.

He nods. *Walked it across the street that next morning*.

So I guess now we know who to slaughter. I give a weak playful smile.

We're not killing. The goal is not to kill, he counters.

Reality check. I point up to my throat. *I will kill whoever or whatever I have to, not to breathe through a straw like that again. And by the way, I think they have a lot worse planned for me. I'll kill them by the herd if I have to—for you and for me.*

And what about for us? His features soften. *Am I losing you?*

My mouth falls open at the thought. Before I can formulate anything coherent to say, he adds, *Well, then,* his amber eyes light up like flames. *I'll have to get you back.*

Logan's Aunt Emma helps me wash off the blood that's already rusted onto my body. She loans me a pink and red scarf, carefully wrapping it around my neck just before Gage drives me home.

This can't go well. My Mom and Tad are going to freak if they see what's under this scarf.

I shoot Gage a look of discontent as we head through the front door.

"Here he is," Tad balks as he passes us on the way upstairs. "Someone warn the refrigerator."

Only once has he ever seen Gage get anything from the fridge, and on that day it was a water bottle. *Water*. Tad's so cheap he can't share water.

My mother rushes up after him.

"Hey you two." She speeds past us in a tizzy.

"You mind if we study up in Skyla's room?" Gage calls after her.

I can't believe how brazen he is. Of course she's going to mind, she—

"Nope. I trust you." And with that, she's out of sight.

My father would have answered with the blast of a shotgun.

Gage helps me upstairs and I briskly shut and lock my door in the event my mother's sanity decides to restore itself.

I grab a notepad and a pen and make myself comfy on the bed with Gage slouching down next to me.

They're going to rut. I spell out.

"Nice." He folds his hands. "Should we?"

No.

He shakes his head slightly while brushing his thumb up against my cheek. "I know." He presses his lips together. "I don't want you to be alone right now."

I'm glad you're here. Which reminds me, this was once Chloe's bedroom and the fact she oddly named Gage as the love of her life still confuses the hell out of me. **You ever kiss Chloe?** I scrawl across the page.

He squints in to read it as though it were written in some foreign language.

"Nope." His cheeks turn pink as he answers.

I drop the pen and take up his hand, press it against my lips. There's definitely something developing here, a progression, something linear pulling me toward Gage. I wish I didn't feel it. I wish I didn't make Logan feel like he had to do something to win me back because he still has me so completely, and I wonder how it could be that my heart has found itself strangely settled in two places at once.

Gage penetrates me with those crystalline blue eyes. He wishes he could read my thoughts as easily as Logan. But it's my face that says it all. He leans in and presses a soft kiss against my forehead. I think he already knows my heart is lying in two very distinct pieces.

8

Read On

I plan on spending all of Sunday in bed losing myself in Chloe's diary. With my newfound sore throat, Mom pretty much agreed I should stay under the covers and simultaneously ignored me all morning. Instead of plying me with hot tea and soup, like old Mom would have done, she's busy holing up in her room coupling with Tad like some baby hungry cougar.

July 5th,

This is going to be tougher than I thought. It's like Gage repels from me the minute I stand beside him. It's really starting to irritate me, so I let Ellis slobber all over me in order to fill him with regret.

I took Ellis on a light drive after. Ellis is like a good little pet, always around when I need him. Too bad I'm not into Ellis. That would make life so much easier in a way, but then, it would suck the fun out of everything too.

I don't know. I haven't really ever had my feelings reciprocated. It's usually me using somebody or somebody using me. I guess you could say I'm unlucky in love. It sort of seems to be this scary theme in my life.

Speaking of scary, I told Lexy I can't deal with Michelle anymore. You would have thought I pushed her in a pool of piranhas the way she freaked out. It's not like losing Logan is going to restructure the landscape of her world. She was never in his league to begin with. So, I told her he was just being nice by hanging out with her. I told her he probably felt sorry for her and couldn't figure out how to ditch her so he just went with it. That's when she slapped me. Yes. Let the record show, Lexy Bakova sealed her own fate by whacking me with an open hand in the Oliver's living room right in front of Gage.

Of course I didn't retaliate. I have something far more interesting in mind.

After the dust settled, Michelle started to arm wrestle with Logan in the backyard, which by the way evolved to include their entire half clothed bodies. Leave it to Michelle to do something like that right in front of Lex.

I took Lexy and left. I told her I felt really bad and would do anything to restore our "friendship". So of course she suggested I help her get Logan back.

You should have seen her, all red with snot dripping down her face, complete with heartbroken tears! I wish I had taken a picture. I'd love to throw darts through her snot riddled face any day, or better yet plaster it all over the walls at West. Anyway, she landed right where I wanted her. I made her promise she'd teach me how to bind Fems without lifting a finger. And she pinky swore she'd do it.

I can't believe Lexy knows about Fems—about *binding* Fems, which I didn't even know was possible. That must mean Lexy is one of them—us, whatever. What if she's Celestra like Chloe and me, like Logan? Maybe that's what attracted her to Logan?

July 6th,
Brushed my teeth.

July 7th,
Found Ellis and some girl from East in a closet at his party tonight. It actually bothered me to see him with someone else. Isn't that weird? I totally thought I didn't care about him. Funny how life surprises you that way. I told him, if he didn't hook up with her, I'd have a treat for him later. He totally thought it was light driving, which I think is quickly becoming one of his many addictions. Anyway, I gave him instructions on how to come through the room in my attic and let himself into my bedroom. I padlocked the door like a Fem was on the other side and let him have his way with me for hours.

I still can't believe I did it. It feels strange knowing I'll never get something like that back, but then again it's over and I don't have to think about it. Plus, it was with Ellis Stoner Harrison, which I don't think really counts. Get it? He's a Count? He's really just a twerp.

July 8th,
Totally regret letting Ellis violate my body that way. At the beach today, he panted by my side all day long. When I showed up at Devil's Peak to hang out, he brought me flowers! It made me want to jump off the cliff.

Obviously sleeping with Ellis has sent the wrong message. Plus, it depressed the hell out of me because no matter how hard I pretended—he didn't magically morph into Gage. Now I'm probably going to have some Count slash

Celestra lovechild because I was too freaking stupid to use protection!!! I swear, I never thought I'd be as stupid as Carly baby-mama-Foster.

So I spent the rest of the night blubbering in a corner to Emily. Honestly, she's like my only one true friend.

July 28th,

OK, so I've let Ellis in a bunch more times. After I got my period and stopped jumping up and down like an idiot who just won some sort of ovulation lottery, I decided that being with Ellis could happen again so long as he brought the proper gear.

Em hacked off all her long black hair today! She totally looks like a guy now, but it's sort of my fault because I encouraged her to do it. That's what friends are for, right?

Anyway. On the Gage front, I went over to hang out tonight. Ellis went somewhere with his family and plus Lexy is out of town, so Michelle practically begged me.

We watched a movie, and after I went outside to hang out by the pool with Gage. We just dipped our feet in the water and sat next to each other real quiet. It was nice. I still wish it were Gage coming down through my attic.

August 2nd,

Ms. Richards knows. Oh freaking shit! I want to strangle Lexy and her big, fat, stupid, mouth!

So I get to sixth period and she goes all psych teacher on me and starts asking about my lineage and shit. Who the heck does Lexy think she is letting people in on our secret? Anyway, Ms. Richards invited me over to her house to check something out that belonged to her great, great, grandmother, like I'm some sort of extra terrestrial expert all of a sudden. The strangest part is that Ms. Richards believed everything Lexy told her. Isn't that weird? Wouldn't a normal person just brush off something like that as though it were coming from a whack job? I don't get it. I really don't.

I'm tired, and it's beyond late, but it's too addicting to stop, so I read through a couple more before turning out the lights. But this is the one that lingers in my mind long after I go to sleep.

August 5th,

So I begged Lexy and Em to come with me to Ms. Richards house, but they both bailed. Lucky for me we just sat on her porch. She gave me sweet tea and had me look through some old family pictures. She mentioned something about stuff in the safe, but thankfully it was blocked with a bunch of crap, so she couldn't get to it.

Anyway, her great, great, grandmother was a freaky looking version of Ms. Richards, but I swear I've seen her somewhere before. Long, red, crazy hair that looked like it was made from copper wires. I bet they put her in the nut house just for looking so bizarre.

In one picture, it was like she was looking straight through me, like she was actually alive and looking at me with her scary bulging eyes. Of course I asked if I could take one of the pictures home, but she said no. So I when she got up to go inside for more tea, I snaked one. Ms. Richards said she was told never to say her great, great grandmother's name. The one I took was marked in chicken scratch on the back. So, of course I said the name like ten times—too funny.

I carefully peel back the next page and a picture slides out. It's of a woman standing in an open field with a familiar wild shag of hair and a solemn, haunting expression on her face. I turn it over and see scrawled in rickety handwriting the name—Ezrina.

9

Friday Night Fight

I'm getting more mileage than I ever imagined from getting my throat slit. On Friday, Gage actually lets me brush my leg up against his and cheat on my Algebra Two test. He was staunchly against the idea just a few weeks ago. You would have thought I had asked him to turn his dog into hamburger, but not this time.

Skyla.

I look up. It's Marshall's voice in the background while Gage is busy processing number nine out of twenty on the chapter test.

I tilt my head at him.

I see you touching Gage. He raises his brows completely unamused. *I'm going to let you slide, but just this once.* He presses his finger to his lips. *I had to hire a cleaning crew to scrub down the house after the near massacre you incurred. I'm glad to see you're feeling better.* He gives a short-lived smile. *Michelle has been asking a whole slew of questions about you as of late.*

Me? I give a puzzled look.

Why don't you meet me here at four-thirty? He gives a sly grin. *It would be my pleasure to go over her concerns with you.*

No, I mouth over at him.

Suit yourself. Don't coming running to me when you receive your next mortal infliction. He turns toward the blackboard.

Next mortal infliction?

Consider yourself warned.

Friday night, Ms. Richards is well aware of my severely sore throat, so she lets me cheer minus the actual cheering, while wearing a white fuzzy scarf that matches my uniform. I don't dare even think of Ezrina when I'm around Ms. Richards. I'm afraid to tell anybody what I read—afraid I might accidentally call her to me with that stupid picture and she might chop off my other arm or my head. Oh my, God, what if it was Ezrina who slit my throat? What if just picking up Chloe's diary was enough to call her? Crap!

The crowd starts to boo. Everyone rises to their feet. Something is happening on the field, but I can't tell what.

"They're brawling!" Brielle shouts, clapping her hands like this is great news.

The air is smoky, filled with the perpetual dense fog that settles over the island night after night. I see bodies streaming in a steady pile, then slowly they get plucked off of one another until just two are left, both in royal blue and white uniforms—number 12 and 44. Logan and Gage.

I cup my hand up over my mouth.

The coach kicks them both about a dozen times before they roll apart and get up.

They cut death rays at one another before walking in opposite directions. I'm pretty sure this has nothing to with the visiting team, the ball, or the game in general. I feel pretty crappy about the whole thing. I'm going to have to figure out a way to put an end to this, but how?

A light drizzle starts in, and we finish the game, frosted with microscopic droplets of water.

We stand in line formation waiting to high-five the team as they run on by. Logan comes first with his lip cut and bloodied. *I need to see you*, he says as we connect. His eyes are filled with sorrow and a part of me wants to run off with him right now.

Gage comes up dead last with nothing to show for the fight, at least not on his face.

"Everyone is hanging out at the falls tonight. Wanna go?" He looks hopeful.

"Falls?" It comes out a little louder than a whisper. I've been trying to use my voice all week like Dr. Oliver instructed. Right after, he broke the news the reason I wasn't healing so well was because I've offed so much blood between the donations for Chloe and having my throat slit. "Is Logan going?"

His eyes dip down with a brief look of disappointment.

My heart sinks at the thought of hurting Gage with my words. I was only asking because Logan mentioned he wanted to see me.

"Of course I'll go."

"Great." He starts running backward toward the gym. "You'll need a bathing suit." He shrugs. "Or not."

Right, like I'm going to skinny dip with all the kids on Paragon.

So technically, I'm wearing my ridiculous white fuzzy scarf, so I'm not really skinny dipping. Plus, it's like pitch black out, sans the full moon, and plus...oh crap, I'm skinny dipping with all the kids on Paragon.

The reality hits me that I actually let Brielle talk me into stripping down and jumping in without any clothes in order to prove that I didn't care what people thought of my body—a demonstration of sheer stupidity on my part. Thank God, Gage and the guys are all jumping off the cliff side, way up the hill, screaming like idiots, or I never would have agreed to it.

"I'm getting out." My teeth chatter in rhythm. My skin is numb from the shock of icy water. You'd think, by the way the rest of the girls lounge around and laugh, that we were sitting in a hot tub.

"Relax. Besides, it's dark out there. Someone might be waiting to hack your head off." She lets out a high-pitched laugh.

"Right, that's not funny." I don't know how she can sit there and joke about it, when she's the one who swore she would never be able to look at a straw the same way again.

Brielle seems unfazed by the sting of the lake. She dips down under the water line and reemerges with her hair washed back, spitting a perfect stream into my face.

"I swear, Skyla, you take life so seriously. For all you know, you might be swimming with the person who did it." She pushes off the rocks and strokes effortlessly into the distance.

What the hell was that supposed to mean? I watch as she shifts onto her back exposing her bare chest. The moonlight casts its glossy high beam over her pale naked body. Brielle has no shame, no remorse for cheating on Drake, *and* she's a Count. Maybe I am swimming with the one who did it?

I back out of the water slowly and head into a thicket of weeds that comes up to my waist. I watch as Kate bumps into Brielle in the middle of the water, and they start to drown each other while laughing. A small part of me wants to warn Kate, tell her Brielle is capable of anything.

The sound of someone clearing their throat startles me to attention, and I spin around creating an x across my chest with my arms.

Logan!

A slow spreading wicked grin appears on his face. He plucks a hand from his pocket and points over at me.

I look down briefly.

Crap! I've managed to flex my arms expertly over my chest to cover up, well— nothing.

He takes off his shirt and tosses it over just shy of where I'm standing.

I snatch it off the ground quick as thief. I can feel the weight of his stare as I pull it on.

"I think that body should be illegal in all 50 states," he says it in a low husky growl.

"Was that an insult?" I slip into my cheer shorts at super sonic speed.

"Why don't we go into the woods, and you can figure it out." There's something hauntingly seductive about Logan under this full squatting moon—something in his eyes, that suggests there are still so many more layers to this person than I could ever imagine.

I circle his waist and rub his bare stomach with my hand—hitch my thumb in through the belt loop of his jeans.

So many more layers, I plan on removing.

10

Alone

Logan rubs his hand up and down over my arm as we make our way into the wall of pine trees just beyond the border of the lake. I remember coming here with him in the summer, back when we were free to be together out in the open—at least we thought.

The forest is heavily scented. The pines release their oils into the night air creating a dramatic, sweet, woodsy scent that awakens your memory, reminds you of all the things you cherish.

Logan's T-shirt and my cheer shorts cling to me like a second skin. I turn to face him and my hair whips around in sopping thick tendrils.

I love being alone with Logan, lost in the shadows, nobody around to distract us from one another. In the distance we hear errant screams, voices sounding off like a riot in some other dimension.

"I miss this," he whispers warm in my ear.

I push him against the trunk of a tree and examine him in this blue filtered light. Logan looks amazing, like he belongs to some noble race.

He gives the slight huff of a laugh and holds our conjoined hands up. He heard, and this makes me suppress a nervous smile.

He pulls me in and offers a sweet kiss. Logan gives powerful kisses. There is nothing that Marshall's body can pulse through me with his feel good vibrations that could ever compare to a moment like this. It more than feels good. With Logan I can feel the love behind it.

"Skyla," he whispers pulling me close.

"Yeah?" I like holding Logan like this.

"You read the diary?" He pulls back a bit. I can see the question circulating in his eyes.

"Just a little. I found out Lexy knows a way to bind Fems."

"What?" He looks disbelieving. "Really? I don't think she's one of us."

"She must be. She told Chloe she'd tell her how to do it."

"Did she?"

"I haven't gotten that far, but if Chloe was taken by Fems probably not."

The whites of his eyes dart around in the dark.

"You think there's a way to bind Fems? She said she could do it without lifting a finger," I say.

"I don't know, but if there is, we need to figure it out fast. That could save us—you."

"She said you were with Lexy." I shrug. It's stupid to hurt over something that's ancient history.

"With Lexy," he says it like a fact. "We hung out." He shakes his head. "But she was never anything more than a friend. I'll try and talk to Lex, see what she can tell me about binding Fems."

I don't like the way he sinks effortlessly into calling her Lex.

"OK. I'll try and see if the diary has anything else to say about it."

The loud shrill cry of a female voice reverberates all around us. Then the very distinct sound of two guys yelling.

"That's Gage." Logan leans in to listen as the shouting intensifies. "I better go see what he's gotten himself into."

We head out of the forest at a decent clip.

"I'll go get my clothes," I say, parting ways with him at the south end of the lake.

It's so still here, scary. Even though I can hear the volatile voices from a thousand manic teenagers, it's freaky being on the dead end of the lake—just me and the moon, an owl sounding off in the distance. I make my way over to the giant rock where Brielle and me left our belongings. It looks like the girls all took off toward the cliffs. Not one soul lingering down at this end of the water, unless of course Brielle drowned them all.

I pluck through the pile of cheer uniforms and pull my skirt over my kick-pants.

"Don't I know you?" A male voice disrupts the silence from behind.

I turn around and take in a sharp gasp.

Crap!

It's a thing! It's covered in mud, or crap, or maybe that's just the texture of its freaking skin?

"I don't think so." The words stutter out of me as I try and make my way around him. I lunge toward the edge of the waterline in an effort to make a break for it, but he snatches me up by the wrist and pulls me in hard.

He bears his teeth and hisses with an awkward smile.

Crap! It's a Fem.

"Lo—" It clasps its hand tight over my mouth and drags me backward into the overgrown brush. I give a swift hard knock to its stomach with my elbow, four or five times, before it clasps both my hands behind my back. Dark slime rubs off all over Logan's white T-shirt and down my legs, thick as grease.

It swipes my feet from underneath me and lands itself on top of my chest, hard.

Can't breathe! I try pushing it off as it crushes me under the weight of its body. I open my mouth to gasp for air as it impales me with its tongue.

A warbled scream gets caught in my throat. Instinctually I bite down hard causing it to writhe and twist away. I try to slither out of its slimy grasp as it struggles to restrain me.

Its eyes glow an eerie shade of yellow as they squint out in pain. I try to harness my anger against Carly, for fuel to fight him like I did when I killed that last Fem, but now that I know she's somebody's mother, it doesn't yield the same effect on me.

My father's face brims to the surface.

I remember the way they accused him of killing those vagrants, the way the Counts had him burn, and I gouge into the Fem's soft neck with my hands, dig in with my nails, and rip at its flesh, shredding it with my fingers.

It gurgles and groans beneath me. I can feel my thumbs connecting in the sinews of his body, touch his spinal cord, feel its veins wrap around my fingers like spaghetti. Logan is right, anger magnifies my strength, turns me into a rabid beast, hungry for the blood of this creature.

Its hands wrap around mine in an effort to pluck me off, but its efforts wane quickly. I've honed in my wrath. I want this to be a warning to others like him. I hope they think twice before trying to violate me. Lexy may know how to bind a Fem, but I know how to kill them.

It falls limp, and I crawl away until I can get back on my feet.

I dart over toward the voices, now jovial and laughing as though the fight that was breaking out had never happened, as though there weren't a dead Fem lying fifty feet away. I scan the crowd for Logan and Gage as everybody starts to move down toward the south end of the lake to gather their things.

Michelle backs into me and turns around. She studies my arms as I hold them out like a surgeon prepped for duty.

"What the hell happened to you?" Her face flickers in disgust. The rose pendant Marshall gave her hangs around her neck from a thin silver chain, catching the sparkle of moonlight like a fractured shard of glass.

If I were nicer, I'd yank it off her. Judging from the severe dark circles under her eyes, she's still having Fem terrors in her sleep unlike me who has them right here in the open.

"Where's your boyfriend?" I ask searching the vicinity. It wouldn't entirely surprise me to see Marshall lingering in the crowd somewhere—nude.

A series of piercing screams erupt from behind.

"Wouldn't you like to know," the words jackknife through her. She slams hard into my shoulder as she makes her way back into the crowd.

"Yes, I would," I whisper as my teeth give way to a hard chatter. Marshall could help me get rid of a dead Fem if I needed him to.

The crowd drains in the direction of the deceased creature. Another round of cries and gasps erupts.

Oh crap. Judging by the look of horror on people's faces he didn't disappear.

Logan and Gage emerge from the mass of onlookers gawking at the Fem.

"Did you see it?" I jog over, fogging up the air with my heavy panting.

"Crap," Gage moans as he inspects my bloodied hands. The moonlight bleeds out all color, leaving a dark, glossy, residue on my skin.

Logan gives a depleted smile.

Someone in the distance shouts that the paramedics are on their way.

"They're going to take the Fem!" My fingers come just shy of covering my lips.

Logan scoops me into his arms and runs us over to the peak just above the deepest portion of the falls.

"What's going on?" I ask. There's something written on his face, a tension I'm not familiar with.

He gives a bleak smile.

"It wasn't a Fem," he says out of breath. "You killed him, Skyla, and now we're going to wash the blood off."

He plunges us both into the icy biting waters.

11

Police

The smoky air illuminates in spasms with alternating shades of soft blue and red. With an escort of flashing black and whites—an entire army of police cars—each one of us is instructed to follow them down to the Paragon precinct for questioning. Dozens of vehicles commence in a line that clogs up the main artery of the island—they even shut down the other side of the highway to accommodate us.

"There are two ways we can do this," Logan says, over the phone.

I'm riding with Gage, but I have Logan on speaker.

"The truth and a lie?" Gage says running his hand over the steering wheel as we wade through traffic.

"Exactly," Logan states.

"I choose the lie." I raise my hand slightly. "It's not like anybody saw me, plus I'm dripping wet, there's not an ounce of blood on me. And it's not like anybody's going to understand what the hell I'm talking about when I say I thought I was being attacked by a Fem."

"If I saw him attacking you, I would have killed him myself," Logan adds.

"Right," I whisper. I sort of wish he did. "Maybe we should hang up now. With my luck this will accidentally get keyed in over the radio," I say, eyeing the barrage of cop cars escorting us like a funeral procession.

"See you there," Logan's line goes dead.

I slip down in the seat and watch the fog swim by like an apparition.

"It's gonna be OK." Gage cups his hand over mine.

"Is it?" I spike up hopeful. Gage has the gift of knowing. He knows all kinds of strange things about the future.

"No, I mean, I'm pretty sure it's going to be OK."

"Oh."

I slump back into my seat.

I don't think it's going to be OK. I don't think you can just kill somebody and have it be OK.

At the station, mass confusion erupts over who exactly the dead body was. Apparently a bunch of guys from East decided to crash the party and douse themselves in mud, because apparently, they're idiots.

I hear names whispered all the way down the long hall as Logan, Gage, and I try and find a place to sit.

"Logan Oliver?" I hear Michelle say as we come up behind her. She turns around and lunges at him with a hug, Lexy follows suit.

"We heard it was you!" Lexy cries in a panic. Her arm lingers up over his shoulder as she cups the side of his face.

"Wasn't me." He turns a bright shade of red from the attention.

Lexy's hair has turned into a giant ball of frizz, her mascara is dripping down the sides of her cheeks and she looks darn right scary. I don't like the way she's letting her arm gather dust on Logan's shoulder, so I squeeze in between the two of them pretending to get out of the way of the crowd.

I've never thought of Lexy as anything special before. Sure she's pretty in her own way, but I've always classified her as more of a bitch than anything human or female.

"Anyway..." She looks over my shoulder at him as though I were invisible. "I'm glad you're OK."

I can see it now, that sad underlying spark in her eyes wishing he was still with her, and it makes me want to vomit on her shoes.

The clock ticks away in morbid slow motion. They have four staging areas set up. We wait impatiently until they finally seat Logan, Gage, and me in a room with the bitch squad where we wait another twenty minutes. Michelle keeps nodding off, hitting her head against the back wall from exhaustion. Strangely, I find this the highlight of my evening. I watch her eyes bolt open as she inhales a scream—all the while that black rose gleams under the harsh light from above.

A woman officer with her hair pulled back in a shiny dark knot asks banal questions about our connection to one another, the party, the location of where each of us were before the body was discovered.

Logan was plucking Gage off some guy from East, the bitch squad was swimming under the third tower of the falls, and I was wandering out by the forest with my hands buried deep in someone's neck. Of course that's not what I say.

"I was over there, too," I say in a whisper, "by the falls."

"No you weren't." Michelle moans half asleep. "I saw you by yourself. You were all dirty wearing some guy's shirt with weeds in your hair. Cheating on Gage much?"

Great. She's perfectly lucid now.

"So why were you dirty, and whose shirt did you have on?" The officer makes a notation in her journal.

"Well, let's see..." Emily bears her canines in my direction. Her dark hair has shrunk four inches and sits on her head like a slimy black helmet. It's hard to imagine Emily with long flowing hair the way Chloe described. "You've got on a guy's T-shirt, and Logan is shirtless under his jacket, which is hot, but weird, and, oh yeah? Weren't you with Logan before you hooked up with Gage?" She dips her finger in her mouth. Her emerald eyes light up from the pleasure of it all.

"That's right." I cut her a long hard look before turning my attention back to the officer. "I was..." My eyes close. I can't look at Gage—Gage who is holding me right at this very moment, nudging me to go on. I'm not going to smash his heart into a million little pieces, in a room full of people, just to save myself from the possibility of prison. And with that reality looming, I say, "I was naked, and I ran into Logan, so he gave me his shirt. Then he took off, and I fell in a puddle. That's when I saw you." I nod over to Michelle. "And then everyone started running around, and the next thing I knew, some jerk pushed me in the water."

Logan raises a brow over at me.

There. I give a big sigh of relief. It feels safe here in the lie, so good. I recline into Gage and relax.

"OK." The female officer taps her pen down on the table. "Now I'm going to have each of you phone your parents, and then you'll be released."

Crap.

I knew this wasn't going to end well.

The bitch squad disbands pretty quickly. Turns out none of their parents wanted to crawl out of bed at three in the morning, dead body or not. I was able to hear Michelle's dad scream over the phone that he wanted her ass home pronto.

Of course, *my* mother insists on coming down herself to see what all this debauchery is about. And since Dr. Oliver gave Logan and Gage the OK to drive home, they hang out until we hear the wild ruckus, which is undoubtedly Mom and Tad, erupting in the hall.

My mother frantically pokes her head into the room.

"She's in here," she shouts. Before I know it, her arms are squeezing the life out of me. "God! You're OK! I'm so glad you're OK." She runs her fingers through my hair. "You're wet."

"You two jokers," Tad jabs his fingers at Logan and Gage. "Get out now."

"See you later." Logan pats my leg as he and Gage disappear into the hall.

"What the hell is going on? You kill somebody?" Tad asks, gripped in a purple-faced tirade. He's wearing pink and white pinstriped pajamas, so it's hard to take him seriously.

"No." Technically yes.

"Let's get out of here." Mom tries to pluck me off the bench just as Tad steps between us, examining me with a curious stare.

"Lizbeth, go get her cleared with the front desk. I'll stay here." His eyes remain locked on mine. Soon as she steps over the threshold he yanks down my scarf.

"Holy crap!" He jumps back. It takes him a full three seconds to catch his breath. "I don't know what the hell kind of satanic crap you've managed to get yourself into, or if this is some new dress in black, stick an earring through every orifice in your body to piss off your parents stage you're going through, but while you're under my roof you're going to knock this crap off. You can save this experimental phase for college for all I care. Got it?"

I pull the scarf back up to cover the tiny neat row of X's that skip across my neck.

He thinks it's some kind of weird piercing I've inflicted upon myself.

"If I see you prancing around with your face made up like a corpse, wearing thigh-high boots and your hair frozen up like the Statue of Liberty, I'm shipping you off to nearest boarding school." He adjusts the invisible tie on his nightshirt in a fit of frustration. "They can deal with you," he mutters mostly to himself.

My mouth falls open. Mom swoops back in and helps usher me into the hall. Something tells me Tad would love for me to be at that boarding school anyway.

He speeds down ahead of us, pushes the door to the precinct open so hard the glass considers shattering from the violent jolt. A frigid blast of air pours over me, reminds me with its bitter fingers that my hair is still wet in the back.

"And that boy you're seeing?" His face ignites with color. "That ends tonight!"

12

Sorrow

His name was Holden.

I carefully peel back another page of Chloe's diary, trying to push away the idea that I was responsible for removing a soul from this planet—that a family was locked in grief over something I had done.

August 7th,

Gage is SO mine. We talked for HOURS at a party, then walked down the road and sat under the stars. I love the fact we can talk about all this angel crap. It's such a relief to talk to someone nice, who's not going to go all psycho or octopus on me any second. I swear Ellis is like some hormonal grenade. Just being near him is enough to pull the pin. Anyway, I think Gage and me are about to have a breakthrough. Something about tonight tells me that we've turned a corner in our relationship. I'm going to give him something. I don't know what, but something special that he'll always have just from me.

Oh, and Lexy the liar reneged on her offer, looks like binding Fems is not in my future. No surprise there.

Lexy is going to have to learn the hard way that payback's a bitch.

August 11th,

I had three late night conversations with Gage that lingered into the wee hours of the morning. I can tell he's just about ready to take that next step. I told him I wanted to have a picnic down by the dunes this weekend and he said YES! I can't wait. Come September when school starts, we'll totally be together. I can feel it.

A light knock erupts at my door. My mother peers in and gives an uneasy smile.

"There's someone down here to see you."

I follow close behind as she leads me to the kitchen. Tad is there with his arms folded tight, staring down Gage like he's some kind of fugitive.

"Skyla?" Tad's eyes oval out like two giant eggs. "I'd like to talk to you alone a moment," he says ushering me out to the back patio.

The sun is already starting to set, and it's just barely after four. I rub my hands up over my bare arms as the chill grips me.

"I want to take this opportunity to make it clear that..." His words get strangled in his throat as he points hard back toward the house, "that hulk of a person...that the two of you are nothing more than friends. The last thing I need is you saddled with a kid before graduation." He turns to head back in then stops abruptly. "Oh, and if I were you, I'd remove that necklace of horror as soon as humanly possible. I don't care if you have to wear a scarf the rest of your natural life. Your mother and sisters are never to see that atrocity." His finger comes just shy of digging into my chest. "Got it?" His eyes bug out, furious and wild.

"Got it," I mouth the words and walk back in the house. "I'm going out with Gage," I announce.

"That's great, Hon. You need some air, you've been stuck in bed all day." My mother lets the paper she's holding slip through her fingers while looking suggestively over at Tad.

Come to think of it, Drake is probably out with Bree, and the girls were at a sleep over last night and still haven't been picked up—OK the implications are pretty gross.

"Don't worry." I restrain myself from picking up the phonebook next to her and swatting her over the head for wanting to procreate with such a moron. "You can have the house to yourself. Gage and I have got things to discuss." I look over at Tad to see if he's buying this load. The only thing we'll be discussing with great sorrow is the fact Tad is in my life—that, and the awful fact I killed someone.

Gage drives us to the base of Devil's Peak. I've never been down at the bottom before. A few cars are parked along the rocky shore facing the ocean. The white caps swirl in a massive fit of destruction, and it reminds me of the night Marshall saved me, as I was getting ready to drown.

"What'cha thinking?" Gage wraps a blanket around my shoulders as we as head over to an embankment.

"About death." And selfishly, not Holden's. I still can't seem to wrap my head around the fact I ended someone's life yesterday all because I mistook him for a Fem. I'm a danger to society—welcome to my new reality.

"He attacked you." Gage guides me high up on a dirt patch and tosses down a towel for us to sit on. We land softly, and I let him hold me while we stare out at the angry, boiling sea. "What were you supposed to do? Let him overpower you just because he wasn't a Fem? You did the right thing."

"I ran my fingers through his esophagus like it was rotten fruit. I went overboard," I say, closing my eyes in disbelief.

"Sorry. I don't know what to say," he whispers into my ear.

I turn to face him. Even in this dim light his eyes radiate a brilliant electric blue. His dimples tremble as though they might ignite full and deep at any moment. I don't really know why I'm here with Gage. He should be my friend when we're not around other people, but something in me wants more. Eventually I'll have to stop blaming Logan for this, whatever it is, and start taking responsibility for my feelings.

"So," I sigh, "Brielle texted me this morning and said it was a kid from East named Holden." I shrug looking down at my fingers.

"Holden Kragger," Gage nods. "He's got a twin brother, Pierce. They weren't identical though. I think Pierce goes out with Nat off and on, not sure."

"Oh." I didn't even know Nat had a boyfriend. "So they're twins—*were*." A horrible feeling comes over me to know that someone has to bury their brother, a son because of me.

"I don't think you should dwell on this." He studies my face intently. "It's not like it was intentional. Even if you confessed, you'd be found innocent."

"What are the police saying?"

"They ruled it a homicide. They think someone hopped up on drugs did it. My dad said it looks like he was mauled by a wild animal."

My fingers come up over my neck. He was struggling to get away. I could have let him go.

"He was forcing himself on me." I can still feel his tongue slithering down my throat like a barbed, rabid snake.

"Don't upset yourself. And don't worry about the cops. My dad said the last person in the world they're going to suspect is a sixteen-year old girl." He rubs his hands gently up and down my back. "Um...I talked to Logan." His voice drops down into his chest.

It seems so trivial now. Me with Logan, me with Gage—none of it matters because we're all still alive and breathing.

"He's pissed." One of his dimples ignite as he gives a slight grin.

"What exactly did you say?" A part of me doesn't want to know, doesn't want to get sucked down further by the undertow of our blossoming relationship.

"I told him I thought you were beautiful." His eyes round out. "That I can't stop thinking about you." He stares me down with those cobalt spheres. "That I don't think I can pretend to be your anything, and that I want to start seeing you." His

Adam's Apple rises and falls dramatically as though he were unsure of what my reaction might be. "I know you have feelings for Logan. I'm not asking you to deny them or tell me you're leaving him. All I want is a chance." It comes out as a fact, but beneath the surface there's a layer of desperation. "Skyla," My name comes out broken, just shy of a whisper. "I'd do anything to be with you. And if that means giving you all the time in the world to make up your mind, I'll do that."

I lean in and press my lips soft against his. We start in with slow, deep kisses—then it erupts into an entire desolate exchange of passion.

Choosing between Logan and Gage would require more time than the world could possibly afford. I'd need two lifetimes, and two of me—both of which reality could ever hope to give me.

13

One Count Down

Monday, on the way to second period, I pass Logan in the hall. He not only smiles in my direction—he holds out his hand to high five me.

Butterfly room at ten? He asks.

It's on, I give a sly smile as I head into Marshall's class.

Gage pretends not to notice the whole skin slapping exchange. I spent all day yesterday trying to figure out how to see one Oliver, without cheating on the other—turns out there's no possible way. I'm going to have to do something, rather drastic and painful, like choose, but I think I'd rather pluck off my fingernails.

I contemplate the finer skills I've picked up since moving to the island—liar, cheat, thief, oh yeah—murderer. At least Paragon is molding me into a well-rounded asshole.

I plop down in my seat. It takes all of my effort not to put my head down, I'm so tired and it's only nine in the morning. Marshall whistles happily while passing out the tests from last week. I find this extremely annoying so I don't bother acknowledging him.

He glides a paper onto my desk with a giant red F scrawled across the top.

That's impossible.

"What did you get?" I lean over to Gage whose paper is sporting a neat little A in the corner. I scan the sheets side by side and none of the numbers match.

"Maybe I confused you when I was repeating the problems," he whispers.

Marshall swoops over to the two of us. "Maybe what confused you, Ms. Messenger, is that you didn't know the answers." His brows sharpen. "I took the liberty of discussing your disposition with your mother this morning."

"What? You said you were going to let me slide." Did I just say that out loud?

"She has agreed to procure my tutoring services." *I charge four hundred dollars a month, and with that I can practically guarantee an A. Oh the fun we're going to have.* He bites down on his lower lip suggestively.

Mom and Tad don't have a spare four hundred lying around. It might just be cheaper for Tad to ship me off to boarding school. And, of course, he'll use me as an excuse to deny Mia and Melissa their self-entitled weekly shopping sprees. Soon, I'll be to blame for all things debt related.

"When do we start?" I spear him with my anger.

"Soon as possible." His cheek pulls into a half smile as he walks away. *And Skyla? Feisty becomes you.*

"I don't like the thought of you hanging around him," Gage whispers, while holding me under the awning at lunch.

A downpour ignited as soon as the bell rang, which leaves ninety percent of the student body huddling en masse like ants under a leaf. You would think with all the rain they get on Paragon, they would offer us more shelter.

Ellis comes over, spilling his backpack onto the ground. "You guys hear they caught some kids going at it on top of the English building?" He laughs into the words. This is obviously the trivia he lives for.

"It was Nat." Brielle closes in our circle. "Pierce came up. He's all freaked out about losing his brother. He lost his sister like a year ago, and now he's the only child. Anyway, I guess Nat has been suspended for three whole days."

My heart sinks. Of course he's all freaked out about losing his brother—dead is pretty much forever, unless you're Chloe.

"Funeral is Friday." Brielle smirks when she says it. "Isn't that weird?"

"Why would that be weird?" I ask.

"It's Halloween," she whispers as though it were top secret. "I don't know, it's just wrong."

"Yeah well, I'm not calling off the party." Ellis growls. "I'm not letting some murderous lunatic ruin life for the rest of us."

Ellis is right—ever since I moved here, I've been ruining life for the rest of them and flat out ending it for others.

"Don't go there," Gage says it hot in my ear. "You made so many things right."

It amazes me sometimes that Gage doesn't have to read my mind to know what I'm thinking. I pull in closer and let my head dip down over his chest. A violent clap of thunder explodes above us, rattling the windows of the surrounding buildings. I tighten my grip around his waist so hard I think I'm going to push through.

I look back and both Brielle and Ellis have disappeared.

"I don't feel right about going to a party that night—any night ever again to be exact." I should voluntarily ban myself from ever having fun again.

"We have to." He tickles my ribs gently. "It's the best party of the year." He rests his lips on the top of my head momentarily. "I'll even wear a costume if you want."

"Really?"

"Really. Anything."

"OK, how about a vampire?"

"Except that." He averts his eyes as though he were rethinking the situation.

"Come on, vampires are cool and super sexy. It's what I really want you to be. I'll be Frankenstein's daughter. I've got the neck, remember?"

"Yeah, well, my dad wanted me to let you know it's time for the stitches to come out."

"I'll leave 'em in until Saturday." I shrug. "Tad saw them and thinks they're some Goth experimental stage I'm going through." I feel better talking to Gage—being with him. He has a way of removing the grime from the world and letting me see things clean and new the way he wants me to, if only for a moment.

Gage leans in and kisses me without reservation. He pulls back and his eyes linger into mine.

"I think I'm falling in love with you, Skyla." His dimples dig into the sides of his cheeks, as though somehow highlighting the importance of what he's saying.

The sky ignites with splinters of lightning that spider across the sky in pink and lavender hues.

I pull him in and lean my head up against his shoulder. Logan catches my eye from the doorway of the building across the way. Lexy is talking to him, but his full attention is locked in my direction.

I close my eyes and listen to the thunder roar over Paragon like a lion on fire.

"I love you," Gage whispers directly into my ear.

"I know." I can feel it, deep, in the marrow of my bones.

As soon as I get home, my mother whisks me away downtown. Turns out I'm *magnificently late*, as she phrased it, for my appointment with Dr. Booth.

Branches whip across the window of his office as we sit across from one another with matching folded hands, somber expressions, which I'm sure reflect boredom more than any other emotion.

"There's rumor of a killer roaming free on the island." He leans back without perforating his bleak expression. Dr. Booth is the psychiatrist I pretend to see in order to appease my mother and Tad.

His dark mat of hair, coupled with his squared off glasses gives him a comical quality I can't quite pinpoint.

"Are you the killer, Skyla?" There's no change in his affect. He may as well have asked if my mother and I plan on picking up fast food on the way home.

I don't say anything, don't dare posture myself, or so much as blink.

His fingers press together at the tips as he rocks back into his seat. "Thought so."

I'm still reeling from my appointment with Dr. Booth. He saw right through me. It's like I have the word killer etched on my forehead or something.

I run my fingers over the tiny paper butterflies pinned to the wall as I wait for Logan. I remember how Gage made them come to life for me, how he let one go and it flew to the ceiling like magic.

Logan shows up close to ten-thirty. For a while, I thought he wasn't coming and started to fall asleep on the floor.

"Hey, sorry I'm late." He gets on his elbows and lies down beside me.

His cologne smells fresh as he brushes my lips with a quick tender kiss.

"I had someone quit tonight, so I had to close." He gives my back a gentle rub. "Heard Gage made his move. He came home and threw the L word around all over the place." He looks startled, afraid, as though it rocked his very existence to witness it.

I don't know what to say to that. Gage is diving in deep, and he's starting to pull me down with him.

"Anyway, I'm not here to talk about Gage." He lets out a heavy sigh. "Just wanted to let you know that I found out a little more about Holden Kragger."

"What?" I'm thirsty to know anything.

"Their family owns a coffee shop out by Rockaway Point. They were always there. That, and the fact he and his brother were infamous for the way they treated girls."

"I heard Nat is dating his brother."

"Sort of. Lots of people are dating Pierce." His fingers twitch in air quotes when he says the word *dating*. "Turns out, there's an entire list of girls from East he toys with on a regular basis."

"Oh," I say, just taking him in. It feels strange with Logan sometimes. As if all this time I've spent with Gage has severely punctured something in our relationship.

"Is that all you have on Holden and Pierce?" I ask biting the tip of my finger then tracing his lips with it.

Logan leans in and gives a slow lingering kiss. His features soften as he pulls away. He studies me with an infinite sadness masked by the weakest smile. "One more thing. I've been combing through the copies from the book of Counts with my uncle. We're able to see some kind of hierarchy. It has a list of regional leaders and locations in the back. There's an infrastructure in place, that's for sure."

"Locations? Like Paragon?" A spike of adrenaline shoots through me.

"Like Paragon," he says without blinking.

"Who's in charge of the Countenance here?"

"A man named Arson."

"Arson? What the hell kind of name is that?"

Logan shakes his head just barely. “Father of Holden and Pierce.”

“Oh no, I killed a Count.”

“Oh yes, Skyla.” He looks at me with a magnetic intensity that seems to weld our souls together. “Looks like our holy war is well underway.”

14

My Ride

Driving rain strums relentlessly against my window, vexing me with its wild tapping thumps, until I manage to crawl out of bed and head downstairs for breakfast.

The lights flicker in rhythm to the storm as the steady hum of a thousand drummers penetrates the walls with its insistent frenetic pace. There won't be any peace in our world today.

"Morning." My mother yawns and stretches, exposing her pink lace negligee from beneath her terry robe. Mia and Melissa speed past me upstairs, already done with their breakfast. "Hey," Mom leans into me as I head to the fridge. "I don't want to say anything around your sisters, but apparently that kid that died the other night was murdered."

"Murdered?" The word feels rugged coming from my lips like corrugated cardboard.

"Yes!" Her eyes widen. "I don't want you going off alone. Make sure to stick with Brielle or Gage."

"Gage?" I ask sarcastically plucking the juice from the counter and filling a glass. "Taddy wants me to break up with him remember?"

She glances in the direction of his office. "I know you really care about Gage—I like him too. Just for the sake of maintaining household sanity, would you please let Tad think you've cooled it on the relationship?"

I examine her up and down. Is this what she's become? Why are we sneaking around behind Tad's back with my relationship status? Shouldn't she stand up for me and tell him I can see whomever the hell I want?

"OK," I reply. Maybe the two of us keeping a secret from Tad is a good thing, in a bonding sort of way.

Tad and Drake meander into the kitchen. I've never noticed until now how much they look alike. Something about this early morning disheveled state makes Drake look like a thinner, younger version of his father.

"Anyway, guess whose seventeenth birthday is right around the corner?" My mother chirps in an effort to change the subject.

Somehow I've managed to push my birthday as far out of my mind as possible. I'm too numb with the recent horrific developments in my life to have any genuine excitement over it. Then a thought hits me, and I take an emotional U-turn.

"You know what?" My mood spikes a little. "I think I'm finally going to get my license. Have I mentioned I already have a car?" I restrain myself from jumping when I say it.

"A car?" Tad echoes, disbelieving. His disapproving tone comes in clear—the one he seems to reserve just for me.

"Yeah, Logan and Gage have some old beat up car they want to get rid of and they offered to give it to me."

"That's right, Skyla," Tad starts in sarcastically. "Let boys run around giving you expensive things, and see if they expect nothing in return. That's exactly how you want to start off in life." He shags out his paper.

"Honey," my mother bites her lip. "He's right. It's not a good idea. I don't think I can let you accept that kind of gift. I don't care how old or beat up it is."

"And who's going to pay for insurance?" Tad cocks his head. "It's bad enough we need to fit Drake on our policy."

"What?" I look over at Drake shoveling in his cereal.

"I found an old hatchback for like two thousand bucks," he mumbles through a mouth full of food. "Plus, I already have my license, so it's a no brainer."

"So Drake can get a car, and you're going to pay for the insurance, but I can't?"

Tad shakes his head with exasperation. "Look, you don't need a car. You don't have anywhere to go that you can't have that giant of a football player take you."

"Oh, so now you want me to use Gage for a ride? He's suddenly become economically convenient to you?" My blood races through my veins, amping me up to the point I could knock a wall out if I wanted.

"You're always with him, anyway." My mother stirs the leftover pancake batter trying to sound impartial.

"My situation is totally different," Drake interjects. "I got a job doing paperwork for Brielle's mom."

I glare over at him. We both know damn well the only thing he'll be doing is Brielle.

"I'm paying Mom and Dad back for the loan they gave me with interest," he continues.

Mom? Since when did he start calling her Mom?

"You gave him two thousand dollars?" I place my hand over my mother's in an effort to stop her frantic mixing.

"We're lending," she corrects.

“I’ll get a job and pay for my own insurance,” I offer. I can feel my heart drop when I say it. If Drake isn’t paying for his own insurance, it doesn’t seem fair that I have to. I don’t ever remember my mother treating me like a second-class citizen before Tad came along.

“If you can get a job and pay for your own insurance,” my mother starts off hesitantly, exchanging glances with Tad as if asking permission to continue. “I don’t really see the problem.”

“Still don’t like the idea,” Tad breathes. “The island is not that big—you can catch a ride with friends or Drake to get around. Besides, now that there’s some serial killer on the loose, I don’t know if I want you driving places alone.” Tad flexes the paper in front of him.

“Serial killer?” I can barely get the words out.

“They think there’s a link between that kid that died and that girl who was killed before we got here.” Tad casts a sharp look. “You two watch where you’re going. I don’t want to be the one to point out the obvious, but you’re right smack in this lunatic’s demographic.”

Drake’s face smoothes over with fear.

“I’d better keep Gage around just to be safe.” I give a sly smile in my mother’s direction.

And I’ll get that car and a job. I’ll gladly spend more time away from this place. I’m sure Logan will be more than happy to employ me.

“Guess we’re going to have to start locking our doors again.” Tad says before losing himself in an article.

I wonder what he would think if he knew the raging lunatic, so-called serial killer, were standing within five feet of him.

"It's all going to be fine." My mother wipes her forehead with the back of her hand.

"I don't know, Lizbeth." Tad moves his gaze over to me and grips me in a fixed burning stare. "You never know who they'll go after next."

15

Get a Job

Marshall insists we begin our first tutoring session at four-thirty, right after I finish up with cheer. I know exactly what kind of tutoring goes on in his classroom at four-thirty, ever since I accidentally exposed myself to Michelle Miller's boobs after walking in on one of his sessions.

I shake out my umbrella and leave it by the door. I find Marshall hunched at his desk, pouring over his laptop. The glow of the screen is the only light available, so I flick the switch and illuminate the classroom.

"Ms. Messenger." He straightens. "You're punctual—precisely the reason I think you'd make a great employee. Are you willing to reconsider the position?"

I look around suspiciously wondering why Marshall bothers to act so strange with no one around to entertain.

"I do need a job, but I'm gunning for something with a little less of you in it." I head over and slide a chair up beside him. The ad for the equestrian school is displayed on his laptop, complete with the picture of me looking very, well, almost naked with the exception of angel wings while lying on a horse.

"I'm inviting the community over in a few weeks to celebrate the opening. Fifty pupils have already signed up." He closes the lid to his laptop. "I stood outside the grocery store with flyers and shook the hand of every mother I could."

"I bet you did." I pull out my Algebra Two book. "My sisters are among the throngs. Don't you dare touch them." I'll find a way to torment Marshall if he even so much as offers a wayward glance.

"I wouldn't dream of such vile things. Besides, the equestrian school comes equipped with competent instructors, none of which include yours truly. I need a stream of real income—teaching provides just enough to keep me on a steady diet of cat food, and I prefer quality meals such as sushi."

"Sushi is cat food, glorified as it may be." I say flipping the pages of my textbook. God, I miss sushi. I haven't had any since I moved from L.A. "You know, I just realized, I don't know all that much about you."

"That's where the disconnect is. Tell you what, I'm going to introduce you to my world. Once you see how wonderful it is, it's doubtful you'll want to leave."

"What's doubtful is the fact I'll be going with you. Besides, isn't death some kind of prerequisite to getting in?" I close the book over my hand and lean into him. "Did you hear about the boy that was killed out by the falls?" I study the blank expression on his face. "It was me...I killed him," my voice shakes when I say it, and suddenly I find myself fighting tears.

His features sharpen. "It was made known to me." He gives a hard blink. "Skyla, it's not your strength or your blood that will ultimately usher your downfall, it's that pit in the center of your face you insist on vocalizing with."

"Then I'll keep it shut." Obviously, I shouldn't have said anything.

"You're incapable." He presses into me with a hard look. "It's your mortal flaw."

I open my mouth to say something, but can't find the words. I've already told both Logan and Gage he's a Sector. If Marshall finds out, he'll hand me over to the Counts. I don't like where this runaway train is headed.

He reaches over and touches my face gently with the back of his hand. That sweet rush I anticipate ripples through me—makes me ache to keep him there just a little bit longer.

I'm so much trouble in this world—maybe it's not the one I really belong in. Maybe, before I kill another human being, I should weigh all my options.

"Does the thought of bringing back your father still intrigue you?"

"Always." But not enough to eternally unite with a Sector.

"Look beyond your hormones, Skyla, before you rack up a body count. You will kill again, and the list grows rather rapidly. If you knew whose blood you were ultimately responsible for, I don't think you'd sit here with that look of indecision on your face." He pauses to clasp my other hand. "I could end this war for you. It's better to decide now than wish you could take it all back once you've fed the grave. There will come a day that you'll wish it were you supine in a casket rather than the ones you put there." He studies my face with an underlying look of malice. "Especially, one in particular."

After the faux tutoring session is over, I convince Gage to drive me to the bowling alley in hopes of seeking employment. Of course, he tries unsuccessfully to talk me out of the idea.

We arrive just as a group of construction workers are taking off. Two of them leer at me openly. Maybe hanging out with a bunch of construction workers for a five-hour shift isn't the greatest idea.

Logan's kitchen remodel is well under way. The floors are done in chalky orange tiles, new stainless appliances are in place with the plastic wrap hanging partially off, and a giant brick oven looks ready to be filled with pizza.

"Nice!" I beam over at Logan. "Guess you'll be needing an extra pair of hands."

"You signing up?" He tilts his head thoughtfully, flirting with me ever so slightly with those sundrenched eyes.

I give a quick nod.

"You're hired." He lets out a smug grin of satisfaction directed at Gage. "Of course, employees aren't allowed to date, but I'll make some allowances." Logan doesn't bother hiding his sarcasm.

"Let me guess, they have something to do with scheduling," Gage says, nodding me over to the table.

"You're a bright boy. That's why I keep you around."

The three of us take a seat.

"He's my ride." I have to work with Gage, besides I want to.

"I'll still bring you, pick you up," Gage offers. "I'm not going anywhere." He slits a quick glance at Logan.

Must change subject.

"Marshall keeps burrowing into my life. How am I going to get rid of him?" I don't tell them that I've added being captured by him to my growing list of paranoia.

"Request a transfer," Gage suggests.

"No... don't." Logan looks lost in thought. "See if you can get him to tell you how to bind a Fem. I'm not getting far with Lexy."

"I guess I can. I just don't like the thought of him wooing me. His words not mine."

"I don't either." Gage picks up my hand and entwines our fingers right in front of Logan.

A distant smile curls the sides of Logan's lips as he glares over at Gage.

"I don't like the thought of anybody wooing you." He doesn't waver his stare from Gage. There's a blackness in Logan I haven't seen before as he intensifies his discontent. His chest rises and falls at a quickened pace. "Celestras are known for erratic behavior when provoked to anger." He leans in a little toward Gage. "We're often justified and rarely caught."

"So you're saying I should watch my back?" Gage clenches his jaw at the idea.

"I'm saying you shouldn't justify my anger."

I wonder how far Logan would take this—if he could do to Gage what I did to Holden. Doubtful. Although something unfamiliar boils deep behind his eyes, and it makes me think just maybe he could.

16

Worlds Collide

Paragon's landscape is dotted with pumpkins—bodies are strung up in trees like Christmas ornaments, and miniature graveyards have cropped up on every other front lawn. There's something about filling this island with all of the glory and horror of wickedness that just feels right.

"You mind if I drive?" I ask Gage on the way home.

"You have your license?" He knows full well I don't.

"No, but I will."

"It's against the law."

His sudden sense of loyalty to law enforcement amuses me.

"Look, this is a tiny island with like two lanes. It's not like I'm asking you to let me zip down an L.A. freeway with a blindfold on. Who's going to care?"

"I'm going to care, and you're going to care when things go wrong."

"Nothing is going to go wrong." I place my hand over his and bat my lashes.

Gage pulls over, and we switch seats.

"Just straight home," he says.

OK, so he's not that enthused with the idea.

"Home—got it." I drive to the intersection where we would usually make a right, and turn left instead.

“Skyla.”

“What? I’m taking the long way.” I stop abruptly as the light turns yellow.

“Geez,” he says, bracing himself against the dashboard. “Ease into it, will you?”

“You wanna go to Devil’s Peak?” It feels so freeing to be behind the wheel. I can go anywhere—do anything.

“No. You might accidentally drive us over the edge.”

“Then let’s go to the beach.”

The light changes, and I pump the gas a few times, sputtering the truck forward in a series of staccato jerks. Then something loosens in the pedal, and it’s almost like the car is driving itself.

It takes about three good miles before Gage looks over with a mischievous half smile.

“I don’t know what happened,” he starts, “but you’ve improved drastically. I think I might actually start to breathe again.”

“Told you it’d be fine. I’m totally getting the hang of this.”

The pedal depresses beneath my foot, and the truck slides into the opposing lane. The truck speeds up unnaturally, and I pass up three minivans in a row and glide right in front of them and back into the proper lane.

“Holy crap!” Gage digs his fingers into the dashboard. “That was an incline, Skyla! There is no way you could have seen if there was a car coming.” He lays a hand over the wheel. “Pull over.”

My heart races feverishly as the gas pedal sinks beneath my foot again. The light at the intersection turns yellow and I try to pump the brake, but the accelerator is sticking.

"Something is wrong." I try to steady the wheel, but it twists and turns, rotating powerfully beneath my fingers as though its got a mind of its own. "Oh my, God!" I close my eyes as the car sails into the intersection just as cross traffic begins to speed into the street.

"Skyla!" Gage takes off his seatbelt and tries hopping over on top of me to gain control of the wheel.

I look up in time to see the whites of someone's eyes just as a dark green Hummer slams into the corner of the hood and sends us spinning out of control. I grab a hold of Gage by the shirt and try to hang onto to him. Another car plows into us just behind the passenger side and stops all movement. Gage explodes through the windshield, through a million tiny fragments of pebble-sized glass, and rolls over to the hood of the Hummer. A trail of blood fills the interim.

"Gage!" I scream, as I snap off my seatbelt. I try to open the driver's side door, but it's jammed. Blue bits of glass litter the seat as I crawl over and get out of the passenger side. "Gage?" It comes out a startled cry as I try to reach his bloodied body.

I'm numb—the world feels as though it's shaking. A light rain begins to pelt me, and I can't feel a thing.

His face...oh God...his face!

Splinters of glass glitter off his forehead, his cheeks. Blood trickles from a thousand different places, covering his flesh completely, despite the rain's best effort to wash it all away.

"Can you hear me?" I say it quieter than intended.

Gage lets out a soft moan and tries unsuccessfully to sit up, only to land back on the hood with a hard thump.

"Don't move!" I hear somebody shout. A woman pulls me to the side.

Sirens cut through the air, as a steady pulse of red and yellow flickering lights blink through the night like a seizure.

I move toward Gage as the air around me turns an ashen shade of grey. I can feel myself falling. The asphalt comes in quick—then the world, and everything in it, disappears.

I struggle to open my lids, the shock of commotion around me is drowned out by a banging headache that pulsates through my ears—it all floods back to me.

"Gage?" I sit up fighting a wave of nausea.

"You OK?" A lady wearing purple-rimmed glasses and a worried expression tries to stop me from getting up.

Gage is being lifted onto a gurney. I can see his eyes moving around frantically.

"Gage!" I bolt over, filled with relief. His face is still covered with pink swirls of blood that dilute with the rain.

"I'm OK." He groans as they load him into the ambulance. I don't wait for anybody to ask if I want to come along, I just hop inside and take a seat near the back where they position his head.

"I'm so sorry. I swear I lost control."

"Incoming!" shouts the EMT as he flexes another body on a gurney into the ambulance.

"I'm not hurt." A boy around our age raises his hand. His face is cut, and there's blood all over. "You driving that car?"

His expression darkens as he bores into me with an accusing stare.

I don't say anything, just sit there wondering how many ambulances are going to be filled and if I've managed to kill anybody in the process.

"This is my girlfriend," Gage hitches his thumb at me. "She was just learning to drive."

"Female drivers, no survivors." He swipes the blood from his mouth. He looks back at me and runs his eyes up and down quickly. "Pierce Kragger."

Gage and I exchange glances.

Oh my, God. I almost killed another one.

"My dad's a lawyer. He'll fix it so you'll never want to sit behind the wheel again." He gives a little laugh before lying back down. "He's good at keeping idiots off the street."

The fact that I killed his brother sails through my brain and I excuse his rude behavior.

Gage reaches back and touches my hand as the ambulance begins to wail down the street.

Did you say you lost control of the wheel? He asks.

"And the gas and the brakes," I say out loud. I don't care how insane I look to Pierce or the EMT sitting at the far end.

I'm starting to think this wasn't an accident, Gage says.

I look over at Pierce lying there—Holden's brother.

Just what are the odds?

17

Survivor

"Well, you're a pair." Dr. Oliver walks into the hospital room as Gage and me inspect ourselves in a hand held mirror. I quickly replace the scarf around my neck.

"Look at you." The horror jumps off his face as he takes in his son's intensely sliced up features. "The intern says it's all superficial with the exception of your shoulder."

"He has a concussion," I add. Not that I should be adding anything. I should be running for the exit—subtracting myself from the equation. I wouldn't blame Dr. Oliver for wanting to throw *me* out a window.

Emma and Logan come in winded. Her hands fly up to her mouth as she lets out a wild gasp.

"What happened?" Logan's anger with Gage has clearly dissipated—although I wouldn't be surprised if it reprised itself in my direction at any moment.

"I didn't see him coming." Gage groans as he attempts to sit up.

"Nice try, but the police report says it was a female driver." Dr. Oliver tilts his head to the side expecting an explanation.

"I think the truck might be haunted," I say. It's true.

The three of them stare back at me as though I had just slapped them all in unison.

"Something was definitely off." Gage scoots in and clasps my hand. "One minute she was stuttering down the road, and the next thing I knew she was ditching in and out of traffic at eighty miles an hour."

God—was I doing eighty?

A great look of sadness comes over Emma as she collapses her hands up near her temples. "It may not have been her," she whispers, "but it was because of her."

In a rare and dangerous moment, Logan offers to give me a ride back home.

"Your aunt hates me."

"She doesn't hate you. I thought she was going to cry when she apologized for like the hundredth time."

"I know, but that's because she's too nice to say what she really means," I pause. "I almost killed her son."

"You didn't." He smoothes his hand over my knee. "If you want, I'll teach you how to drive."

"You will?"

"Yeah, I'll take you to the Black Forest one day, there's a nice clearing. The only thing you'll be remotely capable of hitting is a tree." He flexes a mock smile.

Nice—great time for humor. Then it occurs to me that plenty of people get killed each year by ramming their cars into trees, and I'm perfectly capable of including myself in that statistic.

"There's a party at the bowling alley Saturday night," Logan says, passing my house and pulling in alongside the evergreens that stand guard at the base of our street. The moon is covered in a heavy vale of storm clouds, and if it weren't for the fact Logan's truck is white, we'd blend perfectly into the shadows. Chloe chose a lousy color for his truck.

"Sort of like an after party to Ellis's Halloween bash?" That was stupid. Ellis's party is on Friday.

It feels awkward here with Logan. I haven't been with him alone like this in so long, it feels unnatural.

"Lexy invited me to go on Halloween," he says.

"And you're going to do it?"

"I'll just meet her there." He shakes his head and looks despondent out the window.

A surge of relief pulses through me.

"That party at the bowling alley?" He picks up my hand and pulls me toward him. "It's private."

"Oh, another Lexy event?" Just add it to the list of growing horrors.

"It's very private." He gives the impression of a wicked grin.

"Oh, for me. Of course, I'll be there."

"If you want you can hang out after your shift while I close up. Then we can start the party." The contours of his face are laced with shadows—they define him, make him look strong, hard as marble.

My heart picks up pace. I'm not sure what kind of party Logan has in mind, but I'll definitely be hanging around to find out.

"Sounds like we're dating on the job," I bite down on my lip.

"You know what they say—there's an exception to every rule." And with that he leans in and kisses me, makes me forget rules and accidents and boys named Pierce.

August 12th,

I took Nevermore with me down to the dunes. I had him sit in a tree and wait until Gage met up with me. He was working so I agreed to meet him, plus I didn't want him to see Nev until the big reveal.

Of course, I brought all kinds of great food and was way too nervous to take one bite in front of him. I sat and watched as he ate, as he swallowed, I swear everything that boy does is perfect. Anyway, I had Nevermore come down and Gage tried to shoo him away. Too freaking funny!

I told him it was OK, that it was the guardian my father gave me when I was eight. I took his hand and placed it over Nev. I held them both while I pulled out my knife and cut them. That's the way I remember my father doing it. I remember how my blood beaded on the blade. Now Nev has Levatio and Celestra blood circulating inside of him. He's a prince among birds, literally. Doesn't matter though, he's impressed onto Gage now. I've given Nev to him as a gift. He's Gage's bird now. I hope Gage knows how much it means for me to give up Nevermore. I love that bird more than my brother, hell, more than my mother.

So things didn't go so great after that. I tried to lean in and kiss him and he backed away like I had cooties or something. He says he's real sorry because he's not trying to lead me on, but he's saving himself for someone else. Who the hell saves kisses? And for some girl he hasn't even met yet! He must think I'm repulsive. I'm so stupid for giving him my heart, my bird, my anything.

I miss Nev. I think he was the only one capable of loving me.

-Chloe

Rain beats down against my window. I clutch Chloe's diary against my chest and press my hand up against the cool of the glass, watch as the window lights up in a fog around my fingers.

That was me. I was the girl Gage waited for, and I'll probably be the one to accidentally kill him one day.

A sizzle of lightning electrifies the sky. It slaps against the palm of my hand like a hammer and then produces a violent shatter.

In a moment, the room is lit up with supernatural light and an explosion of flying glass.

18

Follow

Second period Algebra Two.

Outside, it's heaving water like vomit from heaven. It's as though the clouds have malfunctioned and somehow harnessed the power to suction water from the ocean in large, inconsiderate vats.

The entire class sits around talking and shouting while we wait for Dudley the no-show. Oddly, Marshall strolling in late has increasingly become the norm.

"So," I lean into Ellis and Gage, "it didn't go over very well with Tad, that a freak of nature completely destroyed my window."

Gage looks great save for the stray maroon lines dotting his face, and the fact his arm is in a sling.

"So lightning struck your window after you got into a major collision?" Ellis ticks his head at me. "I'm officially revoking your invite to the party."

"Yeah, right. Just having me in the vicinity increases the percentile of Fems that will show up." What's sad about that is it's actually proven to be factual.

Marshall strides in, slams his briefcase on the desk and claps his hands. The entire room falls silent. Something about Marshall today—he looks irritated, maudlin, not his usual annoyingly chipper self.

"Sit quiet for an hour." He gives a dry smile. "Do whatever the hell you like." He snatches up his briefcase before bolting out the door.

"What the heck?" Ellis looks dazed.

The room booms with a mix of laughter and voices. I don't bother saying anything. I just get up and speed down the hall after Marshall, catching up with him as he taps down the stairs.

"Wait, what's going on?"

"This doesn't involve you, Skyla." He bursts through the double doors, popping open his umbrella, cutting through the storm at superhuman speeds.

"Oh, something is definitely happening. And if it's crappy, it usually involves me," I shout, running in an effort to keep up with him.

"Don't flatter yourself. There's plenty of misery in this world that has nothing to do with, Skyla Messenger."

Before I know it, we're in the teacher's parking lot, and Marshall is getting into his car. I sit down on the passenger's side before he has a chance to protest, and we speed away.

Marshall is flying—we're air born—hydroplaning, all of the above. We pass three police cars and not one of them cares to stop us.

"You drive like a bat out of hell," I say, watching the windshield wipers fight a losing battle as I twist and turn with Marshall's erratic driving.

"Really, Skyla? That's so cliché. Sometimes I wonder why I bother with people."

"Cliché? Try accurate." I brace myself against the dash like Gage did yesterday and start pumping the air brakes with my foot.

"Try something a little more original. How about, you drive like an atomic collision?" He grits his teeth as we take a sharp turn. "Or you drive like a sound wave that reaches its destination before the first vibration is felt by the human ear, or..." He drives down the dirt path below Devil's Peak and slows to a crawl as we approach the sheer cliff side. "Hang on." He backs the car up violently before throwing it into drive again and races toward the granite wall as fast as the pedal with allow.

"No!" I scream covering my head with my arms. *Turn left* is my last paralyzing thought before the sheer slate wall approaches. The car starts vibrating in that strange tuning fork manner that Marshall is capable of emitting. We drive right through the granite and land somewhere dark as night, on a forest floor with a low hung moon that gives off a lavender glow.

Marshall gets out in haste. I unbuckle and follow him.

"Where are we?" Looks like Paragon—feels like Paragon, until I see him lift a latch out of the dirt. A brightly lit stairwell blinds me from beneath the ground. It leads straight down into the earth and looks more than vaguely familiar. "Oh no." I try to pull him away from it. "I remember this place. It's that freaky white labyrinth Ezrina took me to. She had me strapped to a metal bathtub and was going to suck all of the blood out of me with a big fat needle."

"You're with me." He continues down the stairs.

"I won't go," I shout after him. My adrenaline picks up, as a spike of perspiration erupts all over me at once.

"Well, I doubt you'll be safe up there," he shouts, disappearing from my line of vision.

Crap!

I run down the stairs, and catch up with Marshall speeding down the hall. I clutch at his waist with both hands. "This is Ezrina's freaking lair," I say in a panic.

"Is that what they're calling it these days?" He eases my arms off and picks up my hand. He's still bulleting down the hall, briefly looking in rooms that have their doors open.

"Here you are," he says to someone curled over the counter with a bevy of glass bottles lying around.

It's her! Crap!

Ezrina straightens and turns around with that dried blood of a thin-lipped smile. She frowns as she observes me from over her glasses.

Marshall lets go of my hand and hops up on the counter next to the clutter.

"I've made a mess of things," he laments. He looks boyish and charming in a humble sort of way.

Damn right I want to say. *Get me the hell out of here* is next on my list, but my vocal chords don't seem to be functioning at the moment.

"You want me to chop off her other arm?" She asks casually while rolling a vial of blue solution between the palms of her hands.

"No, she followed me. I can't shake her—she's like a pet I've come to appreciate." He winks over at me.

"I want to go home." The words stutter out of me as I back into a wall.

"Relax, nobody is going to hurt you, Skyla." Marshall steadies himself. "Remember how I told you the world didn't revolve around you? This is one of those rare moments. I'm the one with the problem."

I study Marshall's face, then look over at Ezrina who doesn't seemed fazed at all by our strange visit. She continues to pick over samples and play with Petri dishes as though it were standard procedure to have me looking over her shoulder.

"What did you do this time?" She asks pulling a long white tube out of a metal hole in the sink with tongs. Smoke rises from the pit as though it were coming from a frozen environment.

"I've impregnated a human." The glass drops from her hand onto the floor and shatters.

My hand rises up over my mouth, and I find myself choking for air.

"Michelle's pregnant?" The words barely escape my lips.

"I'm not here to start rumors, Skyla." He looks annoyed with me for the very first time.

"You'll have an offspring then." Ezrina secures her hands at the hips.

"I will." He drops his gaze to the floor.

This is so freaking insane. I step forward toward Marshall for the first time unafraid of Ezrina until I notice that the bathtub of death is filled with a body. I jump back, startled to see a leg sticking out from underneath a black sheet of plastic and let out a scream.

"Is this the boy?" Marshall asks.

"There's Celestra blood involved." Ezrina plucks the gloves off her fingers. "It's confirmed."

"Well, Skyla," Marshall's mood brightens. "Looks like you've managed to prove your theory correct. All signs of trouble can be directly linked back to you." He hops down from the counter. "You're in more trouble than I am. I feel better already."

"Glad I can help," I whisper.

"Shall I take her now?" Ezrina's wild red mane pulsates as her voice hits the slightest echo.

"Not yet, my love." Marshall glides over to me. "She's mine yet a little while more."

19

Vampire for Sale

I feel rather catatonic the rest of the afternoon. After school, Gage tries to cheer me up by taking me shopping for Halloween costumes. He seems to have completely accepted the fact I was taken to Ezrina's lair as though it were something natural—expected.

"Look, I can tell you're pretty shaken up." He brushes the hair from my face. "Stay away from Dudley. The guy is bad news."

Paragon glows a luminescent orange, as a magnificent sunset tries to penetrate the puff of fog lying over us thick as wool. It gives the impression that inside this mist, the island is on fire—a strange fire that envelopes you, forgets to let you burn.

Gage helps me out of his mother's two-seat convertible. It feels weird driving so low to the ground after mounting over the road for weeks in his tank of a truck.

"So is it totaled?" I feel bad for not asking before.

"Nope. Needs bodywork and some windows. I might get rid of it, though."

"I feel terrible," I say, walking past him as he holds a door laden with fake spider webs open for me.

It's dark in the store. Odd noises emit from the speakers in the form of creaking doors, wild cackles that more than remotely sound like Michelle, and a woman expertly screaming. A strobe light goes off in spasms to our left as a layer of artificial fog drifts around our feet. Gage points up as an entire row of corpses greets us hanging from the ceiling. Probably employees. I'd consider hanging myself if I had to be subjected to this for more than five minutes—seems reasonable.

"You sure you want to do this?" I ask, as Gage speeds us down aisle after aisle.

"I'm sure." He plucks a vampire costume off the rack and holds it up against himself. "I'll let you dress me," He examines the cape at arms length. "Maybe just this once."

"I'm a sucker for a hot vampire. Thank you for being so nice." I circle my arms around his waist. "That's exactly why I love you." I bite down on my bottom lip hard. Crap! I may have accidentally told Gage that I love him while sandwiched between a witch and a scarecrow.

"You love me?" His lips curl as his dimples depress themselves an inch on either side.

Of course I love Gage in the loose sense of the word, but I'm not ready to *love*, love Gage, am I?

"I do." My lips feel as though they're on fire as I give way to a huge grin. I do love Gage. There's a certain relief in hearing myself say it. It feels right.

The air dissipates around us, suffocates us in the reality of our words. Gage stares back at me with wide-eyed anticipation of what it all means.

He pulls me in, rubs his cheek up against mine. "I'm glad you're OK. I'm glad you weren't hurt in the accident," he punctuates it with a quick kiss.

"Me? I'm glad you weren't hurt. I'm glad you're alive."

"I'm glad you're alive." He pecks another kiss. "And I'm alive." He pushes in another quick one. "And that you and I are alive together standing in this tiny space, right here, right now."

My stomach bottoms out, and my heart races for Gage. He presses in with a heartfelt kiss.

It must be real if he can make me feel this way—if I don't want to stop his kisses from lingering.

Gage drops me off at home and I find Brielle lying on my bed helping herself to Chloe's diary.

I snatch it out from underneath her. "What the hell are you doing?"

The window to my bedroom has been boarded up, and it looks like Mom has washed and replaced my bedding.

"Relax. I already knew half that stuff." She rolls over and stretches out her limbs like a lazy cat.

I open it to where I left off and see that the pages thereafter are still sealed shut.

"What are you doing here?" I try to stifle my insane annoyance with Brielle at the moment.

"Drake is getting ready to take me to dinner. I thought I'd come and hang out. Got his new car today, you see it?"

"No." I feel like I've just been bitch slapped. For sure it's starting to feel like Drake is the golden child of the family. If the car was in the driveway, I didn't notice, but then it was dark and I'm still mental from seeing Ezrina.

"Well good for him." I bury Chloe's diary in my underwear drawer before plopping on the bed. "Guess what I heard today?"

"What?" Her eyes widen with expectation.

"Michelle is gonna have a baby."

"Are you freaking serious?" There's a burst of excitement in her voice.

"I shit thee not. And I suppose you know about Carly now." I tick my head back to the underwear drawer.

"I knew about Carly, but Michelle?" Her hands and feet pound the bed with excitement.

"Wait, does everyone know about Carly?" I'm stunned by this.

"I don't think so. I heard Chloe threatening her once in the gym about a baby carriage, plus when she started to sport tents day after day, I got suspicious," she pauses. "So when she left school early, I figured she was going to lay her egg."

"Egg?"

"Yeah, you're full of them. You didn't know that?" Brielle rolls her eyes then burst into laughter.

"Michelle is going to have Dudley's baby. Is that freaking wild?"

"Yeah, that's wild." Brielle gets up on her elbows and gazes out at the wall in front of us. "So," her tone softens, "what are you wearing tomorrow night?"

"Gage picked out a French maid costume for me. Only I won't have to wear that choker thing." I yank down my scarf.

She winces at the sight of my neck.

"That's beyond disgusting." She sticks out her tongue.

"How about you guys?"

"I'm a nun, and he's a priest."

"Oh, I get it—Mr. and Mrs. Blasphemy." I roll over onto my stomach. "So what do you think is gonna to happen to Michelle?"

"Let's see, she'll be wishing she were dead in about nine months when she's trying to squeeze a watermelon out of her ass, then after that, Dudley will wish that he was." She gives a big toothy grin.

It's comfortable lying here with Brielle. Strange how she knew that stuff about Carly and didn't mention it.

I look at her chestnut brown hair falling over her shoulders, her perfect features, that porcelain white skin.

Hanging out with Brielle feels natural, like if she ever did lose her mind and marry Drake one day, I could totally see her as my sister. I sort of already do. There's no way she knows she's a Count or understands the fact she's supposed to oppress me simply because of my lineage. I don't know how I could have ever suspected Brielle of slitting my throat.

She dips her hand down onto the floor and reemerges with a sickle shape piece of glass.

Brielle locks eyes with me, lost in a cold isolated stare. The light refracts off the shard, spraying pale blue dots and shadows all across the room.

"Are you afraid of me, Skyla?" She asks with a slow whisper. There's not a hint of laughter in her eyes, nothing that suggests she might be teasing.

"No." I lie, rubbing my fingers across my stitches. "Should I be?"

"I think you should fear just about everybody."

20

Boo

Halloween morning on Paragon is dark, damp, and blustery. No game tonight, but I decide to wear my cheer uniform to school anyway, minus the scarf I've been wrapping around my neck like a second skin.

Mom gasps as I enter the kitchen.

"What is that?" She makes her way over and taps my stitches with the pads of her fingers. "Looks so real."

"Like it? Gage and me went and got a bunch of cool stuff at the Halloween store yesterday." I turn around toward the fridge so she won't see my face light up like a flame.

Crap! What was I thinking? For sure I wasn't thinking she was going to touch it. Hell, I didn't even think she'd notice.

"So what are you?" Mia comes around the corner and ogles at my neck. Her face contorts in a repulsive manner, and she backs off as though it might be contagious.

"I'm a cheerleader who got her throat slit." I walk over and pull a banana off the counter while considering the irony.

"So how's the baby making going?" Mia asks as she picks her backpack off the floor.

I hold my hand up and shield my face from Mom so I can retch freely in Mia's direction.

Why would she ask that? That's totally disgusting. I'd rather have my throat slashed a thousand times than ever bring up the subject of baby making with Mom.

"You know. It just seems like it was a whole lot less work when you were born." She starts slicing into a grapefruit.

I can't breathe. This is sick.

"Excuse me," I sigh into my words. "It's neither normal nor healthy to be discussing this at breakfast, or quite frankly at any meal with your children."

"Oh, I'm sorry, Skyla," Mom's voice is laden with sarcasm. "Has my desire to produce a beautiful baby brother or sister ruined the digestive process for you?"

"Completely." I push a box of Drake's cereal away to prove a point. "You know, maybe it's just not meant to be."

Her mouth gapes open, and she stands there staring at me in disbelief.

She stops cutting her fruit and walks over at an uneven clip with the knife still in her hand.

"Just because you're rooting for this not to happen, doesn't mean I'm willing to take whatever you feel like dishing. I've got time and money working against me. The last thing I need is your attitude."

"What the hell is going on?" Tad scampers over at a brisk pace. "Is she upsetting you again?"

"What do you mean again? I haven't been upsetting her," I say taking a giant step back. It's too late, I've lit the fuse—I can feel it.

"I'm fine," my mother whispers, shuddering in his arms. The drama is so thick, for a moment I think I missed something.

Tad's eyes hook onto Dr. Oliver's handy work braided across my neck and his face explodes in a crimson ball of anger.

"I thought I told you not to expose this family to the graffiti you've inflicted upon yourself." There's a renewed calm in him.

"It's for Halloween," I say, quietly running my finger across the incision.

"You are pushing the both of us to the outer limits." His voice shakes as efforts to control himself begin to wane. "Is this family some kind of joke to you?" His voice booms across the house creating an unnatural echo. It's deathly silent in the void.

There it is. The explosion.

I can feel Drake pulling up a seat beside me eagerly anticipating the rest of the show.

"Because if you think you're too good for us, we'll be happy to make other arrangements." There is something more than anger inside of him—it's as though the aftertaste of genuine hatred is layered just beneath. Then it hits me. Tad really does hate me. He doesn't want me as a part of this family.

"Mom?" I want to ask if she's going to stand there and let him talk to me like this, but she cowers into him almost as if she agrees.

"Skyla." She pushes her fingers into her forehead and closes her eyes. "Just get to school. We'll start fresh later."

"Right." I take off upstairs.

Something tells me we can never start fresh again.

Gage is all hopped up on the heels of our love as we stand in the overflow parking lot.

There's something charming about the way he smiles and gazes openly, but something alarming about the fact that we've let a fake relationship get so far while I'm still in the midst of a real one. The good thing about being with Gage is that I made a promise to myself that whenever we're in public I'll never pretend my feelings for him. The bad thing is, during moments like this, when it's just the two of us in the woods and there's not another soul around, I should feel far guiltier than I do.

"I dreamed about you," he says. The smile melts off his face ever so slightly.

"Was I naked?" I bite down on my lip and give a playful smile.

"Nope." He loosens into a grin. "Very much clothed."

"So, what happened?" I give a light massage to the back of his neck.

"Can't tell you. It was one of my special dreams."

"Special? As in code for dirty?"

"No." His eyes widen into two large pools. "Special as in prophetic."

"You know something?" I cease all movement and gaze into him. His dark hair lies in thick wet strands—it curls up around his temples and at the base of his neck in neat little coils.

"I know lots of things." He looks down briefly. "Anyway, I like dreaming about you, seeing you even when you're not with me."

I wrap my arms around his waist and sway with him in the breeze.

"I want to know the things you know. Will you tell me what you saw?"

"It's not important what I saw." He gives an apprehensive smile as if trying to hide a mild thread of panic.

"It's important to me. If it concerns my future, I want to know."

"I've done that before, and I swore I'd never do it again."

"So it wasn't good—the dream." My hands drop to my sides.

"I never said that. It was fine, I just...I think we're going to be late." He picks up my hand, and we start in toward the English building.

"Just promise me something." I step in front of him, blocking his path.

"What's that?" His dimples dig in on either side, and I get the urge to drag him into the thicket again.

"One day you'll tell me everything."

He takes in a ragged breath. "Trust me, Skyla, there will never be a day you will want to know everything. Sometimes it's just better to let life surprise you."

21

Oh Wicked Night

Drake drives Brielle and me over to Ellis's party in his newly acquired death mobile. I'm starting to think maybe Mom and Tad aren't so hot on Drake after all. This thing is rife with engine problems, torn upholstery, stinks like a cigarette burial ground, and I swear it hobbles. It has three-car pileup written all over it.

As soon as we hit the driveway, I bounce out of the car.

I tug at my skirt as I make my way up the driveway. Instead of showing off my French maid costume in front of Mom and Tad, and trying to escape their clutches as they attempt to strangle me with my fishnet stockings, I changed over at Brielle's.

Brielle's mom, Darla, lent me a pair of four inch spiked heels with metal studs running down the back. They're totally cute, but hurt like hell to walk in. Darla kept saying they were her favorite pair of FM's, and when I asked what FM's were, both Brielle and Darla laughed.

It's annoying when I don't know things. They've totally lived their lives cloistered on an island—they're the ones who shouldn't know things. I'm from L.A. for God's sake. I'm almost positive I was exposed to every vile thing possible before I was nine, and somehow an entire group of people sequestered from society know more than I do.

Ellis's front yard is littered with gravestones, unearthed caskets, and about a dozen groaning corpses that I'm not entirely sure aren't Fems. I'm expecting anything tonight, and a part of me feels ready—the other part suggests I find either Gage or Logan and hide.

"Knock knock," I say. The front door sits wide open, so I step on in. The house is empty. The hollow click of my heels creates an echo as I traipse over the glossy marble floor in the direction of the kitchen. The thick scent of something baking permeates the air. It definitely doesn't smell like Ellis's house.

I meander on, until I find Ellis himself pulling a gallon of milk from the fridge. It doesn't take long for Brielle and Drake to wander in behind me and make themselves at home on the couch.

"Wow, what's this?" A glass pan of brownies sits cooling on the stove. "You bake?"

"Yes, I bake. All good men bake." He's wearing a football uniform with a tire track across the front of his chest and things that actually look like bloodied entrails hang out of his jeans. "You want one?" He offers me a brownie.

"Sure, I guess. Hey, wait..." I tilt my head suspiciously. "You put your stash in these." I think I just nailed precisely why Ellis Harrison bakes—why he does anything in fact.

"What are you on? I don't share my stash in its natural form, let alone grind it up and waste it on a dozen different people. I just thought it'd be nice to have something around, plus my mom bought the mix."

I wave my hand over the dish. "Ooh, still warm. They're so my favorite when they're warm."

He pours us each a glass of milk in tall cobalt glasses before cutting long rows several inches thick into the pan. We each pick up a strip and indulge.

"These are really good. You should go into business," I muse.

"Check out the nun and the priest." He flicks a finger over at Brielle and Drake. They've gone horizontal and are pushing their faces into one another. "Looks brutal."

"I think it's a part of their costume. You know, sort of a performance piece."

We just sit there stuffing our faces and watch them like it's some sick show on TV until a stream of people filter in through the main entry.

"I better shut the lights off." Ellis takes off and starts flicking switches. Rows and rows of candles are set out in various places all over the house that I hadn't noticed until now.

Ellis's brownies are really freaking good. We've managed to polish off half the pan already, so there's no point in cutting them up and setting them out. I'm practically doing him a favor by downing the rest. Truth is, I only like brownies and cookies if they're fresh out of the oven. There's something about warm gooey chocolate melting in my mouth that I find intensely satisfying.

A swarm moves in. The bitch squad cackles up a storm in my direction. There she is—Mama Michelle. Her hair is curled in tight little ringlets that spring up near her face. She's got on a deep velvet cape that, in this devoid lighting, looks a dark shade of bloody crimson. Of course, she's fully equipped with a clunky walking cast from that flying leap she took off Devil's Peak a few weeks ago. Little red mommy hood. I press my lips together to keep the comment from vomiting out.

Emily looks like a questionable Alice in Wonderland, her fake long blonde hair and overdone face makes it look like she's in drag more than anything else.

Then there's Lexy. Actually Lexy looks good—too good. She's supposed to be the queen of hearts judging by the glorified leotard, mini tutu, and a thousand glittering hearts sprinkled all over. A giant heart on her chest cradles her boobs, sort of gives the impression they're sitting on a tray. She's got her feet pressed into heels twice as high as mine, and they totally look like FM's, and...oh freaking hell. I think I just figured out what FM's stand for, and I don't like those words having anything to do with Lexy on a night when Logan's going to try and get some info out of her.

"And what are you supposed to be?" Emily pulls her bloodstained lips into a snarl while examining me up and down.

"French maid." I point to my neck. "Who just got her throat slit."

The three of them sit and gawk with their arms folded tight.

"It's supposed to be sexy with a Goth flare," I add stupidly.

"You just keep believing that." Lexy swivels her head over her neck and for a brief moment, I'm hopeful it's going to glide right off.

"I don't think you'd know sexy if it walked up and bit you in the face—which I'm sure bears a striking resemblance to your ass." Michelle high fives Emily.

"So where's the big bad wolf?" I ignore her quip, looking behind her, fully expecting to see Marshall. Showing up at a student party isn't beneath him. Apparently knocking them up isn't either.

"Is he coming?" She fingers the rose around her neck.

"How would I know? I'm not his keeper."

Lexy and Emily take off toward the cauldron of bubbling liquid that Ellis just set out, surrounded by towers of red plastic cups that act as an inebriation warning system.

"I saw you." Michelle jabs her finger into my chest with each word.

I slap her hand away. "Saw me what?"

"Get in the car and take off during second. You think your crap doesn't stink? You come into town, steal Logan, break his heart, then take Gage. You disgust me. And now you think you can sleep around with Dudley on the side? I've known Logan and Gage all my life. I'm not going to stand by and watch you slut around while grinding everyone to pieces. I bet that's why you moved from L.A. You slept around town so damn much, they threw you out."

"First of all…" I go to point my finger, and my entire hand feels lighter than air.

Ellis turns on the music, and it's some song I haven't heard in like forever.

"God I love this song!" I really, really *love* this song. "Anyway, I don't break hearts, and I'm not a slut," I pause as I make my way past her. "Besides, they would never kick you out of L.A. for sleeping around. They erect statues and throw parades for crap like that."

22

Bite Me

I start scanning the crowd for either Logan or Gage. It feels so lonely without them. I'm so sick of wanting Logan, wishing I could be with him, stealing a moment just to be together, and never having enough of him. But then there's Gage, those eyes that see right into my soul, the way he protects me, and he just so happens to have the face of a thousand underwear models rolled into one. He's the paragon of perfect. I laugh at my own pun. That is actually pretty damn funny.

Ellis comes down the hall with that scary clown mask he terrorized me with a few weeks back.

I suck in a lungful of air as he charges at me and tries to nip at my neck.

"Get away!" I push him off. I hate clowns, almost as much as I'm hating Ellis right now.

He snatches the mask off and laughs. And strangely I find myself laughing right along with him. Freaking stupid Ellis.

Ellis. I've never noticed before how cute he is in his own right. In fact if I wasn't with Logan and Gage, I could totally see myself with Ellis. I laugh a little louder at the thought. It's sort of gross the way he's always stoned, but I could probably change him if I wanted.

"Would you give up pot for me?" I giggle into him as he wraps an arm around my waist. He's smiling wildly with his seductive half closed eyes—then I see him—Gage.

A tall sexy vampire stands near the roaring fire. I hadn't even noticed how magnificent the fire is, how ferocious the flames look as they lick outside the confines of the hearth, and for a second, I'm mesmerized by the taunting orange blaze.

Gage heads toward me. I push Ellis away, and he drifts effortlessly into a group of girls.

I can't believe this. Gage has his entire face done up—sickly pale skin offset by his dark peaked brows, lips as black as death. God, he's got lipstick on—I'm transfixed by this.

He gives a devilish smile and pulls me along by the hand down the long hall at a quickened clip. We end up in a dark corridor, nothing but rows of closed doors one after another. Gage opens the one at the end with caution before ushering us inside.

It's quiet in here. My ears pulsate in protest to the powerful silence. I stretch my arms in front of me and flail around in the shadows. It feels like I'm about to fall, like the whole world has inverted into an alternate dimension for just Gage and me, and now we're here alone.

I run my hands down his chest and rest my fingers on the rim of his pants. I can feel him brush his lips over my face, light as a feather, and it makes me want him even more.

"Kiss me," I say.

A tremor of laughter rumbles deep inside his chest. He darts a kiss behind my ear and it tickles me mercilessly.

"Stop." I giggle the word out unintelligibly.

He bites down on my earlobe hard. The pain spears through me—hot, like an errant ember, then dissipates into something softer, a more manageable ache.

I gasp for breath as he makes his way down my neck. He grazes and gnaws on my flesh until it feels like I'm being invaded by razor blades.

"Your teeth." I manage the words in a spasm. "So sharp."

"You like that?" He rumbles. "I had them filed." He leans his head back and a thin seam of moonlight catches the tips of his canines.

"That's so hot." I close my eyes as he lunges back at my throat. "Hey." I want to tell him that it hurts, but the words get jumbled in a series of moans. Gage suckles off my neck, pretending to drink deeply. My entire person responds in spasms alternating between pleasure and pain, and I'm starting to feel light headed. I give a halfhearted struggle to push him away, but he lingers for several more minutes before finally coming up for air.

He whispers hot in my ear, "Gotcha."

Gage leaves in a hurry—probably has to get to a restroom fast. Lord knows I've been there.

I filter through the crowd. The party is still going strong when I finally make my way out of the maze of hallways. I swear these houses behind the gates are like self-contained labyrinths.

Finally, I spot Logan and Gage sitting by themselves near the pool and head on over. The backyard is lit up with hundreds of jack-o-lanterns. That must be Ellis's other talent, aside from baking, because each one is expertly carved up with an intricate design.

"We were just thinking you got eaten by Fems. Where've you been?" Gage pulls me into a giant hug.

"I was…" I jerk my hand back at the house and start to laugh. "I was with you, and you took off."

"When were you with me?" His forehead creases, and I realize he doesn't have a stitch of makeup on.

"Just now." Is this like some stupid prank? "What are you guys doing out here? It's freezing." I rub at my arms vigorously—it feels as though my entire body is vibrating from each little goose bump. It almost feels as though Marshall were touching me.

"I was just telling Gage how much I like his dress." Logan nods over to his cape.

"And I was just telling Logan my *girlfriend* asked me to wear it."

"Nice. Hey, where's your make-up?" I'm starting to think that really wasn't Gage back there. Crap. I probably just hooked up with some drunk guy form East. Everyone at West knows I'm with Gage, right?

"I draw the line at face painting." He tightens his grip around my waist and glares over at Logan. "Your strategy of forcing me to listen to your big bad plan of how you're going to battle the Counts, just so I would miss half the party—backfired. And now she was molested by some idiot in a cape."

He looks to me. "You remember what this guy looked like? His name?"

"I thought it was you." I shake my head over at Gage.

"What did he do to you?" Logan stands and gently rubs my arm up and down as his eyes widen with horror. It's only then I notice he's in jeans and wearing his football jersey, looking like his scary hot self.

"He took me in the back room and kissed my neck." I tilt my head to the side.

Logan looks from me to Gage with a clear look of hurt.

Great. Now he's going to think that's all we do when we're alone. Then it occurs to me it sort of is and I feel like hell.

"Here you are!" Lexy comes up from behind Logan. She swings him by the waist, and they both sail into the pool with a giant splash that drenches me from the waist down.

Logan pops up like a cork and shakes back his hair. His teeth glow as he offers me a soft sad grin, but the moment passes too quickly.

Lexy charges at him with open arms and he stops her midflight by playfully dunking her under water. I hope he holds her down at least a good four minutes.

A steady rise of steam drifts on the surface of the pool.

"Feels warm." Gage shakes the water off his hands. He gently lifts my hair back and examines my neck under the paper lantern, wincing. "That's looks like one mean bruise. I'm gonna kill this guy. Are you sure you're OK? Did he do anything else?" His face lights up with worry.

"No. I don't think so." I bite down on my lip to stop the river of laughter trying to bubble out of me.

"It's not funny," he says quietly. "I don't like the idea of some guy laying his hands all over you. You could have been killed."

I set off on a long stretch of titters before holding my stomach and engaging in a full-blown hacking laugh.

"Are you OK?"

I gasp at the one lucid thought that sails through my mind.

"Ellis fed me brownies."

Gage gives an exasperated blink before leading me toward the house.

"Make that two people I'm going to kill."

I look over at the pool and see Lexy ruffling up Logan's hair in the deep end as he attempts to climb out.

I might kill Lexy just for fun. And I laugh.

23

Fight Night

Gage is in a fury. He subdues my incessant need to giggle by vexing me with the truth of what Ellis has done. His rage builds as he pushes through the crowd looking for the perpetrator of my inadvertent high.

The house is crowded, dark—it sways in rhythm to the boisterous music blaring from the speakers. I see Brielle and Drake, gyrating, letting loose on a table with another girl I don't recognize.

The fireplace captures me again. Low blue flames sweep through the air, calling out to me lethargically. They spit out an occasional spark that spears across the hearth like an errant shooting star.

"This him?" Gage thrashes some kid in a vampire costume hard against the metal railing. "Skyla?"

My mouth falls open. He's got the right face paint and the cape...

"I don't know. I don't think so." Gage pushes him to the ground and walks deeper into the house.

"You can't go knocking people around." I try to keep up with him. "You're gonna hurt somebody."

"That's the plan."

I've never seen him caged in so much fury. We scan the living room, kitchen— pan all of the downstairs vicinity.

"Never mind." I pull him back by the elbow trying to abort the mission. "I swear it was probably a misunderstanding. I thought it was you, and maybe he thought I was someone else." I cup his face gently with my hands. Gage is staggeringly attractive with his eyes blazing, his heart thumping wild for revenge. "I want to enjoy the party. Can't we just have a good time?"

"Are you sure you're OK?" His hard expression gives a little.

"Yes, I'm fine. I feel weird, but that's Ellis's fault." I can't believe he lied to me.

Outside the open double doors we hear the faint sound of Ellis's very distinct laughter. It doesn't take long for Gage to bolt in that direction.

I try to trail after him at top speed, but end up flailing and turning my ankles every step of the way. It's strange the way my body feels—relaxed and yet unusually aware of every movement.

I spot Michelle stooped over the porch with her head between her knees. Emily is stroking her back as though she were a cat. I pause to see if she's about to puke or something. Her back jerks in a series of vibrations until it becomes clear Michelle is crying.

"What's going on?" I ask Emily rather impulsively. We are all on the squad together. I did visit her in the hospital after she dove off Devil's Peak, plus evidently I'm stoned, so it reasons with logic that I should inquire about Michelle's almost humanlike behavior.

"Dudley broke up with her." Emily divulges without giving it much thought.

"What?" I'm stunned. "Didn't the Mayans predict this?" A shiver of laughter gets locked in my chest as I try to digest my own absurdity. No sooner do the words fly out of my mouth than Michelle appears in my face. She shoves her fist through my abdomen, knocking the air out of my lungs. I roll into the planter bed—face down. Michelle lands on my back and begins pulling violently at my hair. She maneuvers me around like puppet causing the incision on my neck to stretch every which way, and suddenly I'm acutely aware of the sharp line of pain.

I let out a shrill cry. Before I can turn, or grab her, or close my mouth, she plunges my face into the dirt and grinds it in for good measure.

"Don't let me catch you near him again." Her hot breath sears against the back of my neck.

I roll over in time to see Michelle and Emily ditch into the house. I scan the porch and I'm alone save for a scarecrow sitting on a rocking chair. It seems the entire exchange was witnessed by nobody. I get up and spit into the flowerbed over and over— pretend it's Michelle's face every single time.

She picked a lousy time to get knocked up. I'd love to grind her into the dirt myself, six feet under to be exact.

I see Gage at the bottom of the driveway and run over to him. My ankle gives and twists as I hit the bottom, landing me hard on Ellis.

"I guess she likes me better," Ellis says, helping me upright. "You saved me. He was just about to beat the hell out of me."

"Beat him later," I say toppling over to Gage. "Will you take me to see Dudley?"

The moon squats down low behind him, kisses his black hair with an unearthly glow. He really does look like an angel.

A clear look of exasperation crosses his face as he reaches over and digs his finger into Ellis's chest.

"This isn't over."

Ellis pins him with an evil look I didn't know he was capable of—makes me feel as though I don't know Ellis at all.

Gage is nice enough to drive me over to Marshall's house, in order to help stave off the manslaughter charge I was about to incur.

"Skyla." Marshall pinches at his eyes as though he just woke up. I brush past him, making my way into the house. "Not you." He pushes his hand into Gage. "I choose the guests—and you happen to be the wrong gender. Goodnight." He shoves him outside and begins to shut the door.

"I'm not leaving." Gage swoops back in and appears by my side.

"I don't play this game." Marshall snatches a bowl full of candy from off a small table. "But if you want cavities, I believe you're to stand outside and speak in verse—cast a spell or something." A mild look of annoyance whisks across his face.

"If it's OK, I'd like to talk to Mr. Dudley," I say to Gage. I let him know in the car ride over that I wanted to grill Marshall on leaving Michelle—to let him know it's only going to make my life worse as evidenced by the fertilizer still lodged in my nose.

"I'll wait outside." Gage glowers as he heads out the door.

"Look at you," Marshall marvels at me. "You're filthy and vexingly beautiful." He concludes with a lascivious smile before bolting the door.

"Take Michelle back."

"No." His cheek rises on one side.

"You have to." I take a bold step forward. "I want to kill her—probably will. And if I don't, she's going to put me through a living hell."

"Not my concern." He holds out the dish of candy and rattles it in my direction. "No one showed up tonight."

"It's because you live in the boonies and your porch light isn't on." I push it away indignantly. "Listen, I have enough trouble without adding Michelle to the equation. Just do me a favor, keep doing whatever it is you do with her. It makes her happy." I swallow hard at the thought of concerning myself with Michelle's happiness, but, then again, it directly relates to mine.

"I can't do that. Besides, it's been brought to my attention that it's no way to win you over, so I let her know I've moved on." He gives a devilish smile. "That I'm interested in another student body."

I seize at the thought. "What the hell'd you do that for?"

"Because, Skyla." He lets the candy dish drop rather violently to his feet. "It's the direction I choose to venture in." He gives a hard look. "Now send the twit home, so I can convince you of the same." His sharp features startle me with their beauty in this dim light. Even with all of his fury, there is an amazing attraction he exudes. It feels almost deliberate as though he's trying to seduce me.

I circle around him and make my way to the door.

“You don’t tell me what to do,” I hiss. “If you’re going to turn my life into bloody hell, I’ll return the favor.”

“There you go, Skyla.” His tone sharpens. “Grab the tiger by the tail. See how fast I turn around to bite you.”

I open the door and step out into the crisp night air.

“And Skyla?” His voice sails past me, gets lost in the thicket just beyond the property. “I’ve been to bloody hell. I used to grease the gates.”

“Gage?” I call out. His mother’s car sits abandoned in the driveway, but he’s nowhere to be found. A wild panic surges through me. “Where’s Gage?” I ask accusingly.

“I’ve sent him.” There’s a challenge in his voice.

“Sent him where?”

“To hell of course.”

24

Hot Date

I'm forced to endure an entire session of Marshall's attempt at romance. He promised to return Gage unharmed if I spent the next twenty minutes with him.

I watch as he meticulously lights up row after row of candles.

"How does that look?" He steps back admiring his efforts.

"Great. When's the séance?" I try to ignore the fact he looks glorious in this pale flickering light.

"You slay me." He doesn't look amused.

At his command, the sound of a symphony starts to play from somewhere overhead. He takes up my hand and we start to sway to the music.

"You know," I start, "this would totally be illegal if you were human. Attempted kidnapping, forcing yourself upon a minor—impregnating a minor." Thank God that last one has nothing to do with me. Just as I'm about to continue with his budding list of felonies, he presses his lips against mine and startles me with a kiss filled with ripples of shivering passion.

A vision races through my mind—me with wings, a horse beside me. I'm holding a shield with a marked crack down the center. I see Logan and Gage fighting a war, muddied and tired, as sopping wet clothes cling to their bodies. Logan throws me a long black gun and I dip down to my knees from the heft of it.

Marshall pulls away and leaves me breathless.

"What was that?" I pant.

"Some kiss," he muses with his eyes half closed.

"I saw something." I scrutinize him in his lust-filled glory. "What was it?"

"The future."

"My future?" I'm perplexed. It's only then I realize we're no longer in his home—we're outside somewhere underneath the fat belly of a lavender moon standing on a cobblestone street. "Where are we?"

"Just this side of heaven. Don't worry, you're allowed. I thought I'd give you a taste of my world. Do you like it?"

"Is this some kind of alternate plane?" I try to keep up with him as he moves toward a small shop with tables and chairs set out on the sidewalk.

We take a seat, and a young man appears with two steaming cups of coffee.

"What's going to happen when I drink this?"

"You're going to shrink, and a giant fluffy bunny will begin to chase you," he muses before taking a careful sip. There's a certain charm about Marshall that pulls me in, keeps me interested just enough to keep from strangling him.

"What kind of future was that? I saw Logan and Gage. We were in some kind of war."

"It was the heat of battle. Did you forget you're in the midst of faction upheaval?"

"No." Sort of.

"Are you aware of the fact you've procured a spiritual appendage?"

"A what?"

"You have a ghost, Skyla, lingering by your side. He wants revenge." He motions to my left.

"Crap!" I let out a little scream and bounce my seat closer to Marshall. I see him clear as velum—looks a lot like Pierce, with the exception that his throat is gouged out.

"Relax, he has no dominion here. He's spatial. It's an earth thing. You can bet he's going to manipulate your world, but say the word, and I'll bind him for you."

"It's him." I don't dare say Holden's name. "I've killed him, and now he's going to haunt me."

"That might be the case, but I don't want him ruining our date." Marshall points in his direction and he vanishes. "He says he'll meet you in your bedroom."

I straighten in my seat. "He drove Gage's truck didn't he? He's the reason we crashed."

"You're a bright girl."

"How do I get you to bind him? No wait—don't tell me. If I choose to become a part of your childbearing harem, you call off the haunting?"

"You're much sharper at logic than you are math." He gives a crooked grin.

"There's no logic here." Chloe's face blinks through my mind. I'm going to give blood tomorrow. I'm going to bring her back and she'll fall hard for Marshall. Then he'll owe me. It feels more like a question than a fact at this point. "So when I kissed you and saw the future, was that a fluke?" I've kissed Marshall before and don't remember having any kind of vision.

"It's my gift to you. Anytime you wish to sneak a peek, it's my pleasure." His eyes widen with delight.

"How do I know it's not some fake future you're implanting in my brain to manipulate me?"

"Let's test this theory, shall we? I'll give you a glimpse of something guaranteed to happen within the next twenty-four hours, and when it does, you'll know the power I've laid before you."

How do I know he's not manipulating reality as well? He's a Sector. I don't even get what he's capable of.

"Maybe."

"Here." He helps me to my feet, and we begin to make our way down the street. "I'll show you something of interest while you weigh your options."

That tuning fork feeling, that good vibration that sends my toes curling, jettisons through me, only this time it's not through the hand that Marshall is holding, it feels like it's coming from…the atmosphere?

"This feels so good. What is it?"

"Fruit of the spirit in concentrate. Amazing isn't it? I've let go of it just once to see what it's truly like to inhabit the earth, feels like a car wreck every waking minute."

"I guess it would. Is Gage really in hell?" I squeeze his hand as if to threaten him into telling the truth.

"He's in a holding tank. I'll send him home bright and early in the morning. He won't be happy. I'd stay away."

"I'm sure you'd like me to stay away in general." I'm not going to. I'll never stay away from either Logan or Gage, not for Marshall, Tad or anyone.

He pauses in front of a large cave-like structure. A group of men at least nine feet tall stand outside the mouth looking over me with curious stares. A pale like sheath moves behind them and I notice one of them has wings.

"He—" I pant the word out.

"Yes, Skyla, let's not cause a scene."

"That is so weird." And amazingly hot. "Hey, why aren't there any women here?" I pull in closer to Marshall. I don't like to be the center of attention or leered at like a novelty.

"Pure angels are male. We can breed with women, but it's heavily frowned upon. The practice was nixed just after a few of my brothers took up with the daughters of men. Old news—happened ages past. Still does now and again." He brushes his hand in the air. "Transport tunnels." He slaps the outside of the cave. "Made of pure Jasper, carved from one solid block." The inside looks black from this perspective. "You know what's marvelous about the dark?" He pauses gazing inside with a lost vegetative stare. "The way it allows the light to magnify itself."

I peer in closer and see light in the form of translucent people.

"Fascinating." I run my finger over the soft red wall. "So then, who are you supposed to be with?" Obviously Sectors have a sexual nature, unless of course Marshall is some sort of defect.

"The deceased." He points inside the cave. Two disembodied women appear, both with startled expressions. The man in the cave lets them know they'll be carried upwards momentarily. "Or the Caelestis," Marshall says, flicking a finger skyward as though I should know what he's talking about.

"What's a Caelestis?"

"Angels are men who serve in the divine armed forces, and Caelestis..." He squints into the moon as though trying to figure out the best way to describe them. "They're on the decision council. They make suggestions and assist in the mapping out of peoples lives."

"So the men fight wars and the women decide what to do? How original."

"They decide what *should* be done," he corrects. "When dealing with humans, always lower expectation, then lower it some more."

"Gee thanks." I roll my eyes at the thought. "So are they beautiful?"

"They are, but you my love, are stunning." Marshall takes me in and swallows hard. "Anyway," he says tapping the side of the rock wall. "Transport duty is grueling," he whispers looking back inside the cave.

Another group of disembodied people appear. Two of them go down, the rest go up.

"They're dying?" I'm fascinated by this.

"Dead." Marshall turns to face me, brushes my hair back with his fingers. "I've made arrangements to be on transport duty the day you arrive in that tunnel. I'm going to be the one to bring you safe to your final destination, Skyla." His eyes circle around my face, in a soft sad manner.

Something warms inside me. The thought of death scares me, but knowing Marshall will be there somehow makes it feel all right—safe.

"Thank you."

"Would you like that kiss now?" The words purr out of him. The pale moonlight glides across his face and smoothes away any malfeasance.

"Yes."

Marshall gently cups my cheeks and indulges in a greedy lust-soaked kiss.

In my mind, I see Logan speaking to me. He looks intent on something—sad. I see myself turn away and start to cry. He tries to comfort me, but I shake my head, bring my hands to my eyes and cover my face.

I pull back and stare into Marshall. “What does it mean?” I say out of breath.

“It means you’re one step closer to being my wife.”

25

This Kiss

All night I ruminate over Gage in hell, and that vision Marshall gave me, until my sanity begins to erode.

In the morning, I beg Drake to drive me over to the Oliver's house. I tell Mom and Tad it's mandatory cheer practice, and that afterwards, I'm starting my new job at the bowling alley.

I ring the bell impatiently as Drake backs sloppily out of the driveway taking out an entire row of purple flowers that, moments ago, happily dotted the periphery.

A storm is rolling in. The dark sky looms overhead heavy as a battleship. There's something about the lavender afterglow inside the clouds that reminds me of that kiss from Marshall. A shiver runs through me. I don't dare advertise the fact to either Logan or Gage that I let him near me for a hypothetical glimpse into the future.

The door opens slowly. Dr. Oliver's face brightens as he extends his hand for me to come inside.

"Here to give another pint?"

"Sure. Mostly I'm here to see Gage." I leave out the part about him going to hell.

"He's having a late start today, still in bed. If you want I can take it now. I'm leaving in a few minutes for a meeting."

"OK." I follow Dr. Oliver in the kitchen where he pulls his equipment out from a side pantry and begins to drain my blood into a soft plastic bag. "So this is number five or six?" I'm starting to lose count.

"I believe it's five. Are you feeling alright?" He presses the back of his hand to my forehead. "You look ghastly pale."

"I feel fine." Truth is I'm beyond exhausted. Last night was more than my body could handle.

"There." He removes the needle and quickly replaces it with a band-aid. "Let's remove the stitches shall we?"

"Please." I pluck off my scarf and roll it into a pile next to me.

"What's this?" He gently turns my head to the side and groans. "Which one of my boys assaulted you this way?"

I'm assuming he's looking at the purple hickey the size of Mount Rushmore just below my cut.

"Actually..." God, how do I say neither? "It was an accident."

He rubs his finger gently against my neck and sighs before removing the stitches.

"Skyla, tell the truth, what happened?" His eyes rove over my face deep with concern.

"I thought it was Gage. It was some guy, he...it felt like—"

"You have a puncture wound—several actually, right over your jugular."

"Are you saying I was bit..." I don't believe in vampires, so I stop the thought midflight.

"I'm saying someone, most likely someone who knows you're a Celestra, punctured your neck. Did it feel like they were suckling blood from you?"

I wince when he says the word suckling. Dr. Oliver reminds me of my own dad and it just sounds wrong even if it is in a quasi-medical context.

"Yes."

"I thought you looked pale. I wish I had known—I would never have taken more blood. Do you feel faint?"

"No, I'm fine." Suddenly I feel like hell, but I chalk it up to the thought of someone actually drinking my blood. "You mind if I go up and see Gage?"

"Go right ahead."

I make my way toward the stairwell.

"Skyla?"

I turn around.

"Whoever did this will undoubtedly be back. Prepare to defend yourself."

"I will."

I'm so weak it takes all my strength to make it up the stairs.

I knock gently on his door before entering.

"Morning," Gage says, groggy, pulling a shirt from his dresser. His hair is slicked back, shiny and wet from the shower. He's got on a pair of grey sweats with a small hole near his hip. I'm trying to remember whether or not I've seen Gage shirtless before because I'm perplexed by the hard outline of his abdominals. He tosses the shirt over his shoulder and groans.

"I feel horrible." He walks over to his bed and falls back against the pillow, covering his eyes with the back of his arm.

I make my way over and lie beside him.

"What happened?" I pull his arm off his face, and he drapes it over my shoulders instead.

"I was just standing out front, and the next thing I knew I was in this dirt pit at least ten feet under. It felt like I fell in an oven. I kept thinking I was going to combust." He grips his hair. "And there was all this moaning and screaming...anyway, there was this iron grate up over me and I couldn't get out. I woke up in my bed this morning. When I looked out the window, sure enough my mom's car was in the driveway."

"I bet Marshall wants you to think it was a dream. Remember, he's not a Sector to you, he's just your Algebra Two teacher," I pause. "I'm so sorry. Did you try teleporting yourself out of there?"

"All night. It was useless. Don't worry it's not your fault." He surprises me with a sudden burst of energy and pulls me over on top of him. "You know what I thought of?" There's a seductive quality to his voice. His eyes look a deep indigo in this dull morning light as they warm over me.

"What?" My breathing grows erratic. Something about Gage, something powerfully attractive about the way he seduces me with those barely there dimples, with that hidden beneath the surface smile he refuses to give so freely.

"What you said the other day. That you loved me."

Everything in me clinches. It's true I had said it and I meant it—still do.

I dip down and kiss him ever so slightly. His chest beats under mine in a series of merciless thumps.

"Do you love me, Skyla?"

"Yes," it comes out an inaudible whisper.

His hand pushes in softly against the back of my neck. Gage gives a deep heated kiss that accentuates our feelings. I may be afraid to say it, hesitant to repeat those words, but I feel it, and I know with everything in me that it's true. I really do love Gage.

We lose ourselves in a series of lingering kisses. Gage runs his hands through my hair, down my back, over my jeans. I pull my lips down along his neck and across his chest. He lets out a soft groan and pulls me up until we're sitting. The room spins slightly, and he stops me from falling backward.

"You OK?"

"Yeah." I pull him into another explosive kiss. I'm more than OK.

26

Prophesy

Gage and me arrive at the bowling alley where, evidently, Logan is busy creating a dust cloud with a dust mop.

It's strange to be here so early. The lanes are lit up, and music echoes throughout the establishment, but there's not a patron in sight.

"Morning." I go over and give him a brief hug. I feel so damn guilty about what just happened, I can't look him in the eye. It's like my feelings for Gage just took over. I'd love to blame it on the fact I was worried sick that Marshall had him roasting on a spit, but I'm not sure I could. I'm not sure about anything anymore.

"I've got something for you." Logan gives a soft smile and plucks a nametag off his clipboard. "Ready to work?" Something about Logan feels different this morning. He's melancholy—the spark in his eyes has dissipated.

"Yes! Is the pay decent?" I'd work here for free if wanted.

"Minimum wage." He presses right into me with those expressive amber eyes, reaches in and wrenches me with a look of infinite sadness.

"Minimum wage is totally fine." I'm just glad to be out of the house. I pick up the gold embossed tag that reads Skyla Messenger. "It feels official," I say pinning it up on my shirt.

"What are you still doing here?" His voice hardens over at Gage.

Gage doesn't say anything, just keeps his hands folded tight across his chest.

"Pick you up at seven?" Gage comes over and drops a kiss on the top of my head.

Everything in me freezes. I can't have Gage kissing me in front of Logan. I can't be kissing Gage behind Logan's back. Suddenly, I feel like a giant bag of crap because apparently I am one.

"I'll bring her home." There's a marked aggression in Logan's tone and it racks up the tension in the room immeasurably.

The two of them stand there, staring one another down like they're about to have some high noon showdown, until Gage says goodbye and leaves.

"That was awkward," I whisper.

"Yeah." Logan motions for me to take a seat at the table with him. "Things are getting a bit awkward." He pulls a face.

"So you guys aren't really getting along." As evidenced by every single time they're together.

He shakes his head. "No, but that's not important. I got off the phone with my uncle a few minutes ago." Logan wears a sobering expression. He looks lonely and distant and it badly makes me want to touch him. "He told me about your neck." He presses out a sad smile. "Any idea who it could have been?"

"So I'm guessing, it wasn't you," I say, in a lame attempt to put a cute spin on it.

"My uncle thought maybe a Fem."

"A Fem?" I'm almost amused. "What does that mean?"

"Counts still want them tormenting you—us." He reaches over and brushes his hand over mine for a moment. "What happened to you last night? Michelle said she hurt you."

"She thought it'd be entertaining if she made me eat worms." I can just picture her running around telling everybody she kicked my ass. If she wasn't with child, I would have beat the crap out of her.

An abrupt wave of nausea rolls through me. The room starts to feel like it's spinning as a heavy feeling settles over my bones. I hang onto the edge of the table in order to catch my breath.

"You OK?" He helps steady me.

"I'm fine." I try to shake the feeling away.

Logan rushes and gets me a glass of ice water.

"Skyla, my uncle said he discovered the puncture on your neck after he drew more blood for Chloe. He says your blood levels are way too low, that you're running off minimal reserves. Let me take you home."

"No. It's my first day. Besides, I need the money for insurance and I want to pay for the car."

An easy grin glides across his face.

"Monetarily," I add.

"Of course."

"So did you find out how to bind a Fem?" The thought of Logan hanging out with Lexy makes me sick. "Did she kiss you?"

The smile melts off his face. Something in him darkens before he answers. "No. I wouldn't let her. And no, she didn't tell me, but I made progress."

"What did she say?"

"She said there is a way. It was made known to her by her dad. I guess they're part Nephilim." He shakes his head. "She said she would tell me if..." He looks away briefly. "Anyway, I'm not going to find out. We're back to square one."

"If what?" I think I know, but I want to hear it from him.

The table starts in on a violent rattle.

"What the heck?" Logan struggles to press it down before he stops its erratic quaking.

"Holden Kragger's ghost," I say.

I tell him what Marshall said about my new spiritual attachment and share my theory on the crash.

He lets out a hard breath.

"Marshall said he could get rid of him if I wanted."

"I think I know what he wants in return." Logan doesn't look impressed with Marshall's tactics.

"Is it the same thing Lexy wants?"

"Yes, but I'm pretty sure she doesn't want a race of Celestra, Deorsum children running around."

I twist my lips at the thought. "So Lexy is Deorsum. She never said anything before?"

"She didn't know I was Celestra until after we weren't together anymore."

My stomach sinks when he says it. Lexy and Logan were together once. It's probably only natural for him to still have feelings for her.

"The reason my uncle called was to let me know there's an emergency faction meeting scheduled at Nicholas Havar's tomorrow night."

"What's the emergency?" I'm almost afraid to ask.

"Something tells me you are."

I hang out for three hours after my shift ends and help Logan close up the bowling alley. I'm beyond exhausted—my arms and legs feel like they're going to fall off, and my head feels as heavy as a bowling ball itself.

Logan locks the main exit and turns off the florescent ceiling lights, leaving the alleyways glowing in soft purples and blues.

"You should always keep it like this." I wrap my arms around his neck and peck a quick kiss on his cheek.

He leans in and relaxes into me. His face dims and his brows rise as though he were getting ready to ask me something.

"Well?" A small laugh rumbles from his chest.

"Well what?"

He looks intensely from one eye to the next. "You can't hear me, can you?"

I straighten. I try my hardest to hear him telepathically, but nothing. I study his face intently and shake my head.

"What does this mean?" I'm panicked.

"I don't know. We'll have to ask my uncle." A look of worry slowly dissipates. Logan draws me in and holds me, rocking me safe in his arms. "It'll be OK." He sighs into me and presses a kiss against the top of my head. "You ready to start our date?" A seductive half-smile plays on his lips.

Logan busies himself setting up a picnic right there on lane number five. The music is soft, and the lighting is perfectly enchanting as we take a seat Indian style across from one another with our knees touching.

"Since we had dinner a few hours ago, I thought maybe we could skip right to dessert."

"Was dinner the pizza you catered in and sold to your customers for five dollars extra a box?" I tease.

"That's how I stay in business." He winks. "Kitchen opens near the end of the month."

"Just in time for my birthday."

"And what's the date again?" He brightens as he pulls a mini chocolate éclair from out of the basket.

"Twenty-second."

"Really?" He deflates a little. "I guess you know Gage is the twenty-third."

"No, I didn't know that." I'm surprised, actually. "When's yours?"

"It was the week before you came." He takes up my hand and gently traces my fingers. "You were the perfect present." There's a familiar looking sadness in his eyes. "So you and Gage seem to have a lot in common. How are you getting along?" He massages my hands with his thumbs, staring down at them intently.

Logan is perfect—he glows from the inside with his own special light. I don't think I've ever seen anyone as majestic as Logan.

"Gage is fine." I don't like where this might be going.

"I don't want to ruin our time together, but I want to let you know..." His eyes shimmer with moisture as he looks over at me. "Um, I walked into his room this morning and saw you with Gage." His features smooth over as he depresses out a sigh.

A visual of what he must have seen runs through my mind, me kissing Gage, me on top of Gage. "I..." Crap. "I thought he was hurt. He said he was tired, and he went to lay down, so I—"

"It's OK." He presses his fingers to his lips. "There's nobody to blame, but me."

A spring of tears comes up unexpectedly and I blink them away. I want to say that nothing happened, that it didn't mean anything, but my vocal chords clamp shut, forcing me to swallow the lies.

"I'm not being fair to you or Gage," he starts. "I threw you together and this is something that I'm going to have to live with." Logan nods into this as though he's already considered it.

"You don't have to live with anything. I won't kiss him, I won't be with him."

He tilts his head a little. "I'm not asking you to do that. You need Gage to protect you. I'm not going to give the Counts any extra excuse to hurt you." He swallows hard. "I've been thinking." His eyes light up like sorrowful embers. "I don't think you need the added pressure of me hanging around."

"What are you talking about? Everything is about us. That's why I'm with Gage, so we can be together in private—that's why there's a faction war, so we can knock the Counts off their pedestal and be free to be together. It's going to be you and me, Logan." It comes out more of a question.

"I know that's what we planned and I really do believe you still want that," he pauses pushing into me with an unwavering look of despair. "But I think Gage and I have confused you. I should've known Gage would fall in love with you. It's hard not to." He gives a short-lived smile. "I can't have you with the both of us—it's not right. I'm the one that suggested you be with him, and I think I should be the one to step away, remove myself from the situation. I don't think it's OK for the both of us to pursue you."

"Yes it is." It speeds out of me.

"No." He tugs at my fingers playfully and gives a slow smile. "I love you, but I think your feelings for Gage..." He shrugs. "I think maybe they blossomed unexpectedly." He floats his thumbs over the back of my hands in an even sweeping motion. "It's me you need to keep away from, Skyla, not him. I'm the one who could cost you everything." His eyes glitter with tears as he offers a hesitant smile. "I think maybe for now—we should just be friends."

27

Heartbreak

Alone in my bed that night, I drench myself in tears. It all unfolded just like the vision Marshall had given me.

Logan's rationale meant nothing. They were empty words on a nonexistent platform. He wouldn't admit the real reason he was leaving me was because I cheated. Instead, he shouldered the majority of our demise and pinned the rest on the Countenance.

I apologized beyond reason for ever touching Gage, for ever thinking I might have loved him, but Logan was emphatic we part ways—and that once the faction war was over we could see how things go.

A war. I have to fight a war to even hope to have Logan as a part of my life again. I pull the covers up around my blotchy face, hot from rivers of tears, my chest still heaving with ragged sighs and hiccups.

I listen to the sad drizzle of rain patter against the wood-covered window as I nestle deeper in my bed, feel the arctic breeze snake its way in through the cracks, and meditate on what a mess my life's become.

Unsteady dreams take me captive. Seductive images fed to me in pieces. An entire catalog of events unfold in random order, each one beseeching the next.

I can hear Logan's voice, the tenor lost in perfect octave—the rumble of his chest as he whispers hot into my ear. I am enslaved by his presence. He is magnified by an aura of irrational calm, an undeniable peace as easy as dying.

I can feel his lips. Hear him tell me that it's going to be all right, just breathe. He restrains the sweet ache in my chest to kiss him. It's a temptation beyond understanding.

In the morning I tell Mom I can't go to church, that I'm too tired from working the late shift. Truth is, my wearied body doesn't compare to the Mack truck Logan drove over my emotions last night. It is heartache in acres, trying to imagine my days without Logan.

I fish out Chloe's diary from my underwear drawer and land back on the bed in a heap.

August 14th,

Last time I embarrass myself with a boy. Ever. I've never felt so insecure, immobilized with grief over the way Gage made me feel when he shut me down. Gage said his mystery girl would sail into town soon. I'll be sure to pull out the welcome mat, make her feel like she's my new best friend before I accidentally knock her off Devil's Peak. Oops! People are prone to drinking too much around here and accidents happen.

August 15th,

Perfect night! Carly had a party. Lame as usual. Of course she asked about Brody one zillion times until I finally made something up about him seeing Zoe Topherman. It was priceless to see Carly take off crying upstairs during her own get together. To top it off, Zoe has hair that covers her body like an ape, so of course this really pissed off miss tan and beautiful. It must hurt to think you've been replaced by a circus animal, sort of like it hurts to be replaced by the invisible woman. For all I know she might be a figment of his imagination—wishful thinking.

Anyway, Gage was there, stringing me along with one of his "discussions". I let him fill me in on how Nevermore was doing. I wish I would have cut a little deeper when I plunged that knife into his hand—impaled him two or three times, severed an artery. You should have seen his face drop like a brick when I stopped listening midsentence and went over to talk to Logan. With Michelle and Lex both on vacation, this won't even be a challenge.

August 16th,

I picked up Logan and we went to the south side today over by Rockaway Point. I told him I forgot my bathing suit and stripped down to nothing right in front of him. I swear he's just like Gage. He didn't even try to make a move. He just acted like I was fully clothed and we went out swimming like it was no big deal. There's obviously something wrong with the both of them.

August 17th,

Ellis is driving me insane with these constant midnight visits, not that I'm turning him away. Besides we go light driving after and do fun things like change test scores at school and mess around with Dr. Oliver's corpses. He suggested I mess with Gage, but I have something bigger planned. It involves his BFF Logan Oliver. It is a thing of beauty I tell you.

August 21st,

Look at me. I can't keep you up on things for two days straight. I guess it's not a secret that I have a hard time being faithful. I finally got Logan to kiss me! Turns out there's no invisible girl in his future. Well, Logan doesn't have the curse of 'knowing' so we'll go with the idea that I'm the girl of his dreams. Besides, he's sweet. I like the way he takes up my hand and kisses it.

His aunt and uncle are buying them both trucks. Can you believe it? They are so spoiled rotten. I'll be driving around in that beat up old hatchback for the rest of my natural life and they get brand new wheels right out the gate.

August 22nd,

I think Logan is in love with me. Tonight at the bowling alley I thought Gage was going to piss his pants when he saw Logan and me sucking face for like five minutes straight. Of course, he wasn't the only one having a seizure over the situation, Lexy and Michelle freaked out on me, like I was caught lighting their hair on fire. It's every girl for herself. Don't they know that already?

August 23rd,

Shit hit the fan! Had an encounter with a full-blown army of Fems and I thought I was a goner. Thank God my dad came around and helped me get away. He broke his arm in two places and was in surgery getting pins put in this afternoon. Dad says he doesn't know what they want or what we did to cause this sort of trouble in our lives. Mom thinks we should move, but Dad says they'll just follow us wherever we go. They wanted to know if I did anything to piss off the Counts. I kept my lips shut tight. Good thing dead men (or should I say dead girls) tell no tales. Too bad their brothers do—or threaten to anyway. Maybe I should slaughter their whole family and put myself out of my misery.

There's something to think about.

August 24th,

After cheer practice I got in a knock down drag out fight with Lex, trying to get her to tell me how to bind a Fem. I'm afraid my entire family is going to die if she doesn't spit it out soon.

I bashed her head into my locker so hard it left a dent (my locker not her head). She did get a nasty cut that bled profusely and ruined both our uniforms. Hopefully lockjaw will set in, or she'll hemorrhage internally in her sleep, because she won't tell me a thing. She said she'd die before she did that. I might take her to the mat on that one.

August 25th,

I love that Logan is a Celestra. For a long time I thought he was this stuck-up pretty boy, but he's actually really nice, and kind of shy and quiet. I told him what happened with the Fems and he GAVE me his grandmother's pendant to protect me. I don't think anyone has ever been so kind to me before.

I wish I could get over Gage. Carly swooped in now that Brody and her broke up. OK, I might have had something to do with that, but how was I supposed to know I'd push Carly-let's-have-a-baby-Foster into Gage's arms? Anyway. I asked him if we could get together and talk sometime. I'm hoping there's still a chance for us.

August 27th,

Met up with Gage yesterday after practice and just hung out on the senior lawn. We talked for hours. I finally broke down and told him about how I felt, about how scared I was because of what's been happening with Ms. Richards' grandmother—how I've been seeing her everywhere like a ghost, how she feels so real to me. I think I'm going insane. She actually spoke to me and said it was 'almost time'. Almost time for what?

I feel like I'm losing my mind. Maybe I should go back to Dr. Booth? Obviously giving the Ceslestra files to Holden was a mistake. Maybe telling them they could taste my blood and see how strong it makes them, or how they could read minds and time travel if only for a moment, wasn't the most brilliant idea in order to save my freaking ass. I'll be paying for her death the rest of my natural life. They made me an offer I couldn't refuse, pinned me to a wall and now I'm just screwed.

Oh and have I mentioned I lost Logan's necklace again? Welcome to my wonderful life.

I wonder what kind of deal Holden made with Chloe? She said *them*—I bet his brother knew all about it. What the hell were they doing with Celestra files? Don't the Counts keep track of us anyway? Unless Holden and Pierce were going off on their own, starting their own demonic junior council, with no rules, and no backward code of ethics.

I touch the top of my neck, still swollen and bruised. I wonder what kind of an offer they made her? What could possibly make Chloe whore out her blood to them? And who the hell did she kill?

28

Calling All Angels

"What kind of company meeting?" Tad balks when I tell him and Mom that I'm going out for a few hours and why.

"I don't know. Logan wants to talk to the staff. It's like a production meeting or something. He's buying dinner, so I didn't ask too many questions." Actually I don't know if we're even having dinner. Besides, I can't eat knowing Logan doesn't feel we should be together anymore. The only bright spot in my day is that he'll be at the faction meeting tonight.

A light knock erupts at the door.

"That's for me." I head toward the door with both Mom and Tad hot on my heels.

"Ready?" Gage offers a private smile before saying hello to the two of them.

"So where is this meeting?" Tad cranes his neck looking down the driveway.

Gage presses his lips together. I can tell he's shocked that I might have said anything about the faction meeting.

"At the bowling alley," I say, picking up Gage by the hand and heading into the frigid night air before things get too involved. The last thing I want is to drag Gage into my bed of lies.

"Your friend has a nice ride." Tad ticks his head down toward Logan sitting in the orange beat-up mustang.

"That's actually Skyla's ride," Gage says, as we move down toward the driveway.

"That's the car they want to give you?" Tad rushes past Gage and trots down the stairs to get a better look. "That's a 66 mustang!" He slaps the sides of his heavily pleated chinos. "Lizbeth!" He motions for my mother to come down in her bathrobe.

Logan gets out from the driver's seat and politely says hello.

Tad ignores him. He's too busy asking Gage faux permission before popping up the hood.

"It's got a 289!" Tad's voice echoes through the forest like a boomerang. "Crap!" He smacks his head on the inside of the hood before backing up. "What the hell are you thinking giving her a car like this?"

"I'm going to pay for it," I offer.

"We're working something out." Logan looks back at me and relaxes into a smile.

It crushes me—everything around me stops as our eyes linger. All of the madness of Tad and his bizarre commotion, my mother's bare breast nearly exposed, the fact Drake has appeared and is pulling at his hair like a cartoon character, none of it fazes me.

Logan gets behind the wheel, while Gage and I banter about who's going to sit in the back, but I insist.

I take Logan in, as we head out on the road—drink him down like water. His long muscular arms, his chiseled to perfection features, the strong assurance he exudes without having to say a word, and my heart shatters like glass over and over until it's ground down, fine as sand.

Nicholas Haver lives behind the gates, much further down the road than Logan and Gage. We drive through miles cloaked in darkness, with no streetlamps, and no moon to illuminate our path, just the sterile headlights igniting the evergreens, surprising the world around us with their artificial beams.

Logan parks high on the ridge behind an entire row of SUVs, minivans and sports cars. It's amazing how many people have showed up for this meeting. I crashed one of these meetings this past summer, or tried to, until I was caught sneaking around the periphery with Ellis. Note to self, including Ellis in just about anything will consistently result in deep regret and quite possibly end with me getting stoned.

We get out of the car, and the icy November air slices through my sweater, makes me wish I had the forethought to throw on a jacket. Jackets were something you didn't need in L.A., and rain was something we didn't have. I'm still trying to get used to the violent weather here on Paragon. Between the constant shroud of dark clouds and the continual layer of fog that permeates our world, it's starting to feel like the sun is just a rumor, something that warms the rest of the planet but strategically passes us by.

We make our way to a barnlike structure, lit up like a flame, far behind the main house. The three of us remain unnaturally quiet, dipped in morbid silence until we're just shy of the entry.

"So they know we're coming?" I ask twisting my finger around my hair repetitively.

"They're expecting us." Logan presses his hand into the small of my back ushering me into the well-lit room.

It's probably the last thing I should be thinking, that Logan is touching me, the last thing I need to be doing is focusing in on the electrical impulses that race from his fingertips all the way to my scalp, but my mind refuses to consider anything else. Once again he's the forbidden fruit, not just according to the Countenance, but according to Logan himself.

Nicholas Havar is a heavyset man with a triple chin and pillow-like bags tucked under his eyes. He scoffs when he sees us then gets back to reciting roll call from which the three of us are omitted.

I notice Dr. Oliver and Emma and wave. It's an empty, cavernous room, with chairs set in a giant circle that creates an equitable environment. The strong scent of fresh brewed coffee is thick in the air and I see pastries laid out on a small round table near the back.

"Let's get down to the matter at hand." Mr. Havar leans in, scoops together a loose stack of papers and glosses over them. "In the last four days we've had sixteen brothers who've lost their lives under suspicious circumstances. It's not unusual to have this sort of thing happen, as it does from time to time, but the curious nature of their demise, coupled with the fact the deaths were quarantined to one particular faction, brings this matter to the forefront." He pauses to take a few quick swigs from his water bottle.

"Which faction?" Dr. Oliver asks, adjusting his glasses.

"Celestra," Nicholas answers.

Crap.

I try to make contact with Logan, but his eyes are glued to the front.

“Eleven in suspect fires,” Mr. Havar continues, “three auto accidents, and two beheaded.”

A series of gasps coil around the room.

I take a deep breath and bow my head.

“It has also come to our attention that someone in this room has access to a Sector,” Mr. Havar pauses to allow for another series of echoing gasps. “And I have also been informed that a Civil War has been ordained.” He bounces his water bottle on the table as if to affirm the statement. “The Countenance has clearly taken a progressive step in the conflict already. The C.R.L. has discussed the matter and we feel the potential loss outweighs the devastation that has already taken place. We move to accede for the time being until we can further assess the strategy of the enemy—at that time, we will consider seeking retribution.”

A hushed silence penetrates the room. Nothing but somber faces and dull eyes liter the assembly.

“What’s the C.R.L.?” I ask Gage. I’m afraid if I ask Logan he won’t respond. Although he’s not officially giving me the cold shoulder, I can definitely feel the arctic breeze.

“Council of Regional Leaders. Basically leaders like him from all over the world, excluding Countenance of course.”

“Of course.”

“Excuse me.” A man in a plaid sweater and purple tie knotted just below his chin stands. “Who has access to this Sector? Isn’t there a chasm in place to keep this sort of thing from happening?”

"Chasms are temporal. The Sector involved has expressed interest in one of our own. The young woman's family has requested we not place any focus on her."

About a dozen heads turn in my direction. My cheeks start to burn from the attention.

Of course it's me. Logan, Gage, and I are the only ones under thirty in this entire assembly. And suddenly the overwhelming urge to strangle Marshall seems like a good idea.

"Any questions?" Mr. Havar impatiently pans the crowd. "Meeting is adjourned. Godspeed until we meet again."

A mingling of bodies explodes as the crowd bleeds toward the door.

That's it?

Dr. Oliver and Emma come over and offer me a hug.

"I hope you don't mind that we referred to you as family." Emma rubs my back when she says it.

"No, I don't mind." I cast a heavy glance over at Logan. It feels terrible being separated like this from him. This is way worse than being forced to live a million miles apart. It's an emotional separation, and it's mincing me from the inside.

I hate the brutal awareness that Logan doesn't think we should be together right now. Blaming himself was just a rouse to keep from pointing the finger at me and say that I cheated.

Gage pops up beside me and wraps his arm around my waist. It's beyond uncomfortable knowing that Logan can see—knowing that it's not an act, that there's not a Count around for miles.

"So why aren't they going after whoever did this?" I direct my question at Dr. Oliver.

"It would only incur more deaths." He shrugs as though it were obvious.

"But they killed sixteen Celestra. We're on the verge of extinction as it is," I say.

"Yes," Nicholas Havar steps in. "But they can eradicate the Celestra in an instant given the proper nudging. They're posturing, hoping that a full-scale war will break out so they can have the excuse they've been waiting for, to indulge in genocide. We can't give them that option."

"If this war was fought a long time ago, maybe my father wouldn't have died. It's hard to believe the solution is to do nothing." I try to restrain my anger.

"Peace is a powerful tool." Mr. Haver picks up my hand and cups it between the both of his before walking over to small crowd.

"Peace is an impotent weapon," I say quietly once he's gone.

Dr. Oliver and Emma migrate over to an older gentleman standing near the door.

"You don't like peace?" Gage gives a dry smile.

"I don't like death." A thought comes to me. "We should fight death with death."

Logan steps over and steadies his eyes on me. "And who's going to kill them?"

I give a placid smile. "I am."

29

Struggle

After the faction meeting, Logan drives us back to their house. He asked if I wanted to come hang out for a while, and, of course, I said yes.

In the kitchen Dr. Oliver examines my pupils, my pulse, heart rate.

"You're extremely anemic. It would be irresponsible to extract any more blood for the next several months."

An unexpected sense of relief washes over me. The feeling catches me off guard. Isn't the entire point of donating dangerous amounts of blood, to bring Chloe back, and introduce her to Marshall?

Her diary runs through my mind in snippets. So she has a prickly personality—who doesn't? Anyway, I'm totally relieved.

"She doesn't have her powers anymore," Logan points out.

"Mm hmm," Dr. Oliver throws his stethoscope into his black leather bag. "She's depleted at the moment. Celestra strength lies in the concentration of hemoglobin, and since she's in short supply, she'll need to wait for the bone marrow to generate a fresh inventory. In time, all will return."

"How long?" I pull down my sleeves, almost afraid to ask.

"Could be weeks, but they'll trickle back slowly. I wouldn't recommend time travel unless you're with Logan. You might only have enough to get you one way." He pats the top of my head. “You’ll be fine.” He says a brief goodnight and heads upstairs.

“I’m not going to be fine.” I look from Logan to Gage. “If a Fem comes after me I’m dust.”

“Ask Mr. Dudley for some kind of protective hedge.” Logan looks serious, and this alarms me.

“I’m not asking Dudley. The only way he’ll protect me is if I gift myself to him.”

“No.” Gage helps me up and pulls me in. “I’ll protect you.”

“You’re not always with her. They’ll wait until she’s alone,” Logan glares over at him.

“Then she won’t be alone.”

They bear into one another with something just this side of hatred until finally Logan gives.

“I’m going to bed. Goodnight Skyla.”

He leaves the room and takes my heart with him.

Gage and I head out to the pool. The Jacuzzi is bubbling and sweating into the night so we take our shoes off and roll up our jeans while sitting on the edge. It feels good to have my flesh immersed in a bath of scalding water. It reflects perfectly how Logan scalded my heart.

A blank darkness has settled over Paragon, the light blue glow from deep inside the pool only seems to amplify this.

“I talked to Logan.” Gage scoots in until our thighs are touching and drapes an arm around my shoulder. “I know you’re hurting. I’m sorry.”

It takes everything in me not to sob into him. Hurting would be the tip of this necrotic iceberg, if only hurting were as simple and minimal as it sounds. It's more like I'm regurgitating—eating up the flesh that was our relationship and vomiting it out over and over in one long emotional cycle.

"I guess this is the part where I'm supposed to do the noble thing and step down, too." He nods into the pool.

I take a deep breath and ready myself for it. I've lost Logan, my powers, in a sense the Chloe who I thought I knew, and now Gage.

"But I'm not going to." He pushes into me gently. "I'm going to be with you at school and when we're out, and I meant what I said in the kitchen. I want to protect you."

"Thank you." I wrap my arms around him and give a tight squeeze. "I can't do this by myself. And I love having you around. It would kill me if you shut me out."

"I'd never shut you out." He picks up his class ring dangling from the silver chain around my neck and fingers it before placing it gently back down. "I don't want to scare you, but I really feel like you are my girlfriend—always have been."

I pick up the ring and swivel it in between my fingers while darting a glance up toward Logan's window.

"I am your girlfriend." I can't bring myself to add, *and I always will be* because my throat seems to have solidified with grief. Instead, I lean up and offer a tender kiss that says it so much better.

Gage rubs up against my leg under water and we just sit listening to an owl vibrate through the night with a string of magnetic calls. I never want this peaceful moment—this melancholy magic covered in the shadow of day, to end.

"I read Chloe's diary," I whisper. "Part of it."

"Oh."

"Did you find Chloe attractive?" Maybe he was just using me as an excuse.

"Chloe was gorgeous—it was hard not to look at her."

A spike of heat explodes all over me. I'd rather not hear how gorgeous she was from Gage, but I guess I asked. "So why didn't you go out with her?"

"I went out with her." He relaxes back onto his hands. "Just as friends. It never went anywhere."

"Just friends." I parrot his words, catching his gaze. "She said you rejected her because you were waiting for someone."

His mouth opens then closes. "I was." His lips press together. "I was waiting for you."

Silence cuts through our conversation as obtrusive as thunder.

"Do you regret waiting for me?"

"Why would I regret it?" He reaches over and circles my waist. "You're better than Chloe, better than anyone in every way. I knew that before I met you."

"But how did you know that? Was it a vision?" I'm dying to know if it was the same kind of thing I experienced with Marshall.

"Yes. A whole series of them, sometimes I would dream about you," He examines me for a moment. "Clean dreams, I promise. OK some dreams were a little racy, but that was after you moved here." He gives a tiny grin.

"So your gift of knowing works that way? In snippets?"

"Snippets is a good way to put it. I don't know everything."

"Am I going to kill the Counts responsible for the Celestra deaths?" My blood boils just thinking about the way they tortured my father, and equally that the faction leaders think it's fine to sit back and let this continue to happen. You don't look at cancer and hope it goes away. You cut it out.

"You are," he whispers. "You'll kill many."

My stomach explodes in a hot ball of acid.

"Will you come with me?" I ask.

"I'll always be with you."

30

Down and Dirty

Monday morning, the fog floats around the student parking lot, thick as a cemetery teeming with ghosts. I wonder about Holden as I get out of the car—what havoc he's waiting to inflict on me next, and what it's going to take to get him out of my life completely. That's when I see them.

Logan and Lexy. Even their names are nauseatingly cute together. He holds her backpack as she climbs out of his truck. She pinches down her miniskirt from just above her crotch and laughs into him.

"Disgusting," I mouth the word.

"What?" Gage turns in time to catch the show, and lets out a sigh. "You know it's all an act."

"Yeah, so were we," I say under my breath.

We make our way to the English building in slow easy strides. I've managed to trade my bulky white scarf for a thin metallic grey one that Brielle lent me. The scar still whips across my neck like a thick seam of flesh, looks like it's never going to heal.

Without warning my head plunges backward. A cold hand has me by the hair and gives a few wild yanks before letting go.

"Hey!" Gage barks as he pulls me over to him.

I spin around to see Michelle's swollen, blotchy face. It's evident she's been crying—her makeup is wrecked, and she looks beyond exhausted. She looks exactly how I feel.

Before I can figure out how to respond, she shoves Gage aside and strikes me across the face with an open-palmed slap. The sound echoes through the quad with a deafening finality.

"You bitch," is all I can manage before she takes off toward the parking lot. I don't care if she is having Marshall's baby. I don't care if she's having twelve angelic beings at once. What the hell gives her the right to assault me whenever she's in the mood?

Logan and Lexy walk past me. She's got her hand over his shoulder. Logan's features darken with anger at the scene he just witnessed.

It hurts more to see them together—touching. Michelle could peel the skin right off of me, and it wouldn't hurt half as bad as losing Logan.

I'm fixated on the blackboard behind Marshall. I can't focus in on the lecture or the manic examples he strings out fervently every few seconds. All of this crap with Michelle, and of course the spike Logan drove to my heart is just killing me. Gage reaches forward and traces slow relaxing circles onto my back with his fingers. I can feel his sympathy, but it's drenched in an agony of his own. I'm sure I've made him doubt my feelings for him, while I openly ache for Logan.

What's the matter? Marshall asks, after giving the class an assignment.

I can still hear him, I marvel.

Of course you can hear me, but why can I hear you? He looks perplexed by this.

Crap.

I lost too much blood. Everything is gone. I'm practically less than human. I'm anemic—one step in the grave, all because I wanted to help Chloe. Something in me wanted to blame her. It's as though I've been looking for an excuse to pin all of the problems in the world right on her dead shoulders. *He dumped me.* The swollen river of my heart has finally crested and I want to blabber everything to, of all people, Marshall.

He's touching you. He looks rather smitten, and wait...oh yes, he's fornicating mentally as we speak.

Really? Right now? I turn around and look accusingly at Gage.

It's the male species, Skyla, you have no idea what you're up against. Marshall smolders in my direction.

I have some idea. I picture Logan and Lexy together, her face crammed up against his and it enrages me.

So it's the other Oliver. I can torment him if you like. He offers.

No thanks, but you can torment Lexy. Do you have any other demonic necklaces you'd like to dole out? I'd love to sick an entire legion of Fems on her. And by the way she knows how to bind them, or so she claims. It's the only reason he's letting her drool all over him.

Marshall leans against his desk and squints into me as though he's considering this.

Is it possible to bind a Fem? I ask.

It can be done. He slouches a bit as his features darken.

What's wrong?

Bad memory. His eyes glaze over momentarily. He turns his head as though distracted. *Well then,* He shoots a predatory smile in my direction. *Just had a rather disturbing glimpse into your future.*

I don't like disturbing.

Rain pounds against the wall of windows in the back of the room as though a mass of lunatics were beating their fists to get inside.

Michelle has taken to bitch slapping me on a regular basis, I've lost all my strength, my speed—the Fems could take me if they wanted. Perhaps that's what Marshall knows? If he were to tell me, I could prepare myself—do something to outsmart the situation.

Will you tell me? I'm so desperate to know I feel as though I could break.

You know how to get the information. His head dips down into his chest as he bores into me.

The bell rings. I gather my things and head out into the hall with Gage.

"You know what? I left my History book in the car." I look at the ground when I say it.

"No problem, I'll run out and get it." Gage trots down the hall and makes his way down the stairs.

I step back inside to an empty classroom. Marshall turns around just in time to see me bolt in his direction. I crash my lips into his. Marshall goes off like a radiant bliss-filled grenade, exploding through me with that intense pleasurable sensation.

A picture emerges. I'm with Gage, holding a short silver spear. The blade is covered in blood, and I wipe it down with my finger.

I pull away and stagger back.

"When will this happen?"

"Sooner than later," he says rather soberly.

"Whose blood was on the knife?"

"Whose blood do you want it to be?" There's a challenge in his eyes.

Instinctually, I want to say Lexy's.

"The Counts."

"Which Counts?" There's a slight curve to his lips.

"The ones who killed my father."

"It won't be." His tone sharpens. "The blood on the knife was your own."

31

Animal Attraction

I hate Lexy Bakova. I repeat it like a mantra as I sit at the kitchen counter next to Drake just before dinner.

The strong scent of garlic offensively clots up the air—once again, Mom is abusing the food chain.

Mom and Tad have called us together for another spectacular family meeting. No doubt, to inform us of their procreating schedule or go over graphs they've charted of which positions are the least useful in their impotent endeavors. Or perhaps, it's the big reveal and they'll expose us to Mom's swelling uterus, Tad's microscopic balls. Nothing surprises me anymore.

"Ta-da!" Tad whisks something from out of a baseball cap and places it into Melissa's lap.

Both Mia and Melissa break out into a wild fit of joy.

"Oh my God! It's so cute!" Melissa howls.

Drake and I swoop over to check it out.

I gasp at the sight of it. It's a rail thin looking rat-thing and I can clearly see its ribcage. Maybe those weren't cries of joy. Maybe they're scared spitless.

"What is it?" I ask.

"It's a pocket puppy." Tad's shoulders pull back with pride.

"I think he means a purse puppy," Mom corrects.

"Does it have rickets?" There's not an ounce of sarcasm coming from Drake.

"It needs food," I offer. Sympathy is building within me for the badly neglected creature. Obviously Tad picked it up off the side of the road because he's too cheap to drop a grand on a ball of purebred fuzz, and, for once, I'm glad he's cheap. I reach over and stroke its back. The thin skin moves as I pet it. Its brown frightened eyes dilate with fear as they stare back at me.

"What's the occasion?" I seriously doubt Tad's good intentions.

"I thought this would be a great way for the family to start grasping the kind of responsibility a baby brings into the house." There's something mocking in his tone. I can't put my finger on it, but I can tell it's there.

"So essentially you're readying us for an extremely malnourished child," Drake quips.

"Or maybe they're warning us it won't look human." These *are* Tad's genes we're talking about. I think my mother should voluntarily pull her ovaries out of the simian polluted gene pool while there's still time. Messing with nature like this is bound to have its side effects. She's in very real danger of spawning an anthropoid.

"I won't be disrespected like that, Skyla." Tad's nostrils flare as he says it.

"Drake started it." Lame, but true.

"Both of you upstairs." Tad flicks a finger to the ceiling in annoyance.

"But I'm hungry." And I'm willing to subject myself to Mom's garlic gruel to prove it.

"Now!" His voice explodes in an unexpected fit of anger.

"Tad," my mother chides softly in the background.

I race Drake up the stairwell and he motions me into his room.

"What?"

"Brielle's coming over." He swipes a pair of his jeans up off the floor and sniffs at the ass. "She says you've got a hole in your ceiling where you shuttle guys in all night long."

Crap.

"Bring her to my room about eleven, or I'll tell the sperminator downstairs, and he'll have both the hole in your closet and the one between your legs on lockdown by the weekend." He gives a greasy smile.

"Real nice." I leave the room. The butterfly room is being turned into a portal for Drake and Brielle's sexcapades.

The house is officially part brothel, part infertility clinic.

A riot of wild yapping erupts from downstairs.

Add animal shelter to the list.

Gage suggests we ditch all our classes and hang out for the day.

"Where should we go?" I'm thrilled at the thought of not having to lay eyes on Lexy another minute. I'm so sick of hearing her coo Logan's name during cheer like a song she butchers for an hour straight. Not to mention the mind-numbing hatred I'm starting to feel for Michelle.

"How about I surprise you?" He leans in with a careful kiss.

A warm rush cycles through my stomach. I like this romantic yet naughty side of Gage.

A part of me feels awful, like I'm cheating on Logan. Ironic, since when I was *with* Logan I didn't think twice about kissing Gage—twisted, I know.

We drive down the road, the opposite direction of school. Fog drifts by in a series of elongated strips. It's as though Paragon is unveiling itself to us, removing its mysterious layers one at a time like the unraveling of a mummy. It's the revelation I wait for. The aftermath of what it means.

Gage takes a turn down a familiar looking dirt road.

"Oh no, not here." It's where Carly and Carson abandoned me a few weeks back and I got my arm chopped off by Ezrina. It's a virtual playground for Fems.

"You'll be fine. Besides it's secluded, and that way no one will see us."

"Who cares if anyone sees us? We can go to the beach, or the Falls." Come to think of it, I almost drowned the last time Gage and I went to the beach, and I killed a guy at the falls. It's like I've dusted every location on the island with some sort of demonic patina.

"We'll be needing privacy." He raises his brows suggestively.

The car thumps along the path riddled with branches as we gyrate over every hill and valley.

"I think your mom's car needs shocks," I shout over the sound of the tires grinding their way through the dirt.

We pull into the clearing, and he kills the engine.

"I think I need my truck back," he says, unbuckling himself. "Come on."

We head out as the dust plume settles in our wake. The earth smells sweet and the pines give off their fresh scented oils as an offering to the morning.

"So?" I lean in. "Why the need for privacy?" I bite down on my lower lip, trying to hide the fact I'm reveling in this.

"I thought I'd take advantage of you real quick, then take you out for breakfast." He cocks his head to side.

"Oh? You'll take me right here in the dirt?"

"I was thinking more of that mud puddle over there." His cobalt eyes burn through me like a dare.

"Too bad it has to be real quick." The smile melts from my face as I step forward and graze him with my lips.

"Mmm," He gives a soft groan. "Maybe not here."

"Chicken?" It sort of ruins the moment throwing poultry into a conversation laced with sexual innuendo.

"I think we should save our first time for a special occasion."

"Like our almost shared birthday?"

He presses his lips together and gives a mock smile.

I like testing the limits with Gage this way. It's my new favorite game.

"Like our wedding night," he says.

And I thought I was spoiling the mood with poultry. Then it hits me. This isn't a game to him. He has the gift of knowing, and he's already informed me we're getting married.

Panic rips through me. If I marry Gage that means I lose Logan forever, and now I'm completely derailed from the conversation.

I want to ask him more about the future—everything. But innately I know it will only lead to more questions, an entire ocean of inquiry, a world without end.

I lock onto his eyes, the broad even space between them, his flat forehead, the straight bridge of his nose. In every way Gage is perfect.

He bends over and pecks a kiss on my lips. He pulls me in and does his best rendition of the most romantic kiss known to man while Logan's face brands itself into the recesses of my mind. Logan floats behind my eyelids, settles over my body, adheres to my skin like the scalding hot wax of a candle. He steals the moment from Gage and this infuriates me.

"That's not really why I brought you here." His arm dips in through the open window and he pulls out a rather long knife. He glides it out of the sheath exposing a gleaming pewter blade.

"What are you going to do with it?" I touch the chilled steel tongue of the dagger.

"I'm going to cut you with it."

32

Slash

Gage pierces the solitude with a sharp whistle.

The raven—his bird comes quickly to his shoulder in all its dark glory. It purrs and fidgets a moment before settling down, still as stone.

"Chloe gave her to you." I reach up and stroke its soft black feathers with the back of my hand. It's as tall as a table lamp, and this startles me.

"It's a he—his name is Nevermore." He holds out his arm and the bird bounces down. "I'm giving him to you." Gage gives a soft smile just enough to light up his dimples and spear me with those glowing eyes. "A little nick is all we need."

Marshall's vision makes sense now. I feel sort of jipped with that whole prediction thing. It's obvious he's taking advantage of me. There's nothing disturbing about the blood on the knife being my own. Gage is offering me something beautiful.

"So you cut me and the bird?"

"I promise I won't hurt you."

"Why such a big knife?" Not that I don't like the drama associated with the weaponry. In fact, I wouldn't mind having it around since I'm ready to take on the Counts myself if I have to.

"It's a sacred blade. Chloe gave it to me. Came with the bird." He hands over the knife, and I examine it. It's heavy. The metal handle is carved to look like a rope that wraps around in a smooth coiling pattern. The entire dagger is made of one piece of metal.

"Careful, it's sharp. It'll cut your fingers off before you notice." He reaches for the handle, placing his hand over mine, and the knife begins to wiggle. "Don't do that," he warns.

"I'm not doing that. I thought you were doing that."

The knife twists violently between us—a force so powerful that the two of us start to lose our footing.

"I'm gonna let go," I scream, plucking my hand free from underneath his.

Gage grasps the handle with both hands as it continues to seize combatively in the air. The tip of the blade rises and points in my direction.

"Run," he instructs.

It's a scene from a bad movie playing out before me. Me running from Gage, Gage groaning, slashing through the air to keep from stabbing me relentlessly. My foot catches on an errant branch and I land face first in the dirt. I'm too exhausted to move another inch. It takes everything in me to turn my head so I don't inhale the forest floor and choke to death.

The silver steely blade swipes down next to me. It plunges with the heft of an anvil right through the center of the back of my hand, pinning me to the earth with a forceful thrust.

I squeeze my eyes shut and let out a harrowing scream. The blade is pushed so far down that the base of the handle is the only thing rising up out of my flesh. I'm so thoroughly nailed into the ground it takes Gage standing over me with both hands to yank the knife free.

Nevermore goes wild, pecking and clawing at seemingly nothing but the air nearby.

"Crap!" Gage's voice booms all around us. "What the hell was that?"

"It's my ghost—Holden Kragger." I say his name accusingly. "He's here." I moan nursing my fresh new wound. "He caused the accident too, I'm pretty sure of it."

Nevermore lets out a series of harsh cries before settling back down to the ground not too far away from me.

Gage circles me with his eyes like I've got the plague.

"Looks like Nev just sent him packing," he says. "But how are we going to get rid of him permanently?"

"No clue. With my luck I'll need an exorcism." I try to stop the blood from streaming free from my hand. I press my palm into my jeans and watch the red flower of my existence expand by inches every second.

"Nev." His tone is sharp as he calls the bird.

I pick up the blade and watch my blood rise up on the sides. I swipe my finger down over it and realize I just fulfilled Marshall's prophecy. I look up at Gage as a thought runs through my mind. What if I knew what was coming and refused to comply? Could I change things?

Gage takes the knife and punctures the bird at the base of his wing. Gently he rubs my wound over Nevermore.

"You're bonded now."

"So that's it? Last one bleeding gets the prize?" I ask as the bird hops onto my shoulder.

"Something like that. It understands what you need from it and does what it can to help you, like with Kragger's ghost.

It's more of a messenger than a guardian." Gage takes off his shirt and wraps it around my hand, tight.

"Sort of a prehistoric 911."

"He can't do everything, but he's trained pretty well." He holds out his arm and Nevermore hops over to him. "Say Skyla."

"Say Skyla." It repeats crackled and broken.

"That's amazing!" For a moment I forget about my throbbing bloodied hand.

"I love you, Skyla." Gage says sternly to the bird.

"I love you, Skyla." Nevermore looks right at me when he says it then bolts up toward the upper branches of an evergreen.

"That's sweet," I say. His sincerity and loyalty take my breath away. "Thank you."

"Let's get my dad to look at that." Gage places the knife back into its sheath.

"So is Nev enchanted or something? What's with the whole blood brother thing?"

"It's a bound spirit. It's trapped. Your blood controls its actions. Nothing can happen to that bird while you're still alive."

"What kind of spirit?"

"It could be anything but human. It's a punishment."

"So basically its punishment is hanging around with me? Figures." I lean into Gage. Everything about me feels like a punishment lately.

The morgue is teeming with people. One of the viewing rooms has a crowd nine deep, and it doesn't register until I see Carly Foster twirling her finger around her long blonde hair that everyone here is a teenager.

"Who died?" I whisper to Gage.

"Don't know." He floats me back toward the kitchen in a hurry.

"Skyla." Dr. Oliver sounds disappointed as he adjust his glasses. He picks up my hand and removes the blood-soaked shirt. "You're bleeding again. What happened? A Fem?"

"Holden Kragger happened." Gage says filling him in on the bizarre string of events.

"You need stitches, but I think I'm going to glue you. It's a fixative I use to keep peoples eyes shut, but it'll work just the same. Are you taking vitamins? If not, do. Load up on iron." He cleans the wound before pumping a thin line of fixative on the palm of my hand and pressing the flesh together. "East High is here on a field trip."

"We won't keep you," Gage says.

"I could use your help if you like."

"Doing what?" Gage helps steady my hand while he glues the other side.

"I need one of you to be a corpse—just lie in the bathtub, and pretend you're dead. It packs more punch if it's someone their own age, and I'm fresh out of youths," he says serenely.

"I'll do it," I offer.

Gage stands guard nearby in the event someone decides to pierce a scalpel through my flesh, oh wait—that already happened today.

I keep my eyes shut and take in slow even breaths. I can feel them amassing around me—feel the warmth from their bodies, hear their soft whispers.

I wonder if it really hits home to see someone your own age in the bathtub of death, then I remember the first time I saw Chloe lying here, then seeing Holden in Ezrina's lair. Death happens. It just does. It reminds us of how ephemeral these coats of flesh really are, especially when there's someone your own age involved.

"That's Skyla Messenger!" I recognize Carly's two-year old whine. "She's dead? No freaking way."

"Look at all that blood. Was she like, shot in the leg?" Someone asks.

Laughter begs to bubble out of me, but I manage to resist the urge.

"I never really liked her," Carly says it as a fact.

Before I can pin her with my anger, a shadow falls over me—a dark presence that instinctually makes me want to shiver with fear.

"Too bad." A male voice whispers from just above my head. "I was hoping to kill her myself."

33

I'll Stumble for You

Gage comes into the house and diverts my mother while I run upstairs to change. After, I find him in the family room with Mia and Melissa petting their new dog.

"Does he have a name yet?" I pull my fingerless gloves up toward my wrist. What with the scarf and all, you'd think a blizzard was coming.

"It's between Sprinkles and Cupcake." Melissa picks him up and strokes his back carefully. Her hair is pulled back in a headband, and for the first time, I notice the prominent widows peak on her forehead just like Drake's.

"I suggested Killer," Gage says playfully.

"I like Killer." I bite down on my bottom lip and tickle him under the ribcage with my uninjured hand.

"Oh, come on." My mother breezes into the room. "Girls, don't listen to them." She sets a laundry basket full of clothes on the coffee table. "I hear homecoming is on Friday. You two going?"

"Yes." Gage rubs my back when he says it.

"Great," Mom says. "If you want I can take you shopping, Skyla. I've got at least an hour before dinner." She beams as though she's been waiting for this moment all her life.

"Actually, I'm late for work." That, and the fact she'll want to see me in it without my scarf and gloves on. I know her. She'll strip me down herself if she has to.

"Well, I'm going out with the girls to drop the dog off at the vet. I might hit the mall. If I see anything, I'll pick it up. We can always take it back."

"Good idea." Right. Can't wait to see what pink frosted confection makes its way into my closet. "Make sure you keep the receipt." For sure we'll be taking it back.

Tad walks in and glowers over at Gage before heading into the kitchen. "You two have a good day?"

A sickening feeling comes over me.

"You don't need to worry about a dress." Tad pulls a soda out of the fridge and migrates back over. "I just got a message from the school. Skyla wasn't there today. Guess where else you're not going?" His lips stretch across his face before retracting.

I tried to talk my way out of the fact I was very, very late to school to Mom and Tad. I even showed them the cut on my hand and told them I fell on a metal rod sticking out in the student parking lot. I told them I needed to go to the hospital to get it fixed. Who knew Tad would demand to see medical records? So there's that.

Gage drops me off at the bowling alley almost an hour late.

I'm glad I have the chance to show Logan how dependable I can be. He's probably looking forward to firing me. Getting me out of his life once and for all in every way possible.

"You're fired," Logan says looking over at Gage.

"She's the one who's late," Gage says mockingly.

"Why the gloves?" Logan is immediately suspicious.

I tell him about our time in the forest while he inspects the damage.

"Are you feeling better?" There's a marked look of concern written all over him.

"I'm tired." Even the words come out weak.

Gage takes off, leaving Logan and me enveloped in an awkward silence.

"So, I called someone to cover your shift." He nods in toward the kitchen where I see two older women scrubbing down the stainless steel appliances. "And I called someone to cover mine." He glides over to me with a gentle smile and wraps an arm around my shoulder. "Let's get out of here."

Logan leads us out the backdoor. It's heavily wooded out here, the air is dense with fog, and it feels like we've stepped into some alternate world that belongs exclusively to us.

He flexes a smile in my direction as we head down a dirt path. There's something solemn about him, something quietly accepting, but not too thrilled about the current status of our relationship.

"How are things going?" He asks cloaked in an otherworldly light. It feels as though I'm drifting with Logan's ghost, like he died, and all I have left are memories—makes me miss him even more.

"Lousy. And you?"

"Not good." He dips his gaze to the ground. He pours out all his tenderness in one forlorn smile. "I talked to Gage—he told me that you love him. I know you wouldn't tell him that unless you meant it."

A burst of heat ripples through my body. If I wasn't so achingly tired I'd run all the way home.

He stops and sighs, touches me with his eyes.

"I didn't bring you here to put you on the spot." He takes up both my hands carefully. "Actually I brought you here because I want to teach you to defend yourself."

"Against Fems?"

"Against Gage." He pulls his cheek to the side sarcastically. "And Fems."

Logan spends the next hour teaching me how to get out of headlocks, showing me how to knock someone to the ground by swiping out their feet, kicking them in their balls. It's like cage fighting with Logan, a guy I'd rather wrestle with horizontally in a much more passionate manner.

"Do Fems have balls?" Words I never thought would come out of my mouth.

"We're back to Gage." Logan gives a huff of a laugh and motions for me to take a seat next to him on a patch of pine needles.

I lean up against him for support.

"Your uncle says I need vitamins. I know my mom has some floating around the house." Correction, she's got an entire pharmacy floating around the house.

We lay down on the ground, resting our heads next to one another facing the opposite direction. I snuggle into Logan's shoulder as a pillow. I could easily fall asleep like this.

It's nice. It feels like the old Logan and Skyla.

I look over and see Logan's eyes gleam like melted pools of liquid sunshine.

"I thought he'd back off." He pants the words, still out of breath from our workout.

"He's not going to. Should I?" I throw it out there. I don't know what I would do if Logan said yes.

"No. I know you have strong feelings for him." He exudes a heavy sadness. "And I want to be sure that if you choose me in the end, that you and Gage...that you know, you're over."

How could I ever be over Gage? I roll the thought around in my mind.

"What do you think of his prophecy? About me marrying him? How could that be possible if I feel so strongly connected to you?"

"It's more than possible—part of the reason I backed off."

"So you don't think we're meant to be together?"

"I do." He reaches over and picks up my hand. "That's what I find so wildly confusing about this."

"I think you're turning this into some kind of self-fulfilling prophecy. Is that possible?" Or maybe it's Gage who's doing that?

"I don't think so, but even if it were, how could we test the theory?"

Marshall's face blinks through my mind.

"You're probably right." I try to fuzz out the thought of me kissing Dudley for a glimpse of the future. I won't do that again...unless of course I want to test the theory. "Hey..." I turn to look at him. "You never really mentioned that book of Counts. Anyone we know in there?"

"Brielle, Ellis, Natalie." His eyes widen unexpectedly.

"Yeah," I bite down on my lip and consider it. "I'd like the names of those leaders who OK'd the killing of the Celestras."

"What for?"

"I just want to know."

"I highly advise you don't go around trying to off anybody. Especially since the other factions agreed to stay out of it for now."

"It's my holy war."

"Civil war," he leans over and mitigates me with a soft penetrating grin. "Ours. Yours and mine."

"Well, war and death go hand in hand. Don't you watch the news?"

"Yes, I realize that, and no, I don't watch the news. Say you kill a few Counts, then what? What if they come after you—your family? Nicholas Havar was right—the risk outweighs the benefit."

"They killed my father." The words float out like a morbid song. "I want the names, Logan. I want to know who they are and what kind of lives they live. I'm just curious, that's all. At least let me educate myself on what I'm up against."

"OK." He looks down introspectively. "My uncle was forwarded the names of those who were killed and their locations—we'll work from there in figuring out who was responsible—for educational purposes." He looks mournfully at me before staring off into the ever-darkening sky masked with a veil of precipitation.

A comfortable silence wraps itself around us. The light is swallowed in shadows and the temperature drops, sharpening the air into icy bites.

"I never should have sent you to, Gage," he whispers with his eyes wide open as though he were sharing a private thought. "I really screwed things up."

I place my arm across his chest and hold back tears.

"There was no other way, you couldn't have kept me away from you."

"I don't know about that. I can be pretty creative if I have to." He rolls over and wraps his arm around my shoulders. I can see the hard edge of his jaw clench with frustration. "But it's too late for that. This is how it's going down. You're going to marry Gage, and I drove you right to him."

34

Tutor Time

After school on Thursday, my mother drives me straight to Mr. Dudley's house for a tutoring session. I'm shocked to see Michelle walking a horse back to the barn.

"I stopped seeing her. I didn't fire her." Marshall comes near the window. "You think I'd keep her around for kicks then unemploy her because she's no longer capable of satisfying me? That's Draconian."

"You should marry her. Make an honest woman out of her." Too bad she's wicked. Come to think of it, he's not too far off the mark. "What's this?" I walk over to a silver blade suspended over the fireplace. It has the same metal handle fashioned to look like a rope—it's a twin to the one that stabbed me.

He picks it up and fondles it briefly before presenting it to me.

"Special issue from the King of Glory."

"What does special issue mean?"

"It means not everyone in the celestial sphere is running around with one of these." He points to the back of the handle, at the symbol of a hand. "Tap it, just once, and think about igniting it."

I do, and the knife glows a soft shade of blue.

“Wow. I hate to break it to you, but they sell these things at the mall. I think Drake has a light up sword in his room.” In fact, I’m fairly certain.

“Satan is the great imitator isn’t he? This isn’t light, Skyla—it’s power.”

“Like a laser beam or something?”

“Like a fry you from the inside out, or something,” he mimics. “It’s made for spiritual warfare not humans, but works either way. Disempowers a spirit for days—it’s fatal when it comes to people.” He takes the dagger from me. “Only the original set contains this power. It’s a spirit sword.” He places it back over the fireplace.

“What if you accidentally touch it the wrong way and it goes off and kills you?”

“It won’t. First, you have to know it’s there and use it intentionally. It’s a living thing. The spirit sword won’t kill *you*—its aim is the enemy.”

“Is it a painful death?”

“Quick and complete. Almost instant.”

“You fight in a lot of wars?”

“Everyday is a different battle, Skyla. I’m fighting one right now.” He arches his brows at me.

“You won’t win. Gage wins.” I continue to gaze up at the dagger.

“How do you know Gage isn’t telling you stories?” He steps in front of me, too close for comfort.

I hadn’t thought of that before. What if this whole self-fulfilling prophecy thing is something conceived by his imagination? Doubtful.

“Are you ready to see your dress?” His eyes reduce to smoldering slits.

“I can’t go to homecoming. Tad says so.”

“You’ll be there.” He motions for me to follow him up the wide sweeping staircase. A set of double doors off the main hall leads to an enormous room with a giant bed. The furniture is black and heavily lacquered.

I fall onto his bed backward as he disappears deep inside the closet. Stretching my arms out, I fan them, making an impression of angel wings on the soft brown comforter. Brielle and Michelle have both been up here—so weird. It feels strange being in a teacher’s room, even if he is a Sector.

“I was going to have you try on the dress, but looks like you have a much better idea in mind.” He lands hard next to me.

There’s a light knock at the door, and Michelle steps in looking like she got in a fight with a bale of hay. Her hair is frazzled, and her clothes are covered with pale yellow and green sticks. The look really completes that batshit crazy attitude of hers.

“I thought maybe I could use the shower.” She just stands there looking as though I had slapped her from all the way across the room.

“That would be inappropriate,” Marshall snips. “Would you mind shutting the door? We’re a bit busy.”

She whips out of the room, quick as a poltergeist, doesn’t bother shutting the door.

“Doesn’t follow directions well, does she?” He muses.

“You’re brutal.”

He lays the dress over me like a blanket and I think I could fall asleep.

"Save a dance for me," he whispers.

"Don't you think it'll look bad? You dancing with a student?"

"Nonsense, I'll be dancing with students all night. You'll simply be one of many."

"And if I don't?"

"Well then, there's always hell to pay."

My mother comes into my room in the morning as I'm getting dressed. I've barely had time to pull on my jeans. I snatch the scarf off my bed and fling it around my neck, and hide my swollen hand behind me to ensure no hospital visit lies in my future. I can hardly move my fingers today.

"Morning." She comes in, closes the door behind her. "Just wanted to apologize. Everyone is under so much stress these days, and it's hard when you're trying to have a baby and things aren't moving as quickly as you'd like."

"Does everyone include Tad?"

"Yes," she whispers as if it were a well-kept secret before sitting on the bed. "I know how hard it's been for you, and I know you were really looking forward to homecoming. First year at a new school, great boyfriend, new job... a lot of things are changing for you right now."

She's going to cave! A spike of adrenaline bursts through me.

"I swear if you let me go, I'll never ditch school again. Honest." I hold my hand out like I'm making a pledge.

"I'm sorry, Honey. Tad is firm on this."

"What about you? Are you firm on this?"

"You left school without permission." She shrugs. "You hurt yourself, Skyla." She motions toward my hand. "And what were you and Gage doing anyway? Were the two of you having sex?" Her head tilts to the side as she presses me with those petal green eyes.

Oh my, God.

I'd rather die than have this conversation.

"No." My voice hikes up higher than it needs to. "I've never even done anything. Believe me, I'm as innocent as you can get."

"I don't need details. I just want to make sure you're using protection." Her eyes narrow into mine.

"Geez." I throw my hands up over my ears and close my eyes. "I said I'm not doing it. I don't need protection because there's nothing to protect me from." The only thing I need protection from is Fems, and blood sucking Counts, but that's a different story.

"Well good, I'm glad to hear that. I think a girl your age needs to think long and hard before inviting someone into her body."

A tremble of laughter swells in my chest.

Invite? I picture myself handing Gage a formal invitation with the letters S-E-X embossed in some swirly font across the front.

"I will." I bite down hard on my lip. "I'll think long and hard." And now I want to explode with laughter because I just included the words *long* and *hard* in a conversation about sex with my mother. "I will totally do it." Crap! I press my lips together unable to hide the stupid grin on my face.

She gets up and gives me a warm, lingering hug.

"There is so precious little we can save of ourselves, better to save it for that perfect person. Just think about waiting." She makes it to the door. "And I wouldn't be surprised if your special person was Gage. I think I can really see this." She gives a mischievous smile. "En*gaged*."

"Funny." My features smooth out at the lack of humor in it.

She shuts the door tight behind her.

I press my hand against the plywood that covers the hole where my window once stood. I can feel the world come alive on the other side, the rain needling its intense vibrations.

Even my mother thinks I'm going to marry Gage. It's beginning to feel like a conspiracy.

35

Homecoming

The field is damp from the shower we had earlier, but tonight there's not a veil of fog, not a dark cloud up above, just the crisp arctic chill I've become accustomed to.

Ms. Richards lets us do free style for the rest of the game. It's the end of the second quarter, and the West Paragon Dawgs are up by six. There's only one more game in the season, and it's an away game. I'm so psyched about this I can hardly stand it. Away, as in away from Mom and Tad, away from conversations about weird sexual invites. I totally need to get away.

The homecoming floats are driven onto the field. It's surreal being here knowing I've time traveled to last year's homecoming game with Ellis on more than one occasion. I half expect Chloe to step up on that platform in her powder blue dress.

I'm so winded I stop moving. My arms and legs feel like rubber and it takes everything in me not to collapse on the field.

Principal Rice taps the microphone and a loud obtrusive hum threatens to blow our eardrums out from over the speakers.

She starts in and introduces a row of girls in frilly dresses.

God—my mother could have dressed them. I don't really know who they are, mostly seniors. The principal crowns a king, some guy I don't know either but everyone screams for, then with a bit more fanfare a queen. All the while I can't stop thinking about Chloe. Ellis wants to go back tonight and refresh his stash—odd day to go, if you ask me.

Michelle motions for us to pick up the free kicks, so we do. It takes everything in me to rotate and bounce for the crowd, even a smile seems impossible to produce with this drenching fatigue.

Skyla. Marshall waves briefly from the front row bleachers. *Kick higher, I can't see your panties.*

I turn away from him abruptly. Can't see my panties? What an ass. I'm wearing kick-pants, but information like that seems beside the point with someone like him.

I've offended you. I apologize. Kick-pants aside, I have another vision I'd like to share.

I keep forgetting he can hear me now that I've bled down to a simpleton. I hate the fact I've ebbed away my powers.

No thanks. The last thing I need to be doing is kissing Marshall on a regular basis.

It's about the one who dumped you. It's a rather intriguing scenario I think you'd better see for yourself.

I think I'll pass.

I look across the field and see Logan getting ready to put back on his helmet. He lasers through me with a penetrating stare. I stop all movement and gaze right back at him. Just looking at Logan makes everything else melt away like a bad dream.

The coach whistles, and he's gone, lost in the crowd of bodies once again.

Everything feels so temporary.

I start to feel weak again, the ground feels like it's rolling in waves and I steady myself a minute so I don't pass out. My hands loosen and the pom-poms slip right through my fingers, just like Logan.

Come to me, Skyla. This vision brings you peace, not to mention the pleasure of my company.

No. If Logan would rather I be with Gage then that's what he's going to get.

After the game, Brielle insists on changing at my house for the homecoming dance.

"Brought you something!" She barks out a laugh as though it were hysterical.

"Keep it down." She's already wasted, and it's just barely nine.

Mom and Tad think I'm alone, that I'm already tucked in bed crying over the fact I'm not going to the dance. Brielle screeching and screaming isn't going to help me sneak out any faster. I swear, teaching Brielle how to navigate the wonderful world of the butterfly room has brought me nothing but sleepless nights and well, this.

"Here." She produces a black velvet choker sprayed with smoky grey rhinestones. "It's totally hot, plus it'll cover that thing that looks like a zipper on your neck."

"I got the stitches out," I say, taking off my scarf and trading it for said hot necklace thingy. "This is so awesome!" It glitters with the slightest movement.

I pull on the dress Marshall gave me and turn to look in the full-length mirror attached to my closet door.

"Skyla!" She gasps.

It's form fitting. To call it short would underestimate the actual breathtaking length that cuts off just below my underwear.

"This is not good," I lament.

"Didn't you try it on?"

"No." I give a hard exhale.

"Here." Brielle tugs a little, and it gives enough to look semi-decent.

"At least I won't get arrested." I turn in the mirror and take a look at it from behind. It's backless as far down as it can go, save for rows and rows of dark metallic chains crisscrossing from one side to the other.

"It is so freaking hot on you!" Brielle slaps her mouth after she shrieks the words out.

"It's going to get freaking shitty when my mom busts through the door." I push my finger up to my lips. "Let's get out of here."

Drake left an hour ago, giving Mom and Tad yet more false assurance I wasn't going. Really he's just next door. He parked around the corner to hide his car and he's watching TV with Bree's mom.

We call Drake and let him know we're coming. I push the dresser securely in front of the door before helping Brielle up into the butterfly room.

It's freezing outside. The cold fingers of the wind coil themselves around the chains on my back, and turn them into ice against my bare flesh.

"Hey." She points down to my feet. "You forgot your shoes."

"Crap." That means I have to hurdle three rooflines and crawl all the way back into the attic.

"Don't worry. I've got the perfect pair to lend you." Brielle's whole person ignites with a burst of energy. "I wore them my first time. Maybe you'll get lucky?"

"Doubtful." I haven't sent out the invitation yet.

Logan cycles through my mind. Then again, he probably doesn't want it. I thought he'd at least fight for me—I thought he'd die trying.

36

Put on Your Red Shoes

Red patent leather pumps with four-inch heels. I feel ridiculous.

Drake drives us down to the Paragon Beach Resort through a moonless night. A harsh wind has evicted the fog, and thousands upon thousands of crystalline stars pour out their glory in a choir of radiant luminescence.

The resort is lit up like a jewel, glowing and polished. A trail of limos stretch a half a block long, but in an effort to avoid valet and parking fees, Drake parks at the Jack-in-the-Box across the street.

I pull Brielle in tight as we make our way over to the cobbled pathway that leads to the entrance of the hotel. "There are tons of people here!"

"They're from East. We do all the big stuff like prom and crap on the same night."

"Nice." My stomach does a harsh roll.

The entry is comprised of ornate carved marble. Giant stone lions keep watch on either side with their fixed sterile gaze.

The thick scent of perfume and cologne explode in the lobby and it makes me feel lightheaded as we enter a room marked *Grand Ballroom* to our left. A dim cavernous hall is lit up with thousands of twinkle lights, sheer fabric cascades across an army of chandeliers high up on the ceiling, like rolling waves of pink gossamer.

"Hi!" Brielle screams at someone buried in the sea of bodies before taking off. Drake follows her like the puppy he is and I'm left alone in my ever-shrinking dress and glossy red hooker shoes. Maybe my mother dressing me wouldn't have been such a bad idea after all.

Faces, too many faces—I pan the crowd then pause when I spot Logan standing just shy of the dance floor—a still life in the midst of a riot.

He bows his head slightly and offers a seductive smile. His hair picks up the color from a blue spotlight up above, and it highlights him in an otherworldly way. I'm paralyzed by all his gorgeous glory.

Just as I contemplate going over, someone tickles my ribs from behind and I almost break an ankle jumping in my clown heels.

Gage swoops around, "Good God. This dress should be illegal. You are smokin'! Are you sure you don't want to wear my jacket?" He looks beyond gorgeous in his suit. I don't think I've ever seen him in one.

"Thanks. And it might be illegal. Marshall gave it to me." I'm pretty sure he didn't buy it. Probably plucked it off some celestial vixen or a corpse.

"Normally I wouldn't want you to take things from him, but this happens to be a homerun." He places his hand against my back and I can feel his skin against mine. It feels so intimate a wave of guilt washes over me.

"How's the injury?" He picks up my bloated purple hand and pulls a face. "My dad taught me a few tricks to help get your muscles back into shape once the swelling goes down. He says if it gets any worse, he's got some antibiotics for you."

"I love the way you take care of me. It's so sweet." I pull his gaze into mine.

The music switches gears, slow and steady as the bodies on the dance floor begin to sway hypnotically.

"Come on." Gage leads us onto the crowded wooden platform and digs us deep into the center of the crowd.

He cages me in with those blue flames staring back at me. My stomach bottoms out as he pulls me in, places his warm arm low across my back. The sweet scent of cologne drifts softly from him and the very distinct scent of minty toothpaste escapes his lips.

He grazes me with a kiss, then pulls away to see if it's wanted.

I'm not sure why being this close to Gage makes me nervous, sends butterflies to my stomach—Gage, who I've been melting all over for weeks to prove a point to all of Paragon and the Counts, that we're together.

He comes in again, presses his mouth against mine, and our teeth bump accidentally. I can't hear the music, or feel my feet on the floor, or remember to breathe—I just float in the soft sea of his kisses.

"Break it up." Marshall pushes Gage back rather violently and takes his place. A quick smile appears as he pulls me in tight. An entire orchestra of intense vibrations fills me, and I can't find the strength to protest.

I watch as Gage drifts off the dance floor over to Logan.

"Sunday, the population of Paragon will drain onto my property. Will you wear the wings for me?" Marshall looks past me as though he weren't speaking to me at all.

"No."

"I'll give you five hundred dollars."

"Done." My eyes spring open. I'd wear nothing but wings if he wanted me to, for less.

"I can hold you to that."

"Forget it. I'm not that desperate for money." I lay my head upon his chest. I'm so exhausted it takes everything in me to keep up with the rhythm. It feels like a major workout wearing heels like this. I'm not so sure I'm cut out to be a girl.

"Not the shoes I would have chosen," he says, "but it gives you that edgy flair so many young women gravitate toward these days. They'll be a dozen dressed just like you at winter formal—wait and see."

"It's slut fashion. They're Brielle's."

"That explains it. If I knew you were shoeless, I would have gladly given you a pair."

"Yeah, but they'd probably be magical." As in magically landing me in his bed—more like cursed. "I'm powerless—can you give me an infusion?" I pull back, hopeful.

"I can give you lots of things, Skyla, but that's not necessary. Your blood will reconstitute in time, shortly in fact."

Marshall looks cutthroat handsome in this shadow-filled room. His entire person sparks like a flame. If I chose Marshall—become his wife—my father could live again. If there weren't Logan or Gage…

"You would choose me." His expression sobers.

"Well, don't kill them. I love them."

"You love them both?" He ticks his head to the side considering this. "You know the entire universe frowns on such arrangements. They never work—always someone with a bitter heart. Of course, in this case it wouldn't be you. The single gender is always the victor. Who's the bitter heart? Logan or Gage?"

"Logan." I breathe his name in a demonic whisper.

"I see." His lips twitch. "And that's the one you favor."

My heart breaks for Gage.

"I don't favor anyone." It's true.

"Well, you don't favor me, and that makes you a rare breed." He pulls back a notch, rakes his eyes all over me. "How is this?" His features morph, just barely. They take him across the finish line until he completely replicates Logan in his exact eminence.

"You're still you," it comes out breathless.

Here I am, swaying to the droning rhythm of a very sad love song with a replica of Logan. A small part of it feels right—feels real. My heart tries to reject the idea, but I won't let it. I want this moment anyway I can get it.

Gage taps on his shoulder and evicts Marshall by way of his elbow.

"Thank you for rescuing me," I say, pecking a quick kiss on his cheek.

His dimples push in without a smile. I take in his clean scent as we finish up the tail end of the song. From behind his shoulder, I see Logan leaning up against the table pretending to hear whatever Lexy is saying, all the while staring right at us. To his left Michelle claws at Marshall for attention as desperate as ice in a fire.

Marshall looks over and gives a wicked grin. He still looks suspiciously a lot like Logan.

37

One Enchanted Evening

"Crap!" Carly drops her compact to the floor and slaps her hand over her mouth.

I roll my eyes at Brielle and push past her into the ladies room.

Napkins are laid out on a granite counter with the hotel initials embossed in gold, along with an assortment of perfume and a bin of hair products. A huge burgundy sofa sits nestled against the back wall. I love it when an entire living room acts as the entry to the actual restroom.

"I thought you were dead!" Carly's face bleeds out all color.

"I am," I say, examining myself in the mirror.

"File that under who gives a crap," Carson, the one who served toxic lemonade at her party a few weeks ago, swoops by in a creamy pink birthday cake of a dress that would make my mother proud. "Skank," she hisses as they make their way out the door.

"I hate them," I say staring blankly at myself in the mirror.

Brielle does her lips, then passes me her strawberry gloss. I not only managed to forget my shoes, but my purse and my cell, too.

Brielle's phone goes off, and she squints into it.

"It's Drake." She pulls a face before heading back into the lobby.

I should go out there and talk to Logan. I should ask for the Count file, or see what my hours are next week, or at least say hi, or maybe fall on him in these prostitute specials I've pressed my feet into and accidentally dance with him.

I open the door that leads into the actual restroom and choose a stall near the back. A lengthy battle with the paper seat covers ensues. I swear sometimes it sucks being a woman. Why couldn't God make us so we stand up when we pee? Was that asking too much?

The lights go out, and there's a palpable black silence.

"Hello?" I say stupidly. Obviously someone turned out the lights and left. But wasn't I the only one in here? "This isn't funny." My voice produces a stale echo.

I close my eyes and open them, same effect—it's beyond dark. I hold out my hand and swipe at the air as I try and reach for the stall door.

It's probably just an innocent mistake. There's probably a switch at the entrance that any moron can lean up against or flip on their way out the door. Or maybe the entire facility lost power? I bet they're all out there freaking out—girls screaming, guys scheming. I bet Michelle is taking advantage of this and dry humping Marshall, or worse, Lexy on Logan.

I try to calm my nerves by thinking about how funny this is going to be once I finally make it outside. I clasp onto the metal latch, and the door swings open.

Baby steps. That's all I need to take. I swing my arms out wildly. Every step feels like I'm about to fall down a flight of stairs.

Breathing? I hear breathing!

"Hello?" My arm is yanked hard until I slam into something—a person. The waft of bitter cologne takes over, and before I realize it, my hands are both restrained behind my back.

Lips graze against my choker. One of my hands is violently snatched from behind, and a mouth clamps down hard over my wrist. A sharp injection of pain slides across in a clean line. I can hear him slurping, sucking off my flesh like a bloodthirsty savage.

"Stop!" I try to remember how Logan taught me to take someone down. Who knew it would be in the freaking dark? "Get off!" I end the last word in a shrill scream that rattles the windows. "I'm going to rip your balls off, swear to God, if you don't get off of me!" I'm pinned so perfectly against the cold tiles behind me, it leaves me shivering—nauseated.

He bangs my head hard against the wall, pushes his fingers into my cheeks.

"You going to tell?" He says mockingly. "You let out my little secret, I'll let out yours. The Counts want to know what Celestra on this planet killed my brother. I can make them leave it alone—save you from prison. Or maybe you want to go? Maybe you're up for a jumpsuit vacation?"

It's, Pierce!

I can hear him feeling around his person before a piece of paper gets shoved in my hand.

"That's a copy of the letter I stopped my dad from sending out," he sears the words into the side of my face. "You can thank me later. And you will."

He takes off, leaving a vacuum in his wake. I can hear the roar of the crowd liven then die down as the door opens and closes. I make wild strides toward the exit, slamming into a wall before flicking on the lights.

A big yellow sign sits outside the bathroom, that reads, *Cleaning, do not enter*. I give it a swift kick before heading back into the crowd.

I spot Logan first—embedded three deep in the bitch squad. I try to circumvent the head-on collision by rounding out to the other side, but there's a barrier of tables and chairs interlocked with people, so I turn to face them.

"You're bleeding." He rushes over and picks up my arm.

"Oh my, God! She slit her wrist!" Lexy screams. There's a clear look of disgust on her face, and she starts to retch. Emily pulls her to the side, and they continue to gawk over at me from a safe distance.

"Holy crap!" Michelle plunges the black rose on her necklace back and forth like a nervous twitch. That single action alone is probably calling an entire army of Fems. She's a magnet for them now, sort of like me.

"Ouch," I yell as Logan straps his tie around my wrist, tight as noose. "You're cutting off the circulation."

He tilts his head at the irony. Logan has a calm way about him. Something noble, it's as though he's living out his true age in this younger teenage version of himself.

"How old are you again?" The words swim from my mouth dreamy. It's fuzzy math that involves another place, another time, and I really can't remember.

"Too old for you." His brows peak briefly. "Let's get you out of here. What happened?" he whispers, as we make our way out of the main entry of the resort, into the brisk night air.

I look around suspiciously.

"I don't want to tell you, not here."

He plucks his phone out and texts Gage.

"It didn't look that deep." His eyes sweep up and down. "You look beautiful." He rubs my shoulders, and pulls me in a little.

"I don't feel beautiful." I hold up my hands, revealing the fact I'm still clenching the paper.

"What's that?"

"It's a love letter from my attacker." I hold it close to my chest. "What's taking Gage so long?" My muscles quiver from the cold.

Logan takes off his jacket and swings it around my shoulders. It carries his scent—all of his warmth.

"It's too hard to be away from you," I say. There isn't anything more true in this entire world.

He presses his lips together and leans in close to my ear.

"When the faction war is over, we can be together if that's what you want." He pulls back and lets me see the heaviness in his eyes. He presses out a dry smile. "But according to Gage, you won't choose me."

38

Lead Me

Dr. Oliver is already in bed when we get to the house. Logan runs up to get him as Gage settles me at the breakfast table, the usual spot where I pay my medical visits. I'm starting to think of this place less as Gage or Logan's house, and more like the Oliver free clinic.

"Another infliction?" Dr. Oliver is wearing white and blue striped flannel pajamas and now he's really starting to feel like my own dad—definitely more of a dad than Tad will ever be.

He pulls off the blood-encrusted tie and glances briefly at the slanted incision.

"I'm going to glue you. I like that better than stitches. Let's see the hand."

I raise my other arm.

"It's not infected, just banged up a bit. Skins healing nicely." He pulls down my choker to inspect the wound on my neck. "Skyla, you're incredibly anemic."

"Put some of my blood back in me."

"I'm afraid I can't do that. Besides, your body is working hard to regenerate, just keep out of trouble."

Gage looks at me wild-eyed as though that were impossible.

"I will," I say it with authority. I can believe almost any of my own lies.

Once he finishes pressing my skin back together, he says goodnight and heads upstairs.

Gage helps me over to the family room and onto the navy corduroy couch. I love sitting here, comfortable and warm next to Gage, listening to his steady breathing.

Logan breezes in with a clipboard and wags it in the air before handing it to Gage.

Attached is the crinkled piece of paper I was clutching, complete with bloodied fingerprints.

"What is this?" I'm too far gone with fatigue to read the tiny font, too many letters crammed on one page.

"It's from Arson Kragger's office, Attorney at Law," Logan says that last part drawn out in a sarcastic drawl. "They know you crashed the truck into Kragger's Hummer, or at least believe you did, and they're threatening to take legal action against your parents. They're threatening them with the loss of their home." Logan taps near the line that reads equity at or below five hundred thousand dollars.

"Are you serious?" My entire body goes numb with shock. "It was Pierce. He said he knew I killed his brother, and if I told, he'd turn me in."

"You think he messed with things to keep you out of jail?" Gage doesn't sound convinced.

"That day with Marshall, we went to see Ezrina...she had Holden's body, she found Celestra DNA. Yeah, I think Pierce might be the key to keeping me out of cell block five." I stare into the carpet.

"Crap." Gage pulls me in, warms my shoulder with his hand.

Logan kneels down beside me. He pulls the bloodied paper off the top of the clipboard exposing a list of names, towns, provinces.

"The list you wanted. I did some research and found out where the Celestra that were killed lived." He flicks his finger at the paper. "Regional leaders."

"They're the ones that needed to approve the bloodshed?" I ask.

"Yup." Logan's jaw tightens. He doesn't take his eyes off me, or offer me an out to his bionic stare. There's something surging here, a distinct emotion pulsating between the two of us, and I'm not quite sure how to read it.

"Give me the regional leader's name for the Los Angeles council." I want to nail the bastard who thought it was a good idea to burn my father.

Logan pushes the page back and strums his fingers against the board.

"I'm one step ahead of you."

It reads, D. Edinger

I finally manage to crawl into bed. I don't bother to take off the shoes or the dress two sizes too small, instead, I greedily close my eyes and start floating off to sleep—glorious sleep. A loud hissing sound erupts, and I flip my light on in a panic only to find Ellis standing in my room.

"I thought you were a Fem. You scared the crap out me!" I snap.

"We have a date."

"Why would I want to go back with you? Why would I go anywhere with you after you fed me pot-laced brownies?" Honestly, I'd take Ellis on a light drive, but already this has been one freaking long ass day.

"Nobody forced them down your throat." Ellis gives a low guttural laugh.

People have been forcing a lot of things down my throat lately, like knives, and straws, and fangs, but I guess Ellis is right—the brownies sort of went down voluntarily.

"Come on, we'll be quick," he whispers.

"I don't think I can do it. I've had my superpowers revoked." I try and push him away with my foot.

"What's the matter?" He gives a critical stare.

"I'm anemic."

"Let's try," he insists.

Ellis and his unsinkable spirit. I shake my head and I look over at Chloe's diary sitting there, in all of its malevolent splendor.

"OK, Let's try." I get out of bed and hold Ellis by the hand.

Maybe if I can somehow get us there, Chloe herself can give me the answers I'm looking for.

The night air on Paragon, albeit one-year stale, spears through my dress, turns the chains across my back into icicles.

It all feels rather déjà vu-ish. I don't know if that's because we've been here for what feels like a gazillion times or if it's because only a few hours ago homecoming was reprising itself.

"Give me your hand." I take him by the arm and touch his flesh, not waiting for him to respond. "Say something." I'm so shocked that I managed to land us here—I'm hoping everything is back in working order. I hone in on him and focus on hearing his thoughts.

Ellis raises his brows in a seductive manner.

"You didn't hear me." He rakes his fingers through his hair before taking off.

Ellis goes straight to work. He doesn't bother drawing me into conversations about his duplicate self, hooking up with some girl, or multiple girls from East.

I walk through the darkened house full of partially inebriated bodies.

Usually, while Ellis gets his stash, I'm cowering in the back staring at Logan while he talks to Carly or watching Gage from a safe distance, in the event he tries to make out with me again—although I wouldn't really mind.

The fireplace hisses like a whispering lion. The mouth—the opening is enormous, easily a person can fall in, burn just like my father did, like those Celestras.

The family room expands before me and I see her sitting on the couch with her bare legs hanging over the edge, bright red polish on her toes.

"Skyla?" Chloe crinkles her nose in amusement. "How's it going?" The tiara dangles crooked in her hair.

"Congratulations." I don't bother answering her question.

A boisterous crowd rushes in. Chloe's eyes widen at something behind me, and she spins herself to an upright position.

"What's going on?" A guy with brown wavy hair and giant bee-stung lips, appears by my side.

"Private conversation." Chloe gets up and pushes him away.

"Aren't you going to introduce me?" His eyes are dull as coal.

"Holden." She stretches her hand over him.

Crap!

He looks boyish, harmless, and, of all the things I don't want him to be—nice.

"And who is this mouth-watering piece of ass?" He sneers in my direction.

That's better. I'm glad he was able to eradicate some of my guilt, not that I'm looking for justification. It was a total accident. Or, at least, I believe it was.

"No one you need to know." Chloe sinks her hands in his chest. "Get lost. I think Ellis is running low on supplies, maybe you can conduct business and leave us the hell alone."

Perfect. He's a dealer, too. Add that to his growing list of charming traits. Not that Ellis has needed his services for a good long while. That's what I'm for now.

"I must be dead." He sweeps his eyes over me while circling me slowly. "Because I think I'm looking at an angel."

Right on both counts. "I'm not from around here," I say.

Chloe holds up a finger, advising me to be quiet.

"Alright." He holds his arms out and backs away.

Chloe turns to collect her shoes from off the floor. She bunches up her baby blue gown and it gives the illusion she's encapsulated in a giant storm cloud. Chloe is her own weather system—a hurricane—somehow I find this plausible.

Holden comes in tight, grabs my wrist and massages the incision his brother inflicted.

"So nice to see you, Skyla." He gives the slight hint of a laugh. "We must meet like this again." He pushes his face into mine and presses his lips on the side of my face.

Chloe barrels over and pulls me out toward the door. I turn around and he's gone—vanished like smoke.

39

Into the Woods

I follow Chloe outside as the fog breathes over us in cold jagged sighs. My teeth start in on a violent chatter—I'm not sure if it's because I'm suddenly beyond freezing or the fact I think I just had a formal introduction to Holden Kragger's ghost.

We round out the side of the fence and drift toward the thicket of trees to the left of the house.

"What are you doing?" I break free from her grasp. I know what happens in these woods, and I know damn well I can't stop her from dying thanks to my father's unfortunate demise.

"Are you crazy walking around in there?" Her eyes flash. "You're going to impress yourself on all those people." She continues deeper into the forest.

The shadows of the branches fall to the ground like battling swords.

"I wanted to talk about your diary." My whisper comes out in a series of hisses.

"You didn't finish it," she says knowingly.

"I know you loved Gage."

"Old news." She shrugs into the dark. "Does he love you?" The question floats up in the air and circles my head like a wreath. There's a long pause. "I thought so. I guess the million dollar question is, do you love him back?" There's a hard glint in her eyes.

I can see Chloe a little clearer now that I've read her diary. She's not the kind of person I thought she was, not even close.

"He gave me Nevermore."

"How clever of you to avoid the question by letting me know you stole someone else from underneath me."

"You're not with us anymore." There's just not one nice way to say you're dead.

"I will be."

I cast a glance into the forest. I wonder if I should tell Chloe that I'm too weak to give anymore blood—that I'm afraid I won't be able to bring Ellis and me home tonight.

"You said, Lexy Bakova knew how to bind a Fem," I say.

"So that's what you want?" Chloe creates a steady stream of fog with her sigh. "I promise, you will never be able to bind a Fem, Skyla."

"If it's possible, then I will."

"She won't tell. She'll take it to the grave." She progresses deeper into the dark, crushing the brush beneath her feet.

"What do the Kragger's have on you? Why are you letting them do the things they're doing to you? Did you kill someone?"

She turns and breathes a steady fog of frustration from her lips.

"Turn the page, Skyla."

"And what did you mean that this was going to change everything?" If she only answered one question, I'd like for it to be this one.

Chloe reaches up and caresses the side of my face with her hand. Her warm fingers tug down slowly against my cheek as if she were trying to pull my skin off.

"I know that you'll piece it all together. You're a smart girl and I'm sure you'll figure things out. You love me right now and that's all that matters," she whispers. "Sometimes you have to take the affection others are willing to give you at that precise moment, before they learn the truth about you and revoke it."

My name echoes in the distance. It's Ellis.

"I don't know if I'll get back," I say mostly to myself. "I've lost too much blood."

She pulls her dress up and produces a small pocketknife from a pink frilly garter around her thigh. The blade catches a glint of moonlight before she slits her left arm right up the middle. Without warning, she reopens the slit on my wrist—it peels back effortlessly as though it were thinking of reopening anyway. She rubs our arms together hard, creating an uncomfortable friction. It feels unnaturally intimate, obtrusive, horribly invading. A warm rush pushes through me. Something supernatural is happening, I can feel it.

I hear a hiss just beyond the rim of the forest.

"Run, Chloe," I shout as I head out toward Ellis. "*Run!*" I scream.

I don't hear her footsteps behind me.

Alone in my bed on Paragon, I'm relieved to hear the rain batter down on my wood-covered window as I shrink beneath the sheets. My arm is covered in dried blood, but miraculously I feel better, stronger—infused. I remember that cut from Chloe's arm, the one I wear now as my own. I run my finger over the scar that never healed. It was for me, this one.

I flip the light on and pull out Chloe's diary. *Turn the page,* she says. So many damn pages to turn and a part of me just wants to go to sleep.

September 7th,

School starts tomorrow. Bleh. Went to the bonfire and made out with Logan like the world was going to end tomorrow. I saw Gage shoot daggers at us from across the way. I hope it burned for him to see me with someone else. I know on some level he must care. There was something in his eyes, although with my luck, it was probably smoke.

Pierce texted me. Today was Emerson's birthday, would have been anyway. Wish I never knew her—any of them.

OK, so who's Emerson?

September 9th,

Ellis freaked out. It wouldn't have been all that bad if he didn't choose to unleash his tirade in the quad, in front of Gage and Logan. He totally made me look like a royal bitch when he accused me of cheating. Can you believe it? I don't cheat. I was never with Ellis. You have to be with somebody to cheat.

He pulled me back by the elbow when I tried to flee the scene, told me it was killing him to see me running around with other guys, like there's some long list of people I've been with or something. I think he's got like this competition thing with Logan. Well, anyway, he lost. But really, he didn't, I was never his to begin with.

September 12,

I met up with Gage at the mall of all places. He was at the bookstore reading a magazine and I saw that gorgeous onyx hair that puts the color of Nevermore's feathers to shame. So, of course I stopped in and asked how Nev was doing. We ordered coffee and went out to sit by the fountain out back.

I can hardly breathe. I've been bawling ever since I left. I don't know what happened, but I completely lost it and tried to make him admit to a bunch of stupid shit. I practically begged him to tell me that he wanted me, that he was jealous of the fact I was with Logan of all people, who's like his freaking brother, but he was relentless.

He said he had a vision of the invisible girl—that he was going to marry her. He thinks he cares about her and that he isn't really interested in anybody else right now. Right now, as in me I suppose. How could I be so stupid to fall for the one guy on the planet who wouldn't touch me with a ten-foot pole?

So I asked if he ever had any visions about me, and holy crap was I ever sorry! Get this; I DIE. SOON.

Gage said I was like a caterpillar going into a cocoon. Great. I hope I come back as a zombie butterfly and eat his brain for breakfast.

September 17th,

Mad rush to find another pure me. Handed everything I had, over to Holden, and what I didn't want to give, he took—couldn't resist anyway. I'll always have Emerson to thank for that.

September 18th,

Gage came over. He said he had this vision of my attic room. We sat cutting out butterflies all night long and pinned them to the wall. He says I shouldn't be afraid, that I would be back, stronger, better.

I cried and told him I loved him. I'm such a loser.

So that's how the butterfly room came to be. It was Gage's idea. He made the vision happen.

September 19th,

Finished the butterflies tonight with Gage. He made them flutter and come to life for me. He feels horrible about letting me in on my impending doom—AS HE SHOULD! But, I think I've found a unique way to punish him. He will never see it coming.

Thanx to the crazy Kraggers I've got a plan in motion, one that involves time and space, a death or two, and of course, the 'butterfly' room.

September 20th,

Ellis came crawling into my bedroom to 'talk'. It's official, I guess. I have a stalker. He just barged in and sat on my bed like it was no big deal. Said he wanted to hang out a while, see if we'd go on a light drive. I took him to L.A. Couldn't find Demetri. What a freaking waste of time.

What the heck was Chloe doing in L.A.? And who's Demetri?

September 22nd,

Guess who paid me a visit? The sacred queen herself. Clocked her a good one. If you're reading this BOO!

Oh yeah, guess who got to pick out the color of Gage and Logan's trucks? That would be me. Too bad I can't pick out who I'll spend the rest of my short-lived life with. Maybe, I'll spear both their hearts the second time around.

It was me she punched in the face—clocked me. That was the night of my first visit. I'm the sacred queen. Huh.

September 29th,

Major air gap, since the last entry, I know. SO much has happened. I'm losing control of everything.

Sometimes I wonder if I have it all backwards. If I'm really taking revenge out on someone to prove a point or if the future is just playing out the way it should be. One thing's for sure, I'm determined to change my future and there's not a damn thing anybody is going to do about it.

40

Gather

Marshall's community get together in honor of his equestrian school draws the attention of the entire island. The smoky scent of barbeque ignites the air with dreams of summertime, it smells so good—the food alone is reason enough to be here.

"Feeding the masses." He winks over at me while we walk a decent clip toward the outskirts of his property. "That's my specialty."

Miraculously, there's not a cloud in the sky and the temperature has ratcheted up at least ten degrees. For Paragon, that's practically a heat wave.

Tad and Mom are fascinated by his estate, and, of course, Mia and Melissa find the horses irresistible. It's nauseating the way the entire community drools at Marshall's feet.

"So, I saw Chloe last night, right before she got taken by Fems or Ezrina or Michelle—or whatever the heck happened to her," I say to Marshall.

"Why do you insist on meddling with the past? You'll never change the outcome."

"Can I ask you a question?" I shield my eyes from the sun while looking up at him. "Was she ordained to die that day?"

"Chloe was at a juncture with destiny."

"A juncture with destiny," I whisper, trying to swallow the meaning of his words.

"Your father was ordained—not much of a difference if you ask me. But, I could very well bring him back. It's a soul for a soul. You could take his place."

"Me?" Not the answer I was looking for.

"I could immortalize you."

"Meaning?"

"You die temporarily and I bring you back, then we can proceed with our family. You could have dominion over this world and ours," Marshall clasps my hand now that we're alone in the woods.

"This world *is* my world. I'm not a part of your world and never will be." I free my fingers from his grip. "And no thanks to the offer. Besides, my dad wants me to be happy."

"You'd be more than happy with me." He morphs into Logan just enough for me to see it.

"Stop that. You're making me uncomfortable."

We walk along until we hit a small thicket of trees.

"Are you ready to receive your vision?"

"Nope, not going there." I turn around and see Michelle stalking us from a distance.

"Will the child she's carrying have dominion?" Maybe he could live out his psychotic fantasies with Michelle of all people.

"No. Any other child of mine is a useless human spawn."

"You're going to make a great father," I exude the necessary sarcastic inflection.

"I will—and your children are the ones who will reap the benefits."

OK, I don't want to say that Marshall is starting to creep me out just a little bit more than usual, but his whole kiss me MO, coupled with the suggestion I die to marry him and procreate posthumous is a bit unnerving.

Michelle descends on him like a fly, so I rush back and dive into the crowd looking for just about anybody I know, and the first person I know is Logan.

"Skyla." He actually looks happy to see me. It's the first time in a long while he doesn't greet me with a heavy look. "How's your arm?"

"Gashed it open again, but it was sealed shut when I woke up this morning." I leave out the gory detail about there being a giant brown scab covering the area. I'm wearing long sleeves that come down to my thumbs, so the gauze strip I wrapped myself wouldn't be so obvious. I'm ready to ask Dr. Oliver for a bottle of that adhesive he uses to glue me back together so I can set up a do-it-yourself shop in my bathroom.

Logan clenches his teeth, as if considering how I might have gashed it open again.

"I went time traveling with Ellis—to get his stash." I add that last part, as if now, everything should make perfect sense. Of course it was innocent, albeit illegal, but that's beside the point.

We walk until we hit the wall of pine trees, and we're presented with a labyrinth of overgrown trunks.

"Logan?" I run my fingers over his arm in an effort to slow him down. "Um," I look back to see if Michelle or anyone else saw us ditch into the woods. For all I know, this place is crawling with Counts. "I know you felt like I was cheating on you."

"I would never say that." He places his arm gently over my shoulders. "But as much as I don't like it, I do think you should be with Gage. He's able to protect you."

"How can you want that? Doesn't it kill you that I'm with Gage? That he kisses me?" It would kill me to see someone kissing Logan. A tight knot builds in my throat.

"Yes, it kills me." There's a marked strain in his voice. "But I can't control the facts. The Counts are loose cannons. They want Celestra blood, and they're not looking too hard for reasons to kill," he says in a sorrowful whisper.

"We should kill the ones who did this, send a message to other regional leaders weighing the same decisions." I start to shake just thinking about the Counts in question, Counts just like the ones who destroyed my family.

"Do you really want to kill people?" Logan walks us in between a pair of twin pines, creating the perfect barrier between us and the rest of the world.

"No, but it's a war. People die in wars. It's a given."

"What if they come after someone you love?" he asks, with a sweet depth of concern. "What if you're responsible for the death of someone close to you? At that point you couldn't go back and change it, but you could now."

His words remind me of Chloe's last entry.

"Do you think we shape the future, or does the future shape us?"

"You mean, are there circumstances steering us toward a predetermined destiny? Yes," he says, unwavering. "But I think along the way, we're allowed to make choices, and sometimes we veer off course—badly. I think if we stay on course we'll be OK in the end."

"Do you think we're staying on course? Me with Gage, you with Lexy?"

"You with Gage, yes. As for me, I'm not with Lexy." He sweeps the floor with a solemn gaze. "She gave me a clue."

"About binding Fems?" A burst of adrenaline surges through me. "Tell me."

"She says it has something to do with the stress in your gut."

"The stress in my gut?" I repeat. "And what did you have to do to extract that pearl of wisdom?" I'm not sure I want to know.

He doesn't say anything, just examines me with those eyes of burning fire.

"You kissed her." It comes out a broken whisper. I bite down hard on my lower lip in an effort to hold back tears. A horrible sadness coats me from the inside, heavy as lead.

Logan catches me in a lingering gaze. He doesn't let up, just lets the tension build until I think my insides are going to explode to the four corners of the island.

He shakes his head just barely. "Didn't kiss her. I would never do that."

I blink back the tears that fight to come. He let me think he kissed her just long enough to torment me.

"I let you go, Skyla, because I love you." His eyes glisten with moisture.

"You want me to let you go?" Maybe that's what this is all about, he wants me to free his conscious, so the next time Lexy lunges at him he can go for it like nobody's business.

"I don't want you to hurt anymore because of me." Logan doesn't crack a smile. Instead, he looks at me intently as though there were only one right answer.

I turn and walk out of the forest.

41

If I Leave You Now

Mom and Tad decide the whole family should go on one of Marshall's self-guided horseback tours—only we're not capable of guiding ourselves on six-foot high moving pedestals so Marshall agrees to lead the pack. Drake happens to be M.I.A. so of course Mom insists that Gage come along, especially since she's been having all these weird en*gage*ment vibes.

"Disorient Tad's horse," I whisper to Marshall as he helps me mount the horse.

"I'm one Oliver away from winning the grand prize. Consider it done."

He hops on a white pristine mare and trots to the front of our group.

Everything is a game to him. I'm some stupid prize who he thinks will push out babies like a Pez dispenser. *Isn't that right?* I shout over at him mentally.

Right? I try again. *Marshall?* He can't hear me. Chloe's blood has brought back my capabilities, kick-started me like some old engine. *I'll sleep with you tonight if you turn around and wink at me right now!* I wait for him, but he doesn't turn.

Nothing. Ha! I'm back!

I'm so thrilled, I shoot Gage a huge beaming smile.

The coast emerges as we cross the threshold of what feels like rows of never-ending pines. The sky is so crisp, so surreal today. I don't remember having a single day this beautiful since we've been on Paragon. In fact, it reminds me a lot of L.A., well except for the forest meeting the rocky shore, the Sector, and the horses.

I look over at Gage. His eyes shine with pleasure in my direction.

He ticks his head over to me, and his horse veers off the trail. I pull the reins until my horse goes over and follows suit.

"We'll catch up," Gage shouts over at Marshall.

Not one of them turns around. We we're already lagging, barely keeping up at the back of the train.

"They'll figure it out," he says.

Gage slides his leg over and gets down. He helps me off my horse and we tether them to a sturdy branch nearby.

"Saw you talking to him," Gage says picking up my hand gingerly.

I'm not sure which him he's referring to so I shrug it off. It's not important at this point anyway.

He steps in front of me and I press into him with a tight hug.

Gage wants me—with everything in him.

I still can't believe that Logan is breaking up with me for my own good. It sounds wrong. Maybe it's just some excuse. How do I know for sure that the flame he had with Lexy ever burnt out?

Not Gage. There was nobody else for him, but me. And now here I am. I'm sure I'm nothing like he imagined. I wonder if he had to do it over again if he would.

"I wasn't worth the wait," I whisper.

"You were more than worth the wait." He gives a quick kiss to my forehead. "This is why I didn't really want you reading the diary. I don't know what's in it, but if she recorded things accurately, even semi-accurately..." He lets his words trail off.

"You're afraid I would see how you waited for me?"

His cheeks fill in with color.

"It makes me love you more." I tighten my arms around him. Then it hits me like a thunderbolt. It was for that exact reason Logan didn't want me reading it either—because it would endear me further to Gage.

A filtering sadness ebbs through me, spreads slow like a storm looming on the horizon. I think I know what this means. Chloe's diary is shaping my feelings for Gage, which, in turn, will shape our future, which, in turn, will make his prophecy come to fruition.

I don't know if we have any control. I don't know if Logan was right about that.

Something in me flexes into compliance. I turn and look up at Gage. Those sad watery stones stare back at me. He knows. I can't hide anything from him.

"I want to be all yours. Help me," I whisper. I want to say, help me forget about Logan, but I'm not sure I could ever push those words through my vocal chords. What if I never really get over Logan? I don't like this train of thought—the runaway train, the derailed train, the train gearing up for the big collision.

"I will." He gives a brief kiss. "We'll get there. I promise."

Marshall treats us like convicts when we return.

"Would the horse thieves like some cake?" He holds out two small plates with an exaggerated amount of chocolate icing.

I take one and thank him. He deposits the piece for Gage, right on his light blue T-shirt.

"Oh, did that just happen?" Marshall gives a wistful smile. "You'll have to go home and change immediately. I have a strict no shirts, not allowed policy." *Not for you, Skyla.* He bedroom eyes me a moment before handing Gage a napkin and smearing the mess further around his shirt.

"I should go with you," I offer.

"Nonsense. Your parents are here," Marshall says, wiping the excess frosting off his fingers. *I have yet to make an ass of your stepfather. The horse wouldn't mind me—she's a lot of you.*

"He's right, I should stay," I pull a face at Gage. "My mom would flip out if I took off. It'd be like the equivalent of running away." I lean up on the balls of my feet and press a kiss into his cheek. It feels real now. Like I'm truly with Gage, not pretending in any arena. "We should go on a date. You know, get to know each other better." I mean as a couple, but Marshall is leering in on the conversation as if he belongs here.

After several minutes of awkwardness, Gage finally takes off.

"A little sugar and flour is all it takes to get rid of him. And the other one you're still pining for, proved to be half the challenge." He smirks, as we walk briskly in Tad and Mom's direction.

Marshall claps his hands together, and the horses begin to stir in the corral. My entire family has lined up against the fence like they're waiting for a firing squad. Drake and Brielle have manifested themselves, complete with spikes of hay that stray out oddly from their clothes.

"Who would like to mount a steed bareback?" Marshall calls out. "Tad, you're the man of the family—why don't you show them how it's done."

Tad doesn't even protest. He climbs under the bar of the fence and stumbles into the corral unnaturally.

"The silver one," Marshall instructs.

I recognize that one from the ad. It's the one I took the pictures on, wearing angel wings.

"You didn't have me wear the wings." I'm so thankful, I could actually hug Marshall for letting me off the hook.

"You will," it speeds out the side of his mouth. Marshall bows into Tad as if giving him the go ahead to attempt this moronic feat.

It takes three tries before he hikes his way up the horse, using its mane to propel himself over the top.

"Nice job!" Mom explodes in both laughter and clapping. Her red hair whips in the breeze, and she looks about ten years younger this day. "Third time's a charm!"

The horse jerks a few times before taking off in a full throttle canter throughout the corral. Tad lets out a series of grunts and screams as he latches onto the mane with a death grip.

You approve? Marshall casts a sideways glance at me.

"Very much so." I don't take my eyes off Tad. I want to remember him this way, feeble, with all of the potential in the world of breaking his neck.

It gets better.

Marshall whistles and the horse kicks up on its heels, nearly dislodging Tad in the process. It strides back over, with Tad lying low against its back, frozen with fear.

"Now let's see the dismount!" Marshall calls out.

Tad pulls his leg over the side and slips down under the horse's body landing with a thump on the ground. The back of his head bounces hard before settling.

"Oh my gosh!" My mother gasps throwing her hands up over her face.

"Are you able to breathe?" Marshall calls out rather calm.

A horrid groan emits from Tad.

Before we can react, or my mother can slip into hysterics, it sounds as though a water faucet is going off.

"Oh my freaking gosh!" Melissa screams.

The horse begins to urinate within inches of Tad's face. It's the splash factor that makes this horrifically hysterical. The fact that muddied urine is getting splattered all over his face and neck is priceless.

I shoot a quick look over to Marshall.

I expect full payment tomorrow evening. Your sisters have riding lessons. I suspect it's a good time to go over mathematical equations. He slides into a lazy grin. *I'll have the wings ready. We can discuss your destiny with Logan and Gage. Better yet, I'll show you.*

42

Show, Don't Tell

In the morning, before school, I catch a snippet of Chloe's diary.

October 1st,

Logan took me to the movies and we just sat in his truck afterwards staring out at Devil's Peak. He kept asking what was wrong. I finally just told him I was tired. I'm so glad Gage didn't tell him I was dying. I really want the rest of my life to be normal, well, as normal as it can be.

I saw the crazy redheaded wench again outside of the student parking lot. I was alone and it was just getting dark. I swear to God she came from nowhere. She had a noose in her hand and she tried to lasso me with it. I screamed bloody murder, got in my car and took off. I saw her laughing in the rear view mirror then she disappeared. Is it possible that Ms. Richards' great, great grandmother was a Fem?

October 5th,

I did it. I went to Ms. Richards house Saturday morning and told her I wanted to talk to her. She sat me on the porch and started up with all that angel crap again. I felt like shaking her from across the table. All I really wanted was info on her demonic family, not to debate whether the Nephilim were real or myth. I felt like saying, do I look like a freaking myth to you? Anyway, I casually asked her about her mom and then her great, great grandmother. I asked what kind of person she was. Ms. Richards said that she heard she was a cold woman and clammed up real fast. Then I asked how she died, and Ms. Richards said the weirdest thing. She said she walked into the woods one day and never came out. They never found her body.

I told Ms. Richards that I wasn't feeling so good just before I puked in the bushes.

It's safe to say, I'm more than a little freaked out.

After a long day of school and cheer practice, mom drops Mia, Melissa, and me off at Marshall's house. The inside holds the hypnotic scent of fresh baked bread. I haven't eaten since lunch and I'm half starved, but I'd rather let my stomach digest itself than ask Marshall for food.

He leads Mia and Melissa out back and hands them off to a riding instructor named Julia. She sports a choppy blonde bob and a youthful face even though she's probably in her thirties. Already there are five or six girls riding in the ring with a few other assistants.

I meander over to the black grand piano that sits majestically near the window overlooking the sweeping grounds. A rose garden comes to life just beyond the glass. In this sleepy haze, they show off their colors of blood red and fuchsia, loud as a siren.

My fingers migrate over the keys. It's been so long since I've taken piano lessons. Fifth grade feels like a million years ago, a whole other lifetime. I practiced Pachelbel's Cannon until my fingers ached, until they petrified from the effort. Of course, I called it Taco Bell cannon so I could remember the name.

I start in, plucking at the keys, missing a few until the piece crawls to life.

Marshall plugs in an amplifier next to me and it goes off like a horn. He picks up a shiny white electric guitar and starts to play along.

He starts in slow, pulls out the chords as though each one were the most important. He picks up the tempo and I stop dawdling at the piano to listen. Marshall destroys the piece completely, in every good way. He is a rock god on the electric guitar and his version of this primeval piece, has the ability to grab you by the throat and make you listen with jaw-dropping intensity.

About five minutes later, he places the guitar down carefully and motions me over.

"Let's take a walk," he says, leading me to the back of the property.

"That was amazing! You're a freaking rock star or something."

"I am rather advanced with stringed instruments." His face brims with pride.

It's cold outside. I'm still wearing my cheer uniform and, of course, forgot a jacket. The cheer sweater is more or less a joke, skin tight and cutoff above the stomach.

"I've got something for you in the barn."

"So, I've been wondering," I say as we walk along, "can people change the future?"

"It's a malformed question. Sharpen your focus and feed me the content one more time."

"Well," I try to keep up with him. "If you show me a vision, for example, and say I find myself in that predicament, could I alter what I'd seen in the vision from happening?"

"What did you see, Skyla?" He looks puzzled. "You're beginning to frustrate me. If anything, earth is an exercise in patience—you qualify as one of the chief reasons."

"Gage says I'm going to marry him."

"And you find this stressful because you would rather be with me. Easily remedied." He blinks a smile as he leads us into the barn. It's still pretty cold in here, although the harsh chill has been removed and replaced with the distinct smell of horse crap. "What do you want me to change for you?"

I pull my sleeve up over my face and breathe into it.

"You don't need to change anything for me," I tell him. "I'll do the changing."

"You don't want to marry Gage?" He pauses, dropping his mouth open in a spasm of sarcasm.

"I do." The words fly out and surprise me. "But, right now I have feelings for Logan, too, and I'm plagued with guilt over this whole thing."

"I thought you said he left you? Doesn't that solve the problem? Tell your emotions to leave the party. Only heartache comes from that. Never hang around where you're not wanted."

Alright, so it's obviously best I drop this whole thing. I'm not into analyzing my love life with Marshall anyway.

It's time for me to ease into Gage and get over Logan. Then, when the faction war ends, if I haven't embedded my feelings into Gage completely, I can maybe go out with Logan just to see if anything's still there, that is, if he hasn't embedded himself into Lexy. This whole thing is turning into a pile of relational crap.

"It's just such a mess," I say it soft, mostly to myself.

He pulls the same dirty wings he had me wear for the photo shoot last month, out from behind some equipment. One by one, he helps hoist them onto my back, secured with a metallic brace that hooks over my shoulders. They're heavy—*beyond* heavy, and for the first time, I see they have the slightest blue tint in them.

"Why the costume? Halloween was over five minutes ago."

He strokes his chin with his finger, examines me as though I were missing something.

"Halo?" I ask, half serious.

"Don't be a child. It's simply an effect caused by the inner luminescence we're known to give off. Come." He walks further into the barn and pulls open the door to a huge empty stall.

I walk in without hesitating. It's insane really—playing dress up with my Algebra Two teacher while he pens me in like an animal.

He shuts the door creating a rather strange partition between us and the rest of the world.

"What's going on?"

"I wanted to see you like this. You're the most exquisite creature on earth, Skyla." He gives a thoughtful nod. "This is the part where you reciprocate." He looks dejected as though he knows it's not possible.

"You are the strangest creature on earth." And hot as hell, but I leave that part out.

"I have a vision that you can test out your theory with." He takes a bold step forward and burrows into me with a heated stare.

"I don't have a theory." Never said I had a theory, and suddenly I'm feeling caged in like an overgrown bird. Is this the part where I call Nev?

"You need a foundation in which to test these thoughts that plague you." He takes another step forward and runs his open palm along the rim of my left wing. It sends a sizzle of excitation coursing through my veins.

"What's this constant flow of lightning?" I try to keep my lips from shivering in rhythm to the vibrations.

"Lightning is a good way to put it—passion is another. You felt it when I took you to my home—our home," he adds.

Marshall focuses intently, bears into me with his entire soul—I can feel him pouring into me. His features meld ever so slightly, and he begins to look like Logan's twin again.

"Do you prefer me this way? I don't mind one bit." He gives a wide vexing grin.

"Stop that," I say, but it's too late. I'm already hypnotized. He picks up my hands and takes another step forward.

I have to keep reminding myself this isn't Logan. He'll never be Logan no matter how hard he tries.

"Skyla," he imitates Logan's husky tone with highlighted precision.

I exhale a lungful of air that I didn't realize I was holding. Logan gives a sad smile, the same melancholy look that Gage gave off for so long—still does. We exchange our sorrowful smiles. Everything in me knows this isn't Logan, everything in me knows it's not right to play with the fire that is Marshall. But how will I ever know if the future is immovable, if I don't test it? How will I ever know if I should abandon all fruitless efforts and sever the chords that lasso Logan and me together like a noose on both ends?

Logan comes in and kisses me, deep, masterful kisses that match my passion and intensity. It's that electrical impulse that flies through me, that reminds me this is Marshall. It both detracts and rockets this experience to its zenith, leaves me lingering far too long and far too willing.

A scene emerges—Gage and me, alone in the butterfly room. He plucks one of the paper butterflies off the wall and blows it at me. It energizes and comes to life with its bright blue paper wings, fragile as bougainvillea petals.

Marshall and me are so immersed in our moment, with his arms dropping ever so slowly below my waist, that I ignore the squeak of the stall door opening, chalk it up to the wind, or Holden's ghost.

A shrill scream penetrates the air. It saws through the moment with its serrated buzzing.

I look over and see Mia with her hands clamped over her mouth. Her eyes are locked in fear as she staggers backward and runs away fast.

There was the kill switch—the sharp knife that could split my indecisiveness to ever act on my lust again. It was always reality that ended those feelings in me for Marshall.

I push into Marshall's chest with violent force. He's completely himself again and that's precisely what Mia saw.

"You are ruining my life!" I thunder in his face.

He pulls the wings off me one at a time with no affect whatsoever.

"You don't even care that she saw us." I'm exasperated by his lack of responsiveness.

"She'll get used to it. In the meantime, threaten her. Find something to lord over her. That's what sisters do." He says it like it's some universal truth.

"You looked like Logan to seduce me."

"He's your weakness—don't blame me for the circumstances." He blinks over at me. "I'll play dirty if I have to." The words slit through the air.

I'm sick of Marshall and his head games. It was one thing when Mia wasn't dragged into it, but now this has blown up into a huge freaking disaster. Not only is he my *teacher*, but I happen to have a boyfriend. What worse example could I possibly be to her?

An explosion of anger rips through me. I grab him by the collar and yank him in close.

"You are screwing with the wrong person." I grit the words out in pieces.

He steps back and dusts me off with one swift stroke.

His eyes flare up a vivid glowing copper. He seethes as though I had somehow finally crossed the line.

"So are you," he spits it out with venom—then disappears.

43

Damage

I try to calm Mia down as we wait for Mom to pick us up. I have no idea where the hell Marshall went, but I make myself at home in his living room in an effort to try to quell my sister's hysterics.

Melissa strides into the room. "What happened?" She's alarmed by Mia's blotchy red face, her convulsive hiccupping.

"She fell off a horse," I say it so quickly, I don't have time to process the lie.

"Did not." Mia glares over at me. She goes to open her mouth then shuts it abruptly. "I tripped." She cuts me a hard look.

I mouth a *thank you* as Melissa looks out the front window.

"Your mom is here." She opens the front door and heads on out. Mia speeds out right behind her, leaving me alone in Marshall's living room.

The dagger above the fireplace beckons me. I plan on paying a visit soon to the regional leaders with Gage. I know Logan would never go if I asked. He's too locked up in altruistic illusions just like the rest of them.

I reach up with my left hand and pull it down from the wall. If I took this, then both Gage and me would be well protected. It's ironic that I'm cradling it with my Chloe arm. It was Marshall who had Ezrina hack off my arm for stealing a butter knife. A harsh reminder of what it could mean if I took this from him too. He did say it was special issue.

I drop it in my backpack and bolt outside. I don't bother shutting the front door. Maybe he'll think someone else might have taken it? But deep down I know he'll trace it's absence straight back to me.

Of course, there will be hell to pay.

That night I waste no time and text both Logan and Gage to come to the butterfly room. As soon as I get home, I research the people on Logan's list. I print out a detailed map of the addressees in which the cowards choose to hide themselves.

"What did you need the knife for?" Gage asks trying to pluck a blue butterfly off the wall as he says it.

I pull down his hands. I'm more than curious to see if I can change Marshall's vision, although everything in me says I can't. Logan hasn't arrived yet, so it's just the two of us.

"I took one from Mr. Dudley's house. I want to see if they're the same." I produce the dagger from behind me.

"You took it?" His eyes ignite with horror. "Are you insane?"

I pull the knife Gage brought from out of the sheath.

"Look at this." A small round symbol of a hand is embossed into the top of the handle. I press it with intention just like Marshall said, and it glows a soft shade of blue.

"What's going on?" He scoots over toward me, careful not to touch the dagger.

"It's some otherworldly thing. Marshall said these were special issue." I place it on the floor, and it dies back down. "It fries a person from the inside, almost instant death, just one quick incision."

"You really want to do this?"

"I am doing this." I pull the clipboard toward me again. "And this person?" I point over to the name, D. Edinger. "He's last." I breathe the words out with suspended anger. "I'll cut my teeth on the others and bring my game by the time I get to him."

"Where's Logan?" I'm not all that surprised he hasn't bothered to show up yet.

"Don't know." Gage examines me carefully as though he were assessing my sanity.

"He's not coming." I try to mask the sadness in my voice.

He doesn't care about me anymore. It's obvious the faction war means nothing to him.

I pull out the knife I stole from Marshall and place it on my lap. I fold the addresses of the regional leaders and tuck them into my pocket.

I lean forward and give him a succulent kiss.

"Take me to Barcelona, Gage."

The morning sun warms our backs as Gage and I appear near a bus station behind a group of trees. We secure our weapons in the back of our jeans and head out toward an open marketplace. I don't know how teleportation works or how he can control where we land, but I'm afraid to ask. As long as I don't have the details, I won't have the fear of ending up in some random men's restroom, looming over my head.

"Logan told me, a while back, that if you kill someone in a faction war you're exempt." I look up at Gage hopeful. "You won't get caught, you won't go to prison." It's the last one that terrifies me.

"Yes, the factions have something in place." He shakes his head. "But the emotional consequences—are you ready for those?"

The brilliant blue waters of the Mediterranean jump up behind him and the color of his eyes spring out at me in concert with the sea. Gage is perfectly beautiful in this light. My heart skips thinking about how completely he loves me—how I already have everything I'm looking for with someone, right here in front of me.

"I'm going to do this for all the families like mine. I wish someone would have done this for me. If this Edinger person were stopped before he authorized the killing of my dad, then I wouldn't have to do this. They forced my hand. If I let these Counts off the hook, I let off the person who killed my family as well." And they did kill my family. Tad will never be able to replace what we had before him.

Gage takes us up a steep cobbled path that leads to an ancient looking dwelling made of stone. A gnarled wood frame creates an ornate entry. Large white billowing sheets hang on a laundry line, barricading us from the view of the bustling street full of patrons at the farmers market across the way.

Dominic Savedra lives up on the second floor according to my paperwork. I walk boldly up the steps with Gage tucked close behind and give a power knock on the door. We give it a few minutes before walking downstairs and pounding on the main entry.

A beautiful woman with skin the color of cinnamon emerges.

"Do you know where we can find Dominic?" I point upstairs.

"Working." She says in broken English. She flicks a finger just past the farmers market.

We cross the street in haste. I don't know if we're going to find him. The fact this is all happening in real time, and that we have school in the morning, is starting to make me feel like we're sort of up a creek. Just as I'm about to question a vendor picking through his lot of green peppers, Gage nudges me.

He points over to a sign that reads Dominic Savedra attorney at law in plain English right beneath the Spanish rendition.

I rush up the steps and burst into the office.

"Dominic?" I ask the petite secretary filing her nails. She picks up the phone, but I don't wait for her permission. Instead, adrenaline propels me—cheers me on to complete this very first mission on the war against the Counts.

I burst into the back room and find a heavyset man reclined at his desk, staring off at the television mounted on the wall.

"Dominic Savedra?" I ask a little too loud.

"Yes." He sits up at attention, spreading his fingers flat across the desk.

"Are you a Count?" I ask stupidly.

Gage doesn't hesitate. He plunges his knife in through Dominic Savedra's hand, deep and settled, the way Holden pinned me in the forest. The blue illumination from the dagger quickens through the man's body. And with that, he slumps over onto his desk.

It was the first Count causality in the civil war evoked in my name, and it was Gage who killed for me.

44

Love Like Ours

Venice, Geneva, Cape Town, Taipei, Prague, Tonga, Perth, Dublin, New York City, Cleveland, we hit them all in just one night. There were five more cities we couldn't get to. Five regional leaders who get to see tomorrow because Gage and I were staring down the barrel of first period.

In the morning, Gage picks me up, and we head out to school without saying two words. There's a strangled tension between us as though we were both somehow hoping it were all a bad blood-soaked dream.

A dauntless charcoal cloud stretches across the breadth and width of Paragon.

At school—we move around stiff as robots. It's not until second period that I realize for the first time how much bloodshed we are suddenly responsible for—stunned that I let Gage kill for me. It was Gage who wanted the blood on his hands and he did it for me.

It all feels surreal, too heavy to process correctly. I want to run to Dr. Booth and tell him what a mess I've made of everything—how I've dragged Gage in, yet again.

"Ms. Messenger, can I see you a moment?" Marshall asks with a forced smile. He instructs the students to go over their homework before leading me out into the hall and securing the door behind him.

"Do you love your limbs?" There's a great intensity in him I haven't seen before.

"Yes," I manage to squeak out.

"Do you love your life?" His eyes sweep up and down over my person.

"Yes," my voice is hoarse from being up all night.

"You're covered in blood and have no alliance with me whatsoever."

"I think I need you." I let my gaze fall to the floor. I've done something huge, something horrible, and now I'm going to pay for it. Maybe Logan was right, maybe there was too much to lose going off halfcocked and massacring almost a dozen Counts.

He lifts my chin with his finger. "You've proven yourself a noble warrior, Skyla." He produces a dry smile.

"I changed the future," I say. "The vision never happened." All it took was for me to bat Gage's hand away from the butterfly. It never animated and floated up to the ceiling in a trail of sapphire glory.

"Believe what you like. Are you interested in knowing what the payment for stealing my dagger is?"

"What?" I'm sure it has something to do with spending the rest of my days in Sectorville.

"Why don't I show you?" He pulls me in by the face and indulges in a wild, uninhibited kiss as I try halfheartedly to push him away.

A picture emerges of Mia and Melissa laughing in a crowded room. Mia jumps from off a table and falls into Tad's waiting arms, Melissa does the same. My mother lingers beside them, with Drake and Brielle at their sides.

Table diving? That's what's going to happen?

I pull away breathless.

"I don't get it." I struggle to read his expression. "Is it because I wasn't there—in the vision? Is that what it was about?"

"You'll know when the time comes. Just rest assured it creates a barrier between the lot of you—an impenetrable chasm."

"I'm going to die." My hand comes up to my throat. Marshall is going to remove me from the planet because I stole his dagger. "The chasm is death, isn't it?"

He drills into me with his stare, unwavering—hard as nails. "It will feel like death. Most certainly."

After cheer, Gage gives me a ride to my routine mental exam.

Dr. Booth nurses his coffee, cradles it with both hands, never taking his eyes off me.

"So Logan left you." He reiterates after my lengthy explanation of how it all went down—Marshall with his foresight into the future, by way of his tongue.

I don't nod, or blink—just wait for something profound to come from his lips letting me know this will all work itself out. I want to hear him say that maybe Logan is the love of my life, and that in the end, somehow, it will be OK.

"Fate seems to favor Gage." He indulges in a quick sip. "He knows you'll marry." He shrugs as if to say there is nothing here to mourn, move on, be done with it. Dr. Booth is a Levatio, he shares the gift of knowing—he understands the finality of it all. "And the body count?" He asks as an afterthought.

"I'd rather not say." I lack the proper enthusiasm to own up to the carnage I'm responsible for.

His head tilts as he stares pensively at me. "You will pay for this Skyla. I'm sorry."

"Everyone has to pay for what they've done, that's why I did it."

Dr. Booth considers this, while pinching at his chin. "Slow steps—you don't run into a war." He folds his hands and pushes out a complacent smile. "You might find the thick of the battle a little too long, a little too painful. Better to assess that now before there's no turning back." His eyes rove all over my face as if memorizing it one last time. "There's no turning back now, is there?"

I shake my head.

No turning back.

That night, I curl up with Chloe's diary while waiting for Gage in the butterfly room.

October 11th,

It kills me to see Gage in the quad, Gage on the field, Gage in my biology class, and have to pretend that I'm in love with Logan. I thought by now he'd go insane. I thought maybe because he knows I'm going to die he'd have pity on me and maybe spare one heartfelt kiss. I can't stand to see his face in the halls at school.

Maybe that's what's going to do me in? Maybe I'll die of a broken heart.

October 13th,

I let Logan in through the butterfly room and lured him into my bed. I know for a fact that he and Gage talk about me because Logan mentioned he doesn't keep anything from Gage. He said he's his brother in every way. So, brilliant me, attacked him. Logan was defenseless to my womanly wiles. He was easier to take down than I could have ever imagined.

Invisible idiot visited again. Hi you!

Idiot? Gee thanks.

My stomach turns at the thought of Chloe with Logan—using him like that. Although a selfish part of me feels relieved she didn't love him. I wish she didn't love Gage so damn much either.

Gage shows up in the butterfly room near midnight. I'm beyond exhausted, so when he snatches a butterfly off the wall, and it takes flight in a quiet blue spiral up to the ceiling I don't have the energy to try to change it. Instead, I find a strange comfort in the very secure nature of not being able to alter the future.

"We were destined to kill those men," I speak it softly to him. I think the two of us are going to need Dr. Booth's services for years, psychotherapy, and at least a dozen shock treatments to get over the trauma of ending near a dozen lives. Not to mention we don't know what the fallout will be, but we do know it's coming—consequences that will strike like lightning. This is the storm of our own making. It's going to touch down in our lives and inevitably burn something to the ground—we just have no idea what that might be.

"Come here." He pulls me over. I wrap myself around him completely with my arms and legs around his person as though he were a tree trunk.

I start in with slow measured kisses, then, something inside me gives. It submerges me in the knowledge that Gage will marry me one day. It's a slow build up that pushes me forward in a lust filled haste—Gage, who waited for me, who took me to the Counts to avenge Celestra blood, who ultimately killed for me.

His breathing becomes erratic as he gently lays me down on the floor. I shred the buttons off my blouse in an effort to tear it open—lift his shirt up over his head to feel his bare flesh against mine. It feels magical like this with Gage. Like it was always meant to be.

The overhead latch to the butterfly room bursts open and the hard thump of tennis shoes lands just shy of our heads.

"Whoa!" A voice shouts from above.

Freaking Ellis.

I pluck Gage's T-shirt from off the floor and hold it over my bra. For a dreadful second, I thought it might be Logan—believed it with all of my heart. I think I wanted it to be.

"What?" I hiss perturbed.

"Counts had an emergency faction meeting tonight."

"Are they coming after me?" Everything in me loosens with fear.

"They're coming after all of you."

The next morning before school, I sneak in a few more entries from Chloe's diary.

October 15th,

Went to Emerson's grave. I bought a dozen white roses with the money I took from Mom's purse and placed them in a vase buried in the ground. I like it out there in the cemetery. It's peaceful, so quiet.

I tried to imagine how I might look in one of those long wooden boxes Dr. Oliver has on display. Logan gave me the grand tour today. He kept making jokes about how the bodies are laid in that steel bathtub and that if people knew what they did to you in one of those, they'd rethink this whole dying thing, but I didn't laugh. It took everything in me not to run out of there screaming.

I ran my fingers across Emerson's name carved into the cold black granite until my fingers went numb. If I wasn't so chicken shit I'd go back in time and tell her I was sorry, but I'm not sure I really am.

October 16th,

Holden was a total asshole on the phone today. What else is new?

Anyway, at school, Gage didn't even look remotely pissed during fourth period, so I invited Logan over for a repeat performance. When we were done, I asked Logan if he talked to Gage about us. He got all weird on me and started asking questions, wondering if I was with him just to make Gage jealous or something. I never did say Logan was stupid. Of course, I denied it. Besides, who wouldn't want to be with the second hottest guy at West? Plus, it pisses Lexy and Michelle off. Just watching them squirm makes it all worthwhile.

A storm rages outside the hallowed halls of West Paragon High. The electricity flutters in rhythm, as the thunder rattles throughout the science building like a thousand angry skeletons. Logan sent me a text asking me to meet him under the stairwell at 1:20.

I get a hall pass and leave without telling Gage where I'm headed. After our heated hormonal exchange last night, I know it would break his heart even if it were a purely platonic meeting, which I'm almost sure it will be. But a small aching part of me is hoping for something more—I'm beginning to hate that part of me.

I don't see Logan. He's a no show again, just like the other night.

The door to the janitorial supply closet is open, and I hear a whisper. I lean in to check it out.

I'm yanked in violently and shoved to the back, knocking over a shelf of cleaning supplies in the process.

I turn around in time to see the back of a man in a dull green jumpsuit securing a metal chain between the doorknob and a nail pegged to the wall.

He turns and looks down at me with a strange blank expression.

It's the boy from the party—*Holden*.

"You're not real," I breathe out the words in a panic.

"I'm very real." He knocks over a row of paint cans and flips over a tray of tools as the room explodes in a wild cacophony of bangs and whimpers. "I'm so *damn* real!" He screams, pulling at his arm right below the shoulder and twisting violently until a circle of liquid darkens the fabric. He yanks off his arm and starts wielding it around like a baseball bat, forcing me to whittle myself in the corner.

I'm so frightened I can't breathe. My muscles do their best rendition of rigor mortis, and my brain is completely unable to come up with a plan. Fems die then disappear. How do I get rid of a ghost?

"What do you want?" I shout over his disruptive, one-armed tantrum.

"What do I want?" He thrashes his bludgeoned limb to the floor and charges at me. "I want my life back!" He explodes the words over me in one hot putrid breath.

I couldn't save my father no matter how hard I tried. Maybe it was somehow ordained for me to kill Holden that night? I can't do this, and everything in me knows it as fact. So I do the only thing I can do. Lie.

"I'll do it. I know a Sector." My breathing quickens. "I can time travel..."

"I know a Sector, I can time travel," he mimics, making me sound like a whiny toddler.

"Make crap happen!" His voice booms louder than any human voice possible. He reaches up and grips his face until the flesh rips right off in a slow viscous pull. All that remains, is a wash of blood over muscle—his eyes stare back at me bulging and round as the tissue around his lips pull into a clown-like grimace.

I retch at the sight. The stench sends a fresh rise of vomit shooting up the back of my throat.

The room starts in on a violent rattle, causing a few stray cans to fall from the shelving unit behind us.

A loud pop explodes overhead and the lights go out.

Crap!

My skin starts to pulsate as though one hundred hands have clamped over me at once.

"Having fun yet?" Holden emits a deep guttural laugh as a hand crawls up the back of my shirt.

I want to die. I've never been sure of anything, like I am of this. I'd rather have Pierce with his neatly covered flesh sucking the lifeblood out of me than have anything to do with his brother the bloody ghost.

A scream gets locked in my throat.

I can't think straight. His fingers cinch up my hair. I scream for real this time until it feels like the world could shatter from the sound of it.

A wild panic seizes me as I snatch at the counter. I grab a hold of a small metal cylinder and start thrashing him with it as he struggles to fully seize me.

The door thumps in jags. It opens in one energized burst. I look up at a figure lost in the shadows.

A wild spasm takes place beneath me as Holden bucks and writhes. His fingers claw at me—run right through my chest as he begins to evaporate, slow as smoke.

It's Logan.

He lifts me into his arms and takes me underneath the stairwell.

"It was Holden," I say out of breath.

"Are you OK?" He pants.

"I think so."

I take in his clean scent—try to memorize the flex of his muscle as I run my hand over it, solid, like skin over steel.

"I didn't get your text last night," he says. "Left my phone in the car. I'm sorry. Gage told me what happened." He studies me a moment with intense anguish.

"Gage was there." I try to shrug it off like it's no big deal.

"I'll be there next time and every other time after that."

"Why?" Really, I want an answer.

He brushes the stray hair away from my eyes.

"Because I'm the one who will always love you, even if I can never have you."

45

Rebel, Rebel

Friday morning, I head downstairs overwhelmed by the fact I'm the root of pain for dozens of people in the world. Those Counts we killed had families, and just knowing Brielle, Nat and Ellis—I can tell that not all Counts are out to get me. The fact that some or all of those Counts might have had children makes me seriously question my actions. Logan was right I should have thought things through. Logan is always right and somehow this more than slightly pisses me off.

"Ready for the field trip?" My mother swipes a dishtowel into a glass, then holds it up to the light.

"Oh right." The away game is tonight. After fifth, we're all getting shuttled to the ferry and heading to the mainland.

Drake comes in and sits at the bar looking rather morose over the fact he won't be joining me.

Tad rattles his paper. It's become his way of getting our attention just before something moronic flies from his mouth. Normal people would clear their throats, but then again Tad is not normal so it makes perfect sense. Also, he apparently never got the memo that newspapers have gone the way of the VCR. I'm sure the news he's reading is as stale as his breath.

"The football team going?" He peppers his voice with concern as though the football team going to a football game is cause for alarm.

"It's a football game, so it sort of makes sense." I pull the milk from the fridge and set it on the counter.

Drake's back vibrates as he gives a silent laugh.

"Skyla," my mother groans. "Does everything that comes from your lips have to be drenched with such sarcasm? We're starting to feel attacked." She locks her fists high on her hips.

She's feeling attacked? I'm feeling attacked. Of course, I can't voice that, or I'll get shipped away to an all girls prison, or the psych ward, or the graveyard—all of the above in quick succession.

"I'm concerned, Skyla." Tad ambles over next to Mom with his arms crossed tight. They both wear the same irrevocably pissed expressions.

"What's there to be concerned about? We'll be back Saturday."

"The school has you all checking into the same hotel," he says, laced with suspicion, as if suddenly I'm responsible for travel arrangements.

"Yeah, so? Brielle, Nat, and Kate are sharing a room with me. Boys and girls are on different floors." I get a bowl out of the pantry like it's no big deal. Oddly, I haven't given the away game much thought, but now that they mention it, I think it's going to be pretty damn exciting.

"There's always the elevator," Drake says through a mouth full of cereal.

"That's right." Tad is quick to agree. "Gage will undoubtedly be there. Are the two of you?" He conjoins his forefingers then separates them.

"I gave her permission to keep seeing Gage." My mother sighs into her words as though she were knowingly opening a Pandora's box of grief.

"Oh really?" Tad's voice hits its upper register. "Well at least we'll know who to thank when there's a crib in her room nine months down the road."

My mouth falls open at the accusation.

"Skyla is not having sex," Mom says with a reserved sense of calm. "We've already had this conversation."

Mia and Melissa walk in on cue and take seats on either side of Drake.

"And you know this for a fact, because?" He shouts. "Lizbeth, she routinely lies to us. It's just who she is."

It's who she is? He makes it sound like lying is embedded in my genetic code, or its some pathological condition I've contracted.

"And what about the rest of the kids on this trip?" He directs the question over to me. "Do they *drink* or *drug*?"

A laugh gets caught in my throat. Before I can wrap my head around his stupid phraseology, Mom steps between us.

"Relax," her voice is tethered to a false sense of calm. "The email said there were going to be three chaperones. It's all very well supervised."

I happen to know Marshall is one of them, Ms. Richards and the coach, the other two. Marshall is practically useless, more of a liability than anything else.

"Oh three?" He balks at her. "So three people are going to control fifty or so hormonal teens? They'll probably tie them up and throw them overboard, soon as they hit open waters. Good luck with the delusion that everything is going to be OK with her." He storms out of the room leaving a void of silence in his wake.

My mother spins around with an unexpected look of glee in her eyes. "So! Somebody's birthday is right around the corner." She sings the last word.

"Are you serious?" I hiss. She's freaking insane. "You just let him treat me like I'm some sort of juvenile delinquent who *drinks* and *drugs* and plans on having sex with Gage tonight." I pause in reflection. I did get drunk that one time, and I sort of did engorge myself on pot-laced brownies. I've tried at least twice to sleep with Gage… hey? Maybe Tad's a psychic?

I shake my head.

"Forget my birthday." I abandon the milk on the counter and race upstairs.

I try to remember my family, the way it was before my dad died. I don't ever recall a single argument rooted in my questionable hormonal behavior, for sure no conversations about drugs or alcohol in context with me.

I pull out my duffel bag and throw in a pair of jeans, a sweater for tomorrow, and slide my makeup off my desk and into the bag with a clean sweep of my arm.

There's a light knock at the door before Mia lets herself in and closes it behind her.

"Hey, Sky*la*." She says my name in two equal parts, never a good sign.

“What’s up?” I try not to show any signs of fear as I prepare to be blackmailed into oblivion.

She rolls backward onto the bed. Her long pale legs almost reach the top of my canopy.

“The bathroom was taken so I had to use yours this morning.”

“Oh, that’s fine. You’re welcome anytime.” I get up and snatch Chloe’s diary off the nightstand and stuff it deep into my bag before she gets any funny ideas.

“I wasn’t really snooping or anything, but I dropped my phone in your trashcan, and while I was fishing it out,” she pauses to sit up and pluck something from her pocket, “I found this.” She wands a little pink stick over at me like I should know what it is.

I snatch it out of her hands and examine it.

“What’s this?” I think I know. Looks like a pregnancy test. Inside the urine stained window, there’s a red sign that reads positive. “It’s not mine.”

“You play dumb so well.” She rocks off the bed and jumps in front of me. “So whose baby is it? Is it that teacher’s? I guess it could belong to Gage or even that other guy you were seeing when first we got here.” She itemizes the possibilities on her fingertips.

I stare out at the wall. “Get a grip Mia, it’s not mine. It’s obviously Mom’s. She probably wants to surprise Tad or something, so she took it in my bathroom.”

Mom walks in without knocking, and I hide the test behind my back.

“So when were you going to tell us?” Mia whines, as if she’s honestly offended that Mom hasn’t spilled the news of her cloven-hoofed spawn.

“Tell you what?”

“That you’re having a baby.” Mia’s inflection on the word *baby* makes her sound like one herself.

“Oh, Hon.” Mom lifts her hand up to her chest. “I’m not. Aunt Flow just paid me a visit,” she whispers. “But I promise, you’ll be first to know. I was just stopping in to let *you* know,” she points over at me, “don’t pack your hair dryer, they’ll have one at the hotel.” She squeezes her hand in a mock wave before leaving the room.

Mia gets right up in my face. “Thought so.” She takes off, slamming the door on the way out.

It’s not mine.

I pause considering the alternatives.

Brielle?

Brielle *and* Michelle are both going to have babies? Plus that girl in Spanish, that makes three at West!

Dear God. We’re going to be on the freaking news.

46

All Aboard

All day long I'm a nervous wreck over the fact I've managed to accidentally smuggle Chloe's diary to school. I took it out from the duffle bag, and it's been hitching a ride in my backpack ever since. It feels like I'm walking around with a grenade on my back. Like, at any moment Michelle Miller is going to come over and snatch it out and start reading it out loud in the quad. Not that there's anything really earth shattering in there. That whole *this will change everything* crap turned out to be just a rouse. I mean what did it change really? My feelings for Gage? That was destined to happen.

My heart sinks. That's why Logan broke up with me. Maybe that was all a part of Chloe's plan—break me and Logan up so she could have him to herself when she gets back.

After fifth, Gage and I head over to the bus together. Brielle is already seated with Nat and Kate, so the two of us pick a spot near the back.

The bus is tight, three to a seat, and Logan's yet to get on. I see Lexy craning her neck waiting in anticipation. I feel like craning her neck—twisting it. I wonder how many revolutions it would take before it actually popped off?

Logan steps on. He looks coolly around at the sea of faces. My stomach bottoms out at the sight of him.

"Wave him over," I say to Gage.

"Who?" He looks up. "Oh." He sinks back in his seat mildly irritated. "What for?"

"We can talk faction business." And Lexy won't win.

Gage leans up and waves Logan over.

He's coming. He's about to pass Lexy, and I'll die happy if he does. Logan pauses and whispers something to her before heading back. It was a simple act, innocent really, but it churned up the acid in my stomach in one hot bite.

"What's going on?" He lands next to me, and every bad feeling in me settles. It's blissful like this with Gage and Logan on either side of me—*safe*.

Logan busies himself adjusting his backpack while Gage tries untangling his earphones. I see Lexy pinning me with an aggressive hate-filled stare, and I do what any other girl in my shoes would do—blow her a kiss.

Gage looks up in time to see me do it—makes me feel like I've just thrust a dagger into his heart.

I pick up his hand and hold it in plain view of Logan. This isn't going well. This will never, ever go well.

The ferry ride is so annoyingly boisterous it makes me wish my head would explode and put me out of my misery. Ms. Richards stands at the front and shouts revisions to her latest cheer torture routine over the jutting sound of the engine. Gage and Logan were yanked up deck, with the rest of the guys to go over plays or something. See? Tad had nothing to worry about. Even the boat ride is segregated.

"I need some air," I say.

"Me too." Brielle fans herself spastically.

We head up top, into the wild blowing wind, and my hair flies in a million directions at once.

I pull my hood on and take in the sights. Paragon's coast looks like an emerald illusion veiled in a thin coat of fog. The ocean is frosted with whitecaps, just one violent wave collapsing after another. It reminds me of the first time I saw Marshall, speaking of which....

"Ms. Messenger." He slips in besides me.

Brielle has already migrated over to Nat who—oh my God—Pierce is here!

He's got his arms all over Nat, one on her thigh, the other dancing up and down her back.

Crap!

"What's the matter? Count on board rile you up?"

"Yes." My hand flattens across my chest. "He's a freaking psycho! He did all kinds of bad things to me, and he's like part vampire or something."

"You must taste delicious." He tracks a row of pelicans as they skirt across the water.

"So, what's going to happen?" I pull at his sleeve and that soothing rhythm surges through my bones. "Am I going to be OK? Is this trip going to end horribly?" Sheer panic begins to bubble out of me.

"Do I look like a magic eight ball?" He pulls his cheek to the side mildly amused. "I don't know Skyla. I'm not a voyeur into the future. I let the visions come as they may."

"If I had that gift, I'd want to know everything about everybody." I fold my hands up over the lip of the railing.

"You're vexed with the simple detail of marrying Gage."

"Shhh!" I swat him.

"How do you think you'd handle the rest of the details? The life altering ones? Honestly, I'd have to snatch at your ankles just to save you from tossing yourself overboard, if you knew every last one."

"Wow. You must really know something big." I look up at him somberly. "Anything you'd like to share?"

"You know the rules." He penetrates me in with a smoldering look.

"I don't mean weak stuff like a runaway butterfly. I'm talking earthquakes of my existence—*that* kind of life altering."

"I promise you an earthquake, Skyla." He plucks off his black leather gloves one finger at a time. "Payment is a little higher—room 417, nine-thirty. Be there—prepare to shake, rattle and roll." He walks toward Ms. Richards briskly. Probably rescheduling.

I look up and see both Logan and Gage eyeing me with unsettled expressions.

I wonder which one of them is involved in this earthquake and how strong it will register on the Richter scale.

47

Blood Like Sugar

The game is uneventful. The field sits nestled in a clearing amidst a circle of dense overgrown pines. A fog bank has settled in this bald patch of earth and it feels like we're cheering while perched on clouds way up in the stratosphere. I can't make out the players, for sure can't see the numbers on their jerseys. It's a big ball of confusion, so I focus on my high kicks and scream into the wind.

Marshall happens to be seated right next to my least favorite vampire—Pierce. Nat mentioned they might go out to dinner tonight. He probably has a major artery of hers lined up for dessert, but then again she's a Count, no point in blood suction there.

You like the company I keep? Marshall nods over to Pierce. *I see the discontent on your face when you look over. You're glaring. Do be a little more discreet.*

I try not to make eye contact with Marshall. Pierce will totally misinterpret that and think I'm shooting daggers at him, or worse, lusting after him. He'll think I'm wishing he would drain the life out me as though it were some sensual thrill ride.

I've been reading his thoughts for a while now. Would you like the exhaustive or the synopsized version? Marshall pauses. *He says you've got a great ass. His words, not mine, although I agree. He also likes the way you choreograph your sweater to rise at the precise moment you lift your skirt. He finds that very erotic.*

Again with the sex on the brain. It's every single one of them, I swear.

He's drifting in and out of a fantasy concerning your blood. It's gory and degrading, and I choose to skip the details.

The pom-pom in my left hand starts to wiggle out of control. It takes my arm on a wild ride directly into Michelle's face and smears into her hard.

"I'm so sorry!" I shout.

Crap!

I try to drop the haunted ball of tinfoil, but it sticks to my skin as though it had somehow magically adhered.

Michelle jumps back and clamps her hands over her nose. The black circles under her eyes have impressed themselves as permanent features. For a moment, I think I should take advantage of the opportunity and rip the Fem-riddled rose off her neck.

"You bitch!" She gurgles from under her fingers.

In one quick motion my arm turns, before I can grasp what direction it's about to maneuver, I'm bopping Lexy in the face, fast and repetitive like a cartoon kangaroo.

"Holy crap!" Emily pushes me hard, landing me flat on my back in a patch of orange dirt. Brielle, Nat, and Kate run over to help me to my feet. They're laughing so hard they're dry hacking.

Good show Skyla! Good show! I see Marshall in the stands clapping while gazing out into the field as though the team might have done something worthy of his praise.

If anybody can stop Holden, Marshall can.

Maybe I can cheer *that* in his room tonight.

Dinner theater. No, really. Come to find out Ms. Richards is a theater buff, and the small abandoned town which lies on the outskirts of civilization is putting on a production with all of its thirty-five inhabitants in the cast—that includes an infant.

The play is Romeo and Juliet. The entire tragedy is narrated in verse by a tall, thin, man who looks as though he might have literally been stretched out by Fems.

"Seventh century outdid itself with this one," Marshall leans in and whispers from the table behind me. "The past was much more fun. More rebel rousing, less social death by internet."

"Do you mind?" Gage hisses over at him.

It's not easy to rile up Gage, but I think deep down inside he senses a connection between Marshall and me. Not that I'm even remotely interested in Marshall.

Michelle is practically sitting on his lap, glaring at me with that gaunt haunted expression she wears like a mask. As of late, she's pretty damn scary to look at. Just past her, I can see Logan sandwiched between Lexy and Emily. I should have taken Lexy's eye out while I had the chance.

Logan gives a heartfelt smile. It's the distinct look of longing—that covetous look in his eye when he sees me with Gage that makes me want to forget about everything we're hiding from and go over to him. But it's Gage I'm here with and Gage I'm committed to—Gage that I really do love, so I turn around and try not to let Logan's resplendent face burn a narcotic image into my heart—too late.

The play comes to an end—the actors walk the plank and dip down together in an arm-linked bow.

Natalie whispers something to Pierce, and they laugh in unison. He continues his crooked smile in my direction, but something in his eye glints a challenge.

"What are you staring at?" Gage huffs over to him before taking a swig of his soda.

Something in Pierce hardens. He's handsome in a future frat boy of America sort of way. The arrogance melts off his face and is replaced with a hellish fury. His brows form sharp triangular peaks as he barrels on over.

Gage is ready for a fight. He thrust back his chair and meets him chest-to-chest gorilla style in less than three seconds flat.

"Sit down," I say, plucking at his shirt.

Pierce gives a hard shove and Gage bullets backward into a rolling dessert cart about eleven feet away.

Chaos breaks loose as half the football team rushes over to Gage and the other half try to tackle Pierce.

Marshall snatches Pierce by the back of the collar and escorts him out into the lobby, strangulation style. Pierce's tongue protrudes from his mouth and his face bloats a brilliant shade of purple.

"Everybody calm down." Ms. Richards pats her hands in the air motioning for us to get back to our seats.

Gage cleans the frosting off his arms as the coach tries to calm him down.

I note Logan in the shadows, speeding toward the exit.

"I've got go to the bathroom." I snatch my purse off the table and head on back.

The theater is dressed in deep red velvet. Large black panthers adorn the palatial entry, complete with stickers thrown on by errant children and initials carved, in graffiti style, toward the bottom. The glass doors to the entrance have a lightning bolt shaped crack in one, and a bullet hole in the other.

Over in the corner, Pierce nods to Marshall with feigned obedience. As soon as Marshall heads back inside, Logan pushes Pierce into a darkened alcove.

I run over to the other end of the lobby fast as I can.

I can hear their primal grunting, a series of dull thumps, and a skull bashing into the wall.

A scream dissipates as it fails to make its way out my vocal chords. They're both bleeding. Logan's face is lost in thick tracks of crimson and Pierce's eye is swelling unnaturally.

Logan picks him up and thrashes him down on his back at an increased velocity.

"Crap." Pierce writhes on the carpet as he struggles to get his bearings.

Logan plucks a large picture off the wall and holds it over him in a threatening manner.

"No—let me." I take it from him and heave it over Pierce's body. His flaxen colored waves would look so much better with shards of glass embedded in them. I cradle the gilded frame in my hands. I have my strength back, I could crush him with it if I wanted—kill him like I did his brother. I lift it high and smash it into the ground within an inch of his left ear. His back arches momentarily before he winces in pain.

I kneel next to him and lean in.

"Your brother says, hell is lonely," I whisper. "Touch me again and I'll arrange for you to find out yourself." I bear all of my hatred down over him as I seethe out the words.

Logan pulls me off him, and we head over to a now defunct concession stand. It might have been fully operational, once, like in 1953.

"Are you OK?" His cheek twitches when he says it.

I reach over to the sink and wet a paper towel to give him, but he dunks his head under the faucet instead. A steady stream of pink liquid rinses off his flesh. He pops back up and slicks his hair back in one swift motion, causing a trail of water to shoot up in the air.

"You've got a bad cut." I pat the puff of flesh just under his eye.

"I'm OK." He winces out a smile. A morbid sadness falls between us. An entire sea of strangled words that will probably never be said. "Go ahead and go back in. I'm gonna..." He points toward his cut. Pierce lets out a loud groan from inside the alcove. "Do me a favor and don't leave Gage."

He looks resigned to the fact I shouldn't and never will.

48

Falling

It's only nine-thirty, and I'm already exhausted. Nat left our room to be with Pierce, and Kate and Brielle decided it was too boring to sit around, so they put on their bathing suits and hit the hot tub.

Not me.

I let out a hard sigh as I give a light knock on Marshall's door. I've completely rethought this whole earthquake thing. Marshall is right, I can't just treat him like some magic eight ball.

The door opens, and he waves me in. He's wearing a T-shirt and jeans and looks younger than usual. I'm not used to seeing him so casual, and well, like a teenager. This totally throws me.

A series of wild thumps erupt from inside the bathroom.

"What's that?" I ask. With Marshall around, all of my fear and anxieties are replaced with a natural curiosity.

"I had to meet with a few Fems. Discuss strategies, the implications of subliminal messaging. You'd think after six thousand years they'd get it straight." He takes a seat at the front of the bed and snatches up the remote. A football game is on, and he's totally vegging out, just staring at the TV.

"You seem so—normal."

"Mmm." He appears disinterested in my analysis.

"You're anything but."

"Are you here to argue about my oddities or glimpse into your future?" He doesn't waver his stare from the television.

"Neither. Actually, I wanted to forget about that whole future thing. That, and I sort of promised Holden a body."

"Not your brightest moment."

"Well, I know, but you have to help me. He's really aggravating to have around, and he's completely out of control. He almost killed Gage in that accident."

"Better luck next time." Marshall looks around nebulously as though Holden could hear. "Do you really want to bring him back from the dead? First Chloe the catastrophe, and now him? Leave resurrections to the pros, Skyla. That's nothing you want to specialize in, believe you me."

"Can you help me get rid of him?"

"I can help you do anything." He glides into a malevolent smile. "The *Skyla's* the limit." He grins. "What are you willing to give?"

"Not much. I'm with Gage."

"And you've called off pining for the pretty one?"

"Logan is not pretty. They're both gorgeous. It's like a family curse or something. And yes, I'm working on getting over him. A girl can only have one love interest and I pick Gage." A searing pang of grief rips through me. We're sort of like Romeo and Juliet, Logan and me. Only, it's celestial factions keeping us apart and not family. Our blood is the poison, and we're forced to marinade in it day after day. It's suffering a miserable death this love of ours. How can it possibly survive?

"Have you convinced yourself yet?" He leans back, amused. "That is what you're doing, isn't it, Juliet?"

"I'm convinced. The future is set in stone. Whether I accept it or not, I have a destiny. The funny thing is, I really do love Gage." Tears start to blur my vision, but I won't let them fall. I like it like this, the way they make the world quiver at attention. "We're all arrows, spearing through time in one long trajectory," I say, finishing my thought on the predestination of things to come.

"Poetry in motion." He slides over to me. "The future I'm going to show you is pivotal. The consequences, of which, will be an amazing portrait of your strength, both inside and out."

"I'm not going to kiss you. I'm not kissing anyone but Gage." Logan bullets through my mind.

"The trifecta of misery is written all over your face. Perhaps a tiny glimpse of what lies ahead will help ease the pain—get you from Logan to Gage in a single bound."

From Logan to Gage?

"Will this help get a body for Holden?" May as well kill two birds with one stone.

"No." Marshall's eyes round out momentarily. "Although with much persuading I can resolve those issues as well. Are you ready for your vision?"

"Is it going to teach me something important?"

"Alleviates heartaches and dispenses both knowledge and wisdom. Kissing me is both medicinal and educational."

Marshall doesn't waste any time. He pulls me down in one mouthwatering moment. The rush of energy flows through me like a river of pleasure amplified—no wonder Michelle can't leave him alone.

A picture emerges. I see Gage and Logan near a large banquet table. Gage swipes his finger along the side of a birthday cake and puts a scoop of frosting in his mouth. I see Logan holding up a long serrated knife in my direction. It looks questionable whether it's me or the cake he's ready to cut.

I pull back and take a breath.

"That's it?"

"It's a bit more dramatic in real life."

"That was the last time, I swear." I push past him as I bolt for the door.

"It's not. I've seen this," he calls after me.

When I get back to the room, I'm shocked to see two males slumped over the tiny round table in the room. Crap! It's probably Holden, and he's brought another dead friend, or worse, the Fems that just finished a dress rehearsal in Marshall's bathroom. I accidentally knock into the trashcan and both Logan and Gage sit up at attention.

They're hovering over something. Marshall's dagger sits in front of them, still tucked inside its sheath.

Chloe's diary sits nestled between the two of them, opened.

"You're reading it," I gasp.

"I saw something silver hanging out of your bag," Gage says rather sheepishly. "I thought you brought the knife, but it was your brush. Then I saw this." His face changes colors. "We didn't read it all." He picks up the last few pages still glued in a chunk.

"Let's finish it then." I snatch it off the table and hop onto the bed near the window. Logan and Gage scoot in on either side of me.

More boring, droning days—I leaf through pages of bizarre statements about playing a game of buried treasure, mundane school news, the charting of her period.

October 17th,

Demetri did it. I've fashioned a better noose and the deed is done. Let the record show that the prediction of my beloved shall stand correct. This butterfly will emerge from her cocoon in a blaze of beautiful glory.

October 25th,

I've seen her again—tried to drown her in my dreams.

Counts invited me to their meeting! I'm big time now.

Drown me—she was trying to drown me?

"The Counts," Gage says.

"Logan?" I push the book to my chest. "When we get back I want to go over that list of names."

The two of them exchange glances.

"What?" I ask. They're keeping something from me. I relax the book against my knees. I'll get the list myself when we get back, from Ellis if I have to. "Who was Emerson?"

"Pierce and Holden's sister," Gage whispers. "She was murdered about six months before Chloe died."

"Chloe said she watched someone die, that she had blood on her hands. I bet she killed her. That's what they were lording over her." My breathing becomes unsteady.

Logan twitches his brows and gives a small shrug.

Nothing would surprise me about Chloe anymore.

October 31st,

Michelle has gone psychotically insane trying to figure out what Lex and I are always 'whispering' about. I think in another month I'll clue her in on our little secret, Em too. I'll probably tell her Logan is a demon—although that might actually entice her. She knows enough to stay away from Gage.

Ellis's party sucked just like him. Logan announced that he doesn't want to see me anymore. He doesn't think this is going to work. Well, too damn bad.

I call the shots. I decide the end.

November 2nd,

Demetri freaking Edinger came to town! I almost crapped my pants when I saw him at the gas station. Turns out his grandfather lives here. Weird.

Holden texted me, let me know the Counts have made all the necessary arrangements for Paragon's newest resident. Of course, I put on the finishing touches myself, one well-placed BFF, and one well-placed boyfriend.

I have everyone where I want them—everyone working for me. Death will be like a well-needed vacation.

November 3rd,

Dear Dairy, I'll be signing off for a while. I have this creaky feeling in my bones that I could be headed into my cocoon any day now. I'll be sealing you off as soon as I'm through writing this. I look forward to seeing you again—when I get back.

Chloe

"What's the name of the regional leader in L.A.?" My voice is clenched in a hoarse whisper. It all comes together for me. Chloe looking for someone just like her, bribing the Kraggers for information, giving away Celestra files, doing anything and everything to save her life, clawing her way out of death like a cat at the bottom of a well—Chloe light driving to L.A.

"I don't remember." Logan shakes his head.

"I do. D. Edinger." My fingers shake as I turn the next few pages. Blank. Homecoming came and went and Chloe was busy being tormented by Fems or Ezrina or whoever the heck held her captive for two weeks before dumping her off on the side of the road like the piece of trash she was.

I peel back the final page, written on the inside cover in bold print reads,

People I Hate

Brody Bishop

Emerson Kragger

Lexy Bakova

Michelle Miller

Ellis Harrison

Gage Oliver

Skyla Messenger

49

The Death of You

I flex the diary upside down until the picture of Ezrina floats out, gentle as a leaf. I pluck it from the air before it has a chance to settle.

"I'm going to the bathroom." I push the words out in an effort to ditch both Logan and Gage.

Chloe was the reason my father died. It was an all out hunt for someone like her, someone she could fool into liking her, someone as stupid as me to even think to bring her back. She probably whispered the idea in my sleep. Somehow she made sure I ended up on Paragon, trapped in her world to do her bidding.

I snatch the dagger off the table in one clean swipe and dash to the restroom, locking myself inside.

Chloe was right, this does change everything, although the joke's on her because she is never going to live to see it.

"Skyla!" The door bucks as Logan and Gage frantically scream my name.

I get on the floor and hold the knife close to my chest. I try to remember the last occasion I time traveled alone. For sure I had enough blood in me then. I'm not too concerned with whether or not I'll get back. There's always Chloe's blood—and I plan on shedding quite a bit of it.

Logan and Gage burst through the door, just as I disappear.

Ellis's party is going strong. I walk around back and spy Logan with his arms crossed talking to Carly. Her billowy hair flails in the wind—funny how her being a mom has changed my urge to slaughter her. Although on a night like tonight I fear for anyone who gets in my way.

Turns out Chloe has been hanging around the periphery of my life like a cyclone, ready and waiting for the wind to push her just right so she could knock down my house of cards.

I ditch past Gage just barely. I've impressed myself on him and he hungers to reprise that kiss. Maybe kissing Gage will be how I celebrate this fated night—it seems fitting in oh so many ways.

Then I see her, relaxed, with her feet up over the sofa. She wears a mile wide grin as she talks to Michelle.

I slip the dagger into the back of my jeans—feel the cold steel handle push into my flesh as I pull the picture of Ezrina out of my back pocket. I whisper her name like an incantation.

"Hey!" Chloe throws her legs over the side.

"You have a second?" I force a smile, crumbling the picture in my hand.

"Sure." She looks over at Michelle. "Friend from out of town. Boy trouble. He's a lot like Logan," she sneers as we exit the room.

There's an arctic chill in the air, but my anger has numbed me from the frosty bite of the elements. Dew settles quickly on my skin, my hair, my clothes, but I'm anesthetized from the effects. Hatred has a strange way of stripping your senses away and honing all of your energy into one pure stream of venom.

"Full moon," she breathes the words as we progress toward the woods.

"It's a blistering moon," my voice comes from someplace else, too deep and arid to belong to me. "Can it be that?"

"Sounds like an ominous forecast." She keeps us moving at a frenetic pace. "You better watch it next time. Someone is going to see you." She picks a large stick off the ground as though it were a reflex.

We step into the woods. An entire covering of tall black towers spread over us like a death shroud.

"Let me guess." She bats her lashes. "Logan and Gage are embroiled in a power struggle. The love triangle of doom is about to collapse, and you don't know which one you're going to let deflower you first?" She places her hand up by her face and sighs.

"Mmm," I moan. "The story went down a little different, actually." Our steps even out as we progress deeper and deeper into the black of the forest. "I found a love that grows with Gage, and a love that will wait for me with Logan."

"Aren't you a lucky little witch?" She digs a smile into the side of her face.

"Do you know about love, Chloe?" I pant as the scenery glides by quick and smooth as a dream. "Love, as strong as death?"

"What's that supposed to mean?" Her features darken.

"I read it—right up until the end." I pull her back by the shoulder.

A wild army of thumps land hard on the forest floor, shaking the earth with their disruptive growls.

"So you know?" There's a hint of glee in her voice.

"I know what it changed."

"What's that, Skyla?" Her eyes sparkle with anticipation.

"Everything, between you and me."

I don't tell her that it touched down like a tornado and solidified my feelings for Gage, or that it drove Logan away, or that I may never look at Brielle the same way again.

It feels good razing over the truth, watching it rise and blossom in our conversation, natural as breathing.

"You have my father's blood on your hands. You can't expect to get away with it."

"Well, now we've got a party." She pushes out a smile.

"So Brielle was just a plant?" A part of me can't believe that, even if it's true. "And who's the boyfriend?" Like I don't know it was supposed to be Ellis. "Backfire much?"

"Nothing I do backfires." Her eyes light up with anger.

"You couldn't land Gage. He wants me—always has." I wave his love for me like a banner.

"He'll be mine. Everything I planned is coming true. You standing here is evidence of that."

"I'm not with Ellis, and you're not going to live."

"Ellis?" She laughs when she says his name. "I live, Skyla, and it's by your blood that I do it."

The forest comes alive with a series of thuds and hisses.

"Fems!" A sheer look of panic grips her. "It's happening." She pulls me forward and propels me like a human shield.

"Skyla!" My name booms from somewhere outside the woods.

I can't tell whether it's Logan, Gage or Ellis for that matter.

"In here!" Chloe shouts.

A tall black dog standing upright, with three snapping heads stomps in our direction.

"Crap!" She pulls in behind me.

"You don't get it." I try and fling her in the Fem's direction. "I'm not here to help you. I'm not bringing you back. I'm never going to help you. I'm never not going to try and kill you."

The Fem gyrates wildly, with tongues as long as leashes. Chloe charges at it with the stick in her hand, spears it through the throat. She ducks behind a tree before taking off into the night.

The beast growls and staggers in my direction. Chloe didn't kill it. She only managed to piss it off. It barrels toward me in a fit of wild thrashing, swiping the air, and I run in the opposite direction.

I can hear them—everywhere. Like a bad dream they snap branches from trees as though they were pretzels—groan like dying prisoners.

Chloe screams. I run toward her at a quickened pace dodging trees, hitting trees, twisting in and out of this disorganized maze of nature.

"Skyla!" It's Logan.

I run faster away from his voice. I can hear Gage shouting in the distance. Gage might let me do it, but Logan—I don't know if he'd stand by and watch me kill Chloe— if he'd help if I needed him to.

"Skyla, wait!"

The heavy sound of his erratic breathing propels me forward like springs.

"Get away from me!" I shout, running through a small clearing toward Chloe's cries for help.

"Please, wait!" He snatches at my elbow twice before spinning me around.

We pant out of rhythm, creating a dense layer of fog between us.

"Don't do it." Logan squints into me. There's a genuine anguish in his face that begs me to listen. "She's going to die tonight. It doesn't have to be by your hand."

For a moment I forget about Chloe and a forest full of Fems, instead I shove him hard in the chest.

"You didn't fight for me!" I roar the words from the deepest part of my soul. It's anguish losing him. There aren't enough tears, or I-hate-yous, to convey how terrible he's made me feel.

"I am fighting for you," it comes out strong, genuine and tender.

Chloe's wails of terror light up the night.

Logan steps forward, his amber eyes glow in the reserve moonlight filtering down from the branches. He pulls me in and kisses me full on the mouth, a hot hungry bite of heat that lets me know he's still in the ring, that his love for me is alive and burning— primal in his gut.

I pull back and pant into the dense night air.

Chloe calls my name, begging for my help.

"I have to go." I run into the thick of the woods at breakneck pace. I don't bother looking back.

50

Watch You Bleed

Paragon trembles beneath my feet. Entire explosions ricochet throughout the forest. I see arms and legs moving. It's Michelle. She's trapped by the rotting corpse of a Fem, pinned between two trees. Another Fem covered in thick dark hair claws at her back. Michelle lives. This I know.

"Payback's a bitch," I mutter.

I turn and charge toward Chloe's voice, clutching at the dagger in my hand with bionic force.

"Skyla?" Chloe comes at me bloodied, her bottom lip swelling on one side.

A shag of red hair shoots out of the darkness like a flare—Ezrina. She bolts forward with that strange sense of calm, grips Chloe by the back of the hair and starts to drag her off.

"No!" I pluck Chloe free and pull her over a landmine of tree roots bulging out of the ground like a series of petrified snakes. "She's mine." I secure her arms behind her back and run her into the pit of the forest in an effort to lose Ezrina.

Chloe struggles to get her bearings. She hits me hard in the face with the back of her hand and knocks me to the ground.

I clasp onto her ankles before she has the chance to flee and cause her to sit down hard. The dagger strays near my ribcage, and I pick it up again and touch it. It lights up the night, ethereal—a lovely, deadly shade of blue.

One incision—death without pain. This was far too easy.

Instead, I hike up Chloe's dress and run my hand up her thigh until I hit the pocketknife clipped to her garter.

"Skyla, no!" It sounds like more of a command than a plea.

"This is for my dad." I slash through her arms and legs. I remember where each clean slit was made into her flesh from seeing her in the morgue, and replicate it.

"You can't kill me! I'm coming back." She tries to break free from my grasp. I turn her over, and clutch her hands high up behind her back until I feel the bones bend unnaturally. She lets out a horrid groan, and I relent. "Gage, he told me," she screams. "There's nothing you can do, Skyla. I'll be there."

"There's no more blood for you. I won't give it." I reach over and pat the ground for the dagger, but it's missing. I pat out further, losing my grasp on her wrists.

Before I realize it Chloe thrusts me upside down, flat on my back. The glint of the silver pocketknife shines in her hand.

"First time was practice." She presses the cold steel against my neck.

It was Chloe. Chloe Bishop slit my throat.

The dagger spins over to me by way of a tennis shoe. I look up in time to see Logan topple Chloe off me.

It feels good holding the knife that will kill my enemy. I pulsate my fingers over the handle. This is all the vindication I will ever need to avenge my father's death—a soul for a soul.

Chloe and Logan roll around in the dirt. I wait until she makes one final revolution before plunging the dagger deep in her back, the handle rising just beneath her shoulder like a stump.

Chloe falls over, motionless.

Logan locks me in a tight embrace before we head on out.

"Where is she?" Ezrina looks frazzled. Her voice echoes through the forest like a flock of nervous birds.

I point back at Chloe. A single beam of moonlight underscores her being. She's become a wilted flower, a terrible wasted thing of beauty.

I killed her. It was by my hand.

We changed the future—Logan and me.

51

Happy Birthday

The window in my bedroom has been replaced. A white-framed casement window has been newly installed, and I roll it open and let the pale wisps of precipitation in. It feels good to be back on Paragon in the right time, with my blood regenerating, building its strength back up inside my marrow.

Nevermore comes and sits on the perch outside my window.

"Nev," I say his name sweetly as I usher him in.

He looks majestic—pulsating around my dresser, the bed, my desk.

Chloe's gone like a bad dream I'll never have to reprise. We took the diary to the hotel incinerator last night and watched it erupt in a ball of fire as it met with the flames below.

It feels good to have rectified the death of my father. His blood was spilt for mine, and now the one who depended on it for her survival will never get another drop.

The death, the grief, it moves in a circle—makes a complete hoop of sorrow.

I click my tongue and hold out my hand as Nev jumps up on my arm like a perch. I can feel his heft, feel the weight of his stare as he studies me.

"You're mine now. No more Chloe," I say.

"Skyla and Gage," he calls broken, sounding a lot like Gage himself.

"That's right." I rub the back of my finger over his feathers. "Skyla and Gage," I whisper.

I've changed one scenario from the future, but do I want to change another?

Mom insists the family take me out for an early birthday dinner.

It doesn't feel like my birthday, even though Brielle had everyone sing to me on the ferry ride home. Well, almost everyone. Pierce, Michelle and Lexy kept their mouths glued shut.

"The bowling alley?" I ask my mother as we pull into the parking lot. It looks dark and abandoned.

"I thought it'd be fun. Besides, it's not like you have to work. And we can play a few games as a family. When was the last time we bowled together?" She looks hopeful.

On the bright side, either Logan or Gage will be working and I'll get to hang out with them. I get out of the car and let the white breath of fog cover me soft as fleece. A car whizzes by on the road, stealing the purity from the evening breeze, replacing it with a chemical-filled groan as we make our way inside.

The lights in the game room blink in agitation as we make our way into the bowling alley. Only the reserve lighting is on, glowing in a stream of beautiful pale blues and purples.

"Surprise!" Dozens of voices shout in unison.

The house lights flicker on and off and a sea of faces from West stare back at me.

"Happy birthday." Logan gives a brief warm hug.

"Hey, birthday girl!" Gage swoops in with a hug. "You OK?"

"Yeah," I whisper in his ear. The sign on the wall reads, *Happy Birthday, Skyla and Gage!* "Happy birthday to *you*!" I smile for the first time in what feels like years.

I pull Gage off to the side as Logan rushes back and forth to a giant buffet table set out.

"Um," I whisper. "So, maybe tomorrow we can hang out, just you and me. I mean, I know it's your actual birthday and all, but maybe after you spend some time with your family..."

He looks down at me with a perfect mix of desire and contentment.

"I would love that." His dimples cut in hard on either side. "Maybe we could go snorkeling again? I promise I won't let go this time." He picks up my hand and gives it a light squeeze.

"I won't either. I'll never let go." I don't break our gaze when I say it.

This is a new journey for the two of us, and I plan on giving it one hundred percent. I need to be certain with every cell of my body that Gage is my destiny. I don't know how long the faction war will last, if it will ever end, but something is stirring deep inside my soul—it lets me know that this moment is right for us.

Now that I know the future is governable by our own hopes and desires—that passion can alter circumstances—I want to stretch across the vast expanse of possibilities and discover them for myself.

"Tomorrow." I press in a quick kiss. There is so much hope in that word.

Emma and Dr. Oliver come over quickly and wish us a happy birthday.

I see Marshall testing out the heft of bowling balls with Michelle. She fingers the rose around her neck as she considers her decision. Looks like some things never change.

Logan comes over and asks me to follow him into the kitchen. He waves his hands and presents the fully functioning facility.

"It's open!" I beam. "This is great."

"I wanted to surprise you. What better way to open than celebrating your birthday?" He steps forward, his eyes squint through a mixture of sorrow and gladness. "I have something for you." He pulls something from his pocket and takes up my hand, pressing it gently into my palm without revealing it. "It's a token of my affection. I thought maybe if you doubted how I felt, you could look down and see it—know that I love you even if..." He glances out the kitchen door. "Even if this is your time with Gage." He pulls back revealing a shiny pewter band with a butterfly on top.

"It's so sweet." I place it on the ring finger of my left hand without thinking.

"No," he gives a broken whisper. "For this finger." He helps me place it on my right hand and gives the ring a quick kiss. "When the war is over, I'll buy another ring." The apples of his cheeks liven with color.

There's something inexplicable in his tone, a taste of something forthcoming, something as true as a promise.

"One more thing." There's a mischievous look in his eyes. He pulls a key from his pocket and dangles it in front of me. "Your new car. Whenever you're ready." He places it gently in my hand.

Brielle comes in like a hurricane. "Get out here! I'm taking pictures and I want you in them."

Logan nods and ticks his head out the door. His eyes glitter when he does it and I know if I stay one more minute I'm going to fall apart.

I follow Brielle out into the boisterous crowd. Most everyone is bowling and there's a ton of food set out on a long table, buffet style.

I'm pretty sure this isn't the venue in which I want to confront Brielle about being one of Chloe's plants. It's so hard to believe Brielle isn't genuine. A part of me never wants to ask.

"So, when were you going to tell me?" I shout up over the music that just kicked in through the speakers. I mean about the baby, but I'm curious to see what comes out of her mouth.

"Tell you?" Brielle gives a blank expression before rolling her eyes back into her skull. "You found it?"

"Mia found it. She thinks it's mine."

"Ha!" She shags out her hair like it's no big deal. "We'll discuss later, right now lets get some pictures of you with people."

"Me first." Marshall appears. He walks me briskly toward an empty corner.

We smile back at Brielle just before Drake yanks her away.

"So she tell you?" He creases his brows with disappointment.

"You know?" I gasp.

Marshall nods looking forlorn.

"About the baby?"

"Yes, about the baby," he whispers *baby* until it's almost inaudible. "The faculty is going to frown upon this."

"Faculty?"

"I'll lose some of the prestige I've managed to acquire the short time I've been here." He shrugs. "I've seen this kind of thing throughout the ages. It has its way of working itself out."

"Are we talking about Brielle and you?" I'm slightly amused.

"Who'd you think we were talking about?"

Michelle lets out an irksome cackle with the bitch squad. They're all in uniform. I bet they're here for Gage or because Ms. Richards has a way of turning non school functions into extracurricular activities.

"No—not, Shelly." His head ticks back a notch.

"Shelly? We've advanced to pet names have we?" So, Michelle isn't pregnant. It was Brielle all along.

"It's hardly a pet name." His tongue presses into the side of his cheek.

"I killed Chloe." It stammers out of me. It was begging to dive off the cliff of my tongue and I let it.

"And where's the dagger?"

My fingers fly up to my mouth.

"That's right you left it in her back. It was returned to me by Ezrina. Do refrain from your kleptomania the next time you visit." He leans against the railing looking rather bored with the entire scene.

"So..." I spot Brielle walking over to Drake and my family at one of the lanes adjacent to us. "Did you get me a present?" I bat my lashes up at him.

"In part. I'm about to give you the rest." He nods over to my family.

"Oh, it's the vision you showed me," I say, feeling light about the whole thing. I changed what I needed to, so I don't feel an overwhelming urge to run over and stop Tad from catching Mia and Melissa as they table dive into his arms. Although, if I were to do it, I'm sure Tad would have me locked up on assault charges.

The music stops and the lights flicker.

"Cake!" Gage shouts from the kitchen.

"Ready for your gift?" Marshall whispers.

"Always." It's probably another hot dress, or a...

Marshall picks up my hand and presses a soft kiss against the back before cradling it in both of his. My entire person ignites in the bliss that only Marshall can give. It's the perfect gift, a gift anyone on the planet wishes they could have twenty-four hour access to. Marshall is lucky he hasn't been kidnapped by street gangs, or....

I look over at my family. Brielle and Drake, my mother, Tad...Mia and Melissa—they're blue. Blue—the entire lot of them.

"Counts are blue," I say, breathless. I'm confused. Marshall is playing tricks on me. "This can't be right."

"It's right, Skyla."

Gage comes out of the kitchen carrying an enormous birthday cake with both our names encircled in a heart—no doubt my mother's doing. I hold my breath at the thought of who my mother might actually be.

Gage runs his finger down one side of the frosting and slips his finger into his mouth. Logan comes out of the kitchen and heads toward the cake carrying a long handled knife.

Dear God.

He motions toward me with a wave of the blade.

"He's blue," I breathe out the words.

Logan—*my* Logan—Celestra Logan.

I reach out in front of me and pat the air as if I were blind. I want to feel my way over to him, touch his face.

Dr. Oliver claps his hands together as he makes his way toward me.

"I have something for you." He takes my hand and whisks me over to the arcade. "Now!" He shouts.

A girl steps out in a white sheath, her hair pulled back neat in a long sleek ponytail. She holds a bouquet of red roses that stand out like a bloodstain.

"The hemoglobin began to regenerate itself. All we needed was the five pints." Dr. Oliver trembles the words out in excitement.

Chloe.

I can't breathe or move or feel the ground beneath me.

Dangling from her neck is the pendant belonging to Logan's grandmother. The stone sparkles an iridescent blue.

She gives a wicked grin.

"Happy birthday, Skyla."

Thank you for reading **Burn**.
Look for **Wicked** Book 4 in the Celestra series, available now!

About The Author

Addison Moore is a *New York Times, USA Today,* and *Wall Street Journal* bestselling author who writes contemporary and paranormal romance. Her work has been featured in *Cosmopolitan* Magazine. Previously she worked as a therapist on a locked psychiatric unit for nearly a decade. She resides on the West Coast with her husband, four wonderful children, and two dogs where she eats too much chocolate and stays up way too late. When she's not writing, she's reading.

Feel free to visit her at:

http://addisonmoorewrites.blogspot.com
Facebook: Addison Moore Author
Twitter: @AddisonMoore
Instagram: @authorAddisonMoore